Wings Over the Mountains
- Book Two -

Brian —

I enjoyed being in your "Bats in the Band"

CAPITOL CRIME

audience at the Riverside Library!

JERRY PETERSON

WINDSTAR PRESS

Copyright 2014 c Jerry Peterson
Windstar Press

All Rights Reserved.

ISBN-13: 978-1495930362
ISBN-10: 149593036X

Cover Design c Dawn Charles at
bookgraphics.wordpress.com

April 2014

Printed in the U.S.A.

DEDICATION

To Marge, my wife and first reader.

To the members of *Tuesdays with Story*, my writers group. My colleagues are sharp-eyed readers and writers who demand the very best of me in craft of writing telling.

To a friend and one-time colleague who prefers to remain unnamed.

ACKNOWLEDGMENTS

This is the eighth book I've published as indie author, the third under my Windstar Press imprint.

We indie authors depend on a lot of people to make our stories and books the best that they can be. Cover designer extraordinaire Dawn Charles, of Book Graphics, worked with me on this volume as she has on several of my previous books.

A knock-out cover grabs potential readers and says to them buy this book; it's a great read. That's essential. Nearly as important as the front cover are the words on the back cover. For these, this time I turned to mystery and horror writer J. Michael Major. Here's what he wrote in a note to readers after he read my manuscript: "(Jerry) Peterson's vivid characters jump right off the page, and his sharp detail and snappy dialog puts you, the reader, right in the middle of Prohibition-era action and one of the wildest schemes ever to take down a bootlegging ring. Buckle up. You are in for a helluva ride."

Oh my. But Mike's right. In *Capitol Crime*, you are in for a helluva ride.

Readers often wonder where the author got the idea for the book they are reading. I do.

So I'm going to tell you where the idea for *Capitol Crime* came from.

My first wife, Sallie, was a Kentuckian. One day, she told me her father had bought a still for me. He may well have, but I don't remember the contraption. The still that I do remember is a part of an exhibit at the West Virginia

Historical Museum. Real country engineering. I studied that still for a long time when I was there.

Connect that now with Jack Manning, a Fayette County, West Virginia, sheriff I knew back when I was a reporter for Beckley Newspapers. Jack was death on stills, destroyed a lot of them during his career. But he was highly respected by the hoochmakers because he jailed only the worst, those who either were violent or made bad whiskey. The hoochmakers who were just trying to feed their children, he found ways to cut them some slack.

A crime novel about a sheriff who goes around busting up stills is routine. It's been done. But what if I were to up the ante?

Instead of a still, what if it was a factory cranking out illegal whiskey by the tanker load that the sheriff was after?

This would be big money.

Big danger.

And, with a twist, a capitol crime.

I always close with a note of appreciation to librarians here and around the country. They, like you and your fellow readers, have enjoyed my James Early mysteries, my AJ Garrison crime novels, my short story collections, my John Wads Crime Novellas, and now my *Wings Over the Mountains* series. The librarians are not only boosters, they buy my books and put them on the shelves of their libraries so their patrons can enjoy them, too.

If, after you finish reading *Capitol Crime*, you agree, hey, shoot me a note. You can find me on the web.

JP
Janesville, Wisconsin, April 2014

ALSO BY JERRY PETERSON

Early's Fall, a James Early Mystery, book 1. . . "If James Early were on the screen instead of in a book, no one would leave the room."
– Robert W. Walker, author of *Children of Salem*

Early's Winter, a James Early Mystery, book 2 . . . "Jerry Peterson's *Early's Winter* is a fine tale for any season. A little bit Western, a little bit mystery, all add up to a fast-paced, well-written novel that has as much heart as it does darkness. Peterson is a first-rate storyteller. Give *Early's Winter* a try, and I promise you, you'll be begging for the next James Early novel. Spring can't come too soon."
– Larry D. Sweazy, Spur-award winning author of *The Badger's Revenge*

A James Early Christmas & Other Stories of the Season . . . "The James Early Christmas stories are charming, heart-warming, and well-written. It's rare today to see stories that unabashedly champion simple generosity and good will, but Jerry Peterson does both successfully, all the while keeping you entertained with his gentle humor. This should definitely go under your tree this season."
– Libby Hellmann, author of *Nice Girl Does Noir*, a collection of short stories

The Watch, an AJ Garrison Crime Novel, book 1 . . . "Jerry Peterson has written a terrific mystery, rich in atmosphere of place and time. New lawyer A.J. Garrison is a smart, gutsy heroine."
— James Mitchell, author of *Our Lady of the North*

Rage, an AJ Garrison Crime Novel, book 2 . . . "Terrifying. Just—terrifying. Timely and profound and even heartbreaking. Peterson's taut spare style and truly original voice create a high-tension page turner. I really loved this book."
— Hank Phillippi Ryan, Agatha, Anthony and Macavity winning author

Iced, a John Wads Crime Novella, book 2 . . . "Jerry Peterson's new thriller, *Iced*, is a thrill-a-minute ride down a slippery slope of suspense and shootouts. Engaging characters, spiffy dialogue, and non-stop action make this one a real winner."
— Michael A. Black, author of *Sleeping Dragons*, a Mack Bolan Executioner novel

The Last Good Man, a Wings Over the Mountains novel, book 1 . . . "Jerry Peterson joins the ranks of the writer's writer—that is, an author other authors can learn something from, as in how to open and close a book, but also in how to run the course."
— Robert Walker, author of *Children of Salem*

Capitol Crime

CHAPTER 1

The call

"SHERIFF? SHERIFF? It's something awful."

To Quill Rose, the voice on the telephone sounded like it was coming from the far end of the earth. He pressed the receiver tighter to his ear. "Who is this?"

"Oakie Brown, teacher out at Pistol Creek."

"Oakie, you gotta speak up."

"Sheriff, three people out here. They're dead."

Rose spilled his coffee. He motioned to his deputy for a rag to wipe it up. "What did you say, Oakie?"

"Three people, dead I tell ya. At the old Whitlow farm."

"Oakie, where're you calling from? There're no telephones out on Pistol Creek."

"Asa's, in Rockford."

"Why are you calling me instead of the undertaker?"

"'Cause they been kilt."

"Oak, stay where you are. Tommy and me, we're on the way out." Rose snapped the receiver down on the hook of his candlestick telephone. He glanced up in time to snatch a rag that came flying from Tommy Jenks, his chief deputy. Rose went to mopping at the coffee dribbling down the side of his desk into a half-open drawer. "Oakie Brown, do you think he's been drinking again? He's seen some strange things in the past that weren't real."

"Best I know he's still on the wagon. Why?"

"Says he's come on three people dead at the Whitlow place. You better grab your jacket."

Quill Rose had dealt with nine murders in the years he had been sheriff of Blount County, Tennessee, all singles. If this telephone call was right, he was in for his first triple. He headed for the office door. "We'll pick up Doc Stanley. If we've got dead people, we can at least get the paperwork right the first time."

Jenks hustled along. "Taking your gun?"

"You got yours?"

"Yup."

"Then we're fine."

Rose rarely went armed. He preferred wits over weapons.

The lawmen made an odd pair. Rose, tall and lean, with a mustache no one could be proud of, came out of the Tuckaleechee Cove in the high mountains east of Maryville, the county seat. As the only son of parents who had died poor, Rose determined early to get a job at the courthouse so he'd have a steady paycheck. Now he had stood for election six times, the last four unopposed.

Tommy Jenks, wide as a door and weighing the better part of two hundred fifty pounds, was a brawler who had worked for most of the logging crews in the mountains. When Rose got tired of arresting him, he hired him.

Over time, the two had become so close that courthouse regulars said they shared the same toothpick.

JENKS STOPPED the county's new cruiser, a Ford Model B, in front of Hershel's Drugstore. "You want me to come up?"

Rose eased his lank out the passenger door. "We're not going to have to drag him out. This is Doc's shining opportunity to escape from the office. He does love working on dead bodies."

"He's a ghoul."

"Our ghoul and a nice one."

Rose strode off across the sidewalk to the staircase beside the store. He took the steps two at a time. At the top, he banged on an office door.

"Yeah?" a voice called out.

Rose leaned in.

"I'm in the back," the voice said.

Rose peered around Doctor Gallatin Stanley's waiting room. Two women sat at the side, paging through long out-of-date Collier's magazines. Rose gave them a casual wave as he went to an inner door. This he also opened. There before him sat Stanley on a stool, the town's medic prodding at a man's mouth.

Stanley swore. "Wilson, keep your mouth open. I've gotta see back in there."

Rose rapped on the door jamb.

Stanley snatched a quick look over his glasses. "Quill, come here. Look at this."

Rose came around. He leaned down on Stanley's shoulder and gazed where the beam from Stanley's flashlight pointed, into the mouth of Everett Wilson.

Stanley maneuvered the beam to spotlight something at the back of the man's throat. "Doesn't that look like tonsils to you, kind of red and swollen?"

"Uh-huh."

"That's what I thought, but old Wils here says another doc yanked his tonsils when he was a kid. Frankly, I think the quack swindled his parents. I'd say they're still in there—Wilson, keep your mouth open—whadaya think, Quill?"

"Sure look like tonsils to me."

"Suppose I shoot 'em off."

The man bit down on Stanley's tongue stick, snapping it in half.

Stanley waved his half in front of his patient's nose. "Dammit, Wilson, now the sheriff's gonna have to arrest you for destroying my property."

"Come on, Doc, I'm not about to do that. You better tell Everett what's really going on."

Stanley glared at Wilson. "You've got a sore throat, that's all. It's a little red back there, but you don't have tonsils. Now get outta here. Go home and gargle with salt water."

Wilson spit his half of the tongue stick into his hand. He opened his mouth, but Stanley jabbed a finger at him before he could speak. "Is your hearing bad, Wils? I said get out of here. You'll get my bill."

Wilson closed his mouth. He got up and shuffled away, the only sound the scuffing of his heels on the pine plank floor.

Rose raked his fingers through his mustache. "Doc, the way you treat your patients, I'm surprised you have any."

"Hell, if I treat 'em nice, they just keep coming back. It interferes with my fishing."

"And your work as a coroner."

Stanley swung around, his eyes dancing. "You've got a dead body for me?"

"I've got three."

"What is it, old age, murder, or did they get run over by one of those damn-fool aluminum haulers?"

"You get to make the call."

"Hot-damn. Quill, let's go." He bolted to a closet for his black bag and coat. His fedora he snatched off the skull of Old Bones, his skeleton standing guard by the inner door. Stanley dashed past the reading women on his way out. "Sorry, Ethel, Min, dead people are calling. You stop back tomorrow, wouldja? And kill the light when you leave."

Rose trotted after Stanley, chuckling. He clattered down the stairs, the coroner well ahead of him. When Rose hit bottom, Stanley was already across the sidewalk, huddled with Jenks, admiring the cruiser. "New, huh?"

Jenks held the backseat door open. "Quill got it last week."

"Red wheels, whitewall tires, my oh my. If I brought this home, my wife'd call it the cat's pajamas. And here I thought the county was broke."

Rose came up. He put his arm around Stanley's shoulders. "Thank our county's moonshiners. They bought it for us. Hop in."

Stanley took the backseat, Rose and Jenks the front, Jenks driving.

Rose motioned ahead. "Take us by way of Rockford–Asa's–so we can pick up Oakie."

Stanley pulled himself forward. "Oakie the one who called this in?"

Rose gave a thumbs up.

"Gawd, he's not drinkin' again, is he?"

"Tommy doesn't think so."

"How about you?"

"Me? I hope he is. If Oakie's just seeing some wild things, we'll have had a nice afternoon in the country and the fresh air that goes with it. I swear the county's got

Satan's helper shoveling coal in the boiler down at the courthouse."

"Hot?"

"Like July."

"My, and in the middle of March. The moonshiners really buy this for you?"

"Yup. We bust up a still, we get to keep the copper and anything else we can sell and then the money when we sell it. The still busting business has been really good to us this winter."

Stanley settled back. He ran his hand over the fabric of the seat. "Sure beats that old T-model the fiscal court judges stuck you with all these years."

"That it does.

Jenks glanced in his side mirror as he swung the cruiser north onto the Knoxville Turnpike. "Doc, help me out here. What's your fascination with dead people?"

"Money, it's as simple as that."

"I don't get it, Doc."

"Look, the county always pays me. With the live ones, I'm never sure I'm gonna get my money. And there's something more."

"What's that?"

"The dead ones, they never complain."

OAKIE BROWN, a tightly built little man with a wild thatch of hair that poked out in all directions from beneath his cap, stood with Rose, Jenks, and Stanley, all gazing down at the body of a dog.

Brown poked the toe of his shoe at the carcass. "This is where it starts."

Stanley knelt. He ran his hand over the dog's side, then riffled the hair back under its jaw. "Cut his throat.

That's what you do when you want to kill the animal's family at your leisure."

Rose rubbed at his elbow. "You're the expert, now?"

"It's what I'd do."

"So, Oakie, what caused you to come by anyway?"

"Simmy. She didn't come to school today. She'd just started on Monday. I was worried."

"They're all in the house?"

"Yeah."

"We'd better go in then."

Rose and Stanley stepped out ahead of Brown and Jenks. They went across the yard toward a one-story that listed to the east, its paint little more than a memory.

Brown stepped up on the porch. "I found the woman in the main room. The man's back in the bedroom."

"And the girl?"

"Simmy? I almost didn't see her until I looked up. Her arm was hanging over the edge of the loft, blood everywhere. Sheriff, all I touched was the door."

Rose, with his elbow, pushed the door open, and the smell of death rolled out. The afternoon light spilled across the body of a woman clothed in a flannel nightgown, crumpled on the floor, one leg twisted back.

Stanley got down on his knees. "Cut her throat." He put a finger on the edge of a blood stain in the middle of the clothing. "There's a gut wound, but I don't think that's all. Can I roll the body over, Quill?"

"Go ahead."

"Give me a hand, Tommy."

Together, Stanley and Jenks rolled the woman onto her stomach.

"Tommy, look at this." Stanley swept his hand along a tear in the back of the nightgown that exposed a gash in the woman's back. It began high on the rib cage and carried almost to her buttocks. "A slash like that, she was running from him. What's this?" He stared at the stump of a right arm, where the woman's hand should have been. "He cut off her hand? Why the hell would he do that?"

Before Stanley could answer his own question, he glanced up, toward the loft, to an arm and the top of a head, and something else. "There's two up there."

Brown twisted away. "Oh, Jesus, not the baby."

Rose also looked up. "There's a baby?"

"Simmy said she had a little brother. Two, maybe three years old."

Rose went to the ladder. He climbed the rungs, stopping when he could see into the loft. "Tommy, the boy's here. He's back in the corner. Doesn't appear to be hurt."

Rose climbed higher, high enough that he could reach the child. He caught him under the arms. "How you doing, little one? Oh phew. Tommy, he's got a load." Rose lifted the boy over the edge and down to Jenks. "Take him and find him some new britches."

Jenks grimaced at the stench. "It's a good thing I love children. Others wouldn't do this job." He hiked off to the kitchen, Oakie Brown with him.

Stanley hefted himself up. He took out a pad and pencil and scratched down some notes. "What's the girl look like?"

Rose lifted her shoulder. "Throat's cut. Slashes on her arms. She's missing a hand, too. What in the world's going on?"

He let the shoulder back down and worked his way down the ladder. "Oakie said the man's in the sleeping room. What's your bet?"

"One hand."

In a side room, from where Rose and Stanley stood in the doorway, they could make out a form in the bed, but couldn't see details because curtains shut out the afternoon sun. Stanley took a small flashlight from his bag. He flicked it on.

They made their way to the bed, one man on either side, Stanley leaning down. "He was asleep, Quill. He never moved. Man cut his throat without ever waking him up."

"Or a woman cut his throat."

"Possible, but I don't think so."

"So you're thinking the wife woke up and ran. Have I got that right?"

"Had to. I know I would have, and as tough as you are, Quill, you would have, too. Only thing that makes sense with her out there and that back wound she's got."

"And the girl?"

Stanley massaged behind his ear. "The woman screamed when she was cut. Wouldn't you if you were being killed?"

"So the girl woke up. She saw what was happening and screamed, too."

"So he had to kill her."

"Then why didn't he kill the boy?"

"I don't know." Stanley twisted on the balls of his feet as he peered around the room barren except for the bed, a caned chair, and a small chest of drawers. "Maybe the boy was under the blanket and God kept him from moving. The man didn't see him."

"Maybe he didn't know there was a baby to look for. You see any toys around? Anything that says baby to you? These people were too poor to have toys for their kids."

"Well, should we look at his arms?"

"I expect we'd better."

Stanley untangled the blanket, then lifted it back. "Lord a mighty, hacked right through the wrist."

"You'd have to have an axe to do that, wouldn't you think?"

"Or a stout knife." Stanley held the stump up, his light on it. "See this? He didn't cut the bone. Just sliced through the tendons and the wrist joint came apart."

Jenks and Brown came back, Jenks carrying the child whose bottom was now swaddled in a diaper made from a flour sack with the Martha White brand on it. "Got him cleaned up, Quill. He's a happy little kid. What're we gonna do with him?"

"What do you think, Doc? We could give him to the nurses at the hospital until we find some relatives."

Brown fidgeted. "Sheriff, open to an idea?"

"Sure."

"Asa's wife would take him, and I could look in on him there for you."

Stanley glanced up from the body. "For God's sake, she's already got six of her own, Oakie."

"But she's always taking in strays."

Rose gazed at the child playing with the flap of Jenks's jacket. "Doc, I gotta admit Addie's a good woman. Tommy, go ahead, take the boy down to the store and see what you can work out. And call Roy. Tell him to get out here with his hearse, that he's got three bodies to get ready for the ground."

"He's gonna want to know if the county will pay."

"Tell him yes."

Jenks and Brown left with the child while Stanley took up a seat on the edge of the bed. He continued writing notes on the condition of the bodies for his coroner's report.

Rose rummaged through the bedroom, then the kitchen and the main room. He threw up his hands. "Doc, these people have got next to nothing other than their clothes, a couple dishes, and a skillet. That's it."

Frustrated, he took hold of the front door, to close it. "What the hell?"

Stanley peered up.

"Doc, get in here. You gotta see this."

CHAPTER 2

The find

ROSE STARED at the words scrawled in blood on the back of the door, *You wouldn't leave.* "Doc, what the hell do you suppose this means?"

Stanley hustled up. He put his flashlight on the words, traced over the letters with the flashlight's beam. "You're the detective, I'm just the coroner. But let me ask you, how much do you know about fingerprints?"

"Enough that I bought my own kit. It's in the car."

"Fiscal court wouldn't spring for it, huh?"

"Nope."

"Look at this at the end of the *e.* Your man left you a fingerprint. See it right there in the blood? Likely the index finger of the right hand."

"He could be left-handed."

"Not likely. See the slant of the letters? He's right-handed."

"The fingerprint, could it be one of theirs?"

"Jesus, Quill, I suppose it's possible, just possible, the killer took one of the hands he cut off and used its index finger to write this. But I tell you that's a picture that gives me the heebie-geebies."

Rose cocked an eyebrow as he gazed at Stanley.

"I can tell you this," Stanley went on, "whoever did these killings, he had to be some kind of hell-born person."

"Agreed."

"You've got your spy glass with you?"

Rose pulled a small magnifying glass from his inside coat pocket.

Stanley took the glass. He held it as close to the print as he could, working the glass back, then forward to bring the print into focus, all the time keeping his flashlight's beam on the letters. "Your kit's not going to help you."

"Why not?"

"I read up on this. You've got to have special stuff to get a print up when it's in dried blood."

"The State Police keep a lab man in Knoxville. I can get him down here tomorrow."

"Better get him down tonight. You wouldn't want anything happening to this."

By the sound outside, a car had driven into the farmyard. Rose leaned around the door. "It's Tommy. I'm going to send him back to Asa's to make the call."

"That'd be good." Stanley returned the magnifying glass.

Rose dropped it into his pocket and trotted out to the car. "Tommy?"

Jenks leaned out the driver's window.

"Tommy, we've found a fingerprint in some dried blood."

"Is it a good one? Can we use it?"

"I hope so, but we need Will Kaufmann to lift it for us. Go back to Asa's and call him at the State Police post. It's important." Rose rapped on the roof of the car for one more thing. "How'd Addie go for the boy?"

"Like a broody hen that came on one of her missing chicks. Made a real big fuss over him."

"Well, I guess a little good has come of the day. You better go on now."

Jenks wheeled the Ford around. He bounced it through the ruts leading up to the road, Rose watching the dust rise as Jenks sped away.

A Model A pickup, coming from the opposite direction, pierced the dust and made the turn into the farmyard, a mariah with an enclosed box on the back for transporting bodies and coffins.

The driver—Roy Pinckney—backed the truck up to the porch, then hopped out of the cab. "Tommy tells me you got a bad 'un, Quill."

"Yeah, and people new to the community to boot."

"Any relatives I need to contact?"

"None that I know of. I'll track down where they moved from and give you a call with what I learn."

Pinckney opened the back of the hearse. "I'll do my usual, get 'em ready for burial. I'll hold 'em a couple days. If there's no family to mourn 'em, I'll get me one of the preachers to pray over them at the cemetery."

"Roy, I know you'll take care of everything. You always do."

"They ready to move out?"

"If Doc gives the say-so."

Pinckney hauled out a stretcher. He followed Rose inside and laid the stretcher on the floor near the body of the woman. The undertaker snatched off his duffer's cap. "Cut her bad, didn't he?"

Rose glanced at Pinckney.

Pinckney rolled his cap in his hands. "He—whoever did this."

"Could have been a woman."

"What's the doc say?"

"He's guessing a man."

Stanley came in from the kitchen, a bunch of papers in his hand. "Hey, Roy."

"Hey, Doc. Ready to let 'em go?"

"I've got everything I need."

Pinckney slapped his cap back on his head. "Help me with her, Quill?"

Rose bent down as did Pinckney. When they got their hands under the body, Pinckney blanched. "What happened to her hand?"

"Missing. Someone cut it off. Did the same on the other two."

"Souvenirs?"

"Maybe. It's gawd-awful strange, that's for sure."

They lifted the body onto the stretcher. After Pinckney and Rose slid the stretcher into the hearse, Pinckney toted back a second.

Rose climbed up into the loft. There he lifted the body of the girl down.

Together, Pinckney and Rose placed that stretcher on the floor of the hearse, next to the one that bore the woman.

With the third stretcher, they brought out the body of the man. This they hefted up on a shelf above the others.

Pinckney closed and latched the rear doors of his mariah. "Quill, I can hide the fact that each is missing a hand. We got any decent clothes for them?"

"Just rough work clothes and those pretty well wore out. That's all I've found."

"Not to worry, I've always got some laid back."

"Roy, these people, they should have something better than secondhand. You go to Proffitts, and you buy them some decent clothes. The county will stand the bill."

Pinckney peered at Rose, doubt writ large on his face. "Those penny pinchers on the fiscal court? They'll never go for new clothes for dead people."

"If they won't, I will."

"Quill, it's not right you pay outta yer own pocket. You're always doing that."

"These people deserve a little something."

Pinckney raised his hands in surrender. "Have it your way." He tugged the bill of his cap down. At the door of the mariah's cab, Pinckney swivelled back. "You got names?"

Stanley came out on the porch. "The girl's Simmy. The man's Harrison—Harrison William Noland. The woman, she's Beadie Headrick Noland."

Rose raised an eyebrow at Stanley, and Stanley returned the eyebrow gesture. "What? I found the family Bible you missed."

"Find anything else?"

"This."

He held out a letter.

CHAPTER 3

The home front

ROSE, SITTING ON THE BACK PORCH, pulled off a shoe. He massaged his foot, and, as he worked his fingers under his arch and around his toes, his black lab, Fletch, parked himself on his butt in front of Rose and whined.

Rose stared at him. "What, you want me to massage your feet, too?"

The dog let out a soft woof and rocked, shifting his weight from one front paw to the other and back again.

"You gotta do your business, is that it? Well, you don't have to wait for me for that, hound. Just go out in the garden. Fertilizer, we appreciate that."

Martha Rose, a head and a half shorter than Quill and a bit more flesh on her frame, stepped out the back door. She watched her husband and Fletch for a moment. "Your old dog, he misses you when you work these long days."

Rose pulled off his other shoe and went at his freshly freed foot. "I 'spose he does. How about you? You miss me?"

"Sometimes, when you're late, like two and three days late. I hate it when you don't call. I worry, and I get upset." She leaned against the doorjamb.

"Martha, when I'm up in the mountains on the track of a shiner, there are no telephones up there."

"You could call me before you go."

"We've been over this."

"We have, haven't we? You just don't change, do you?" She slipped up behind him. She pulled off his hat and kissed him on the top of his head. "There are some things about you I do like. You do know that."

"I always hoped so."

"So what was it today that made you late?"

"A bad one."

"Want to talk about it?"

"No."

"Doc Stanley called."

"He did?"

She caressed his hair. "He told me."

"That man is a gossip."

"That little boy—the Noland child—why didn't you bring him home, here? We've got this big house."

"And no children."

"I suppose that's my fault."

"Martha, it isn't anybody's fault. It's just the way it is."

She moved her hands down to his shoulders and massaged at the tension she sensed was there. "We could have that little boy, for a while at least, until you find some family, if there is any. Addie Clarke, she's got her hands full with that brood of children of her own."

Rose shook some talcum powder into his shoe before he pulled it back on. "That's a fair point, but Addie's a good momma."

"I'm step-momma to all the kids in the neighborhood, you know that, Quill. They're always here in the afternoon for cookies and to play on the piano in the front parlor and to romp with your dog."

Rose tied his shoe. When he finished, he gazed up at his wife for the longest time. "You really want him?"

"I wouldn't be nearly so lonely when you're out late. And maybe I wouldn't worry so much about you, old man, and get so angry with you I could spit nails."

CHAPTER 4

Lenoir City

LOUDEN COUNTY SHERIFF Marcellus Briskey sensed someone standing in front of his desk. He peered up from a folder of paperwork that had held his attention for the last several minutes. "Quill Rose, whatcha doin' in my town?"

He scooped a pile of wanted circulars out of a chair and motioned for Rose to sit. While the Blount County sheriff did, Briskey went over to the stove for the coffeepot. He poured his brew into a chipped porcelain cup and handed it to his guest.

Rose ran his thumb over the chipped area. "Still not got the fiscal court to buy you decent china for your company?"

"Hell, our county's broke. The depression's still on, didn'tcha know?"

"Marcellus, you just need the hoochmakers we've got. I capture a still, I get to sell the equipment and keep the money for the department."

"Uh-huh. Quill, you drove twenty miles over here and not because you love my coffee. What kin I do ya fer?" Briskey poured a cup for himself before he returned to his chair.

Rose studied the big man. Briskey, sloppy fat, gave the impression of someone who wasn't overly bright and certainly not ambitious, but he was a friendly soul who knew everyone in his county. That had gotten him through four bitterly fought elections.

Rose handed him the letter Stanley had found. "Know the name on the envelope?"

"H.W. Noland. Wild Willy? Yeah, we shipped him and his family over to yer county a couple weeks ago. What about him?"

"He's dead. So's his wife and little girl."

"Oh gawd. What happened?"

"Knife attack in the house where they were living."

"Know who done it?"

"Not a clue. It can't be anybody local. They'd not lived there long enough to get anybody riled. Thought maybe you could tell me something about who these people were."

Briskey went to rubbing at his stubbly whiskers. "A lot of people over here was mad at Wild Willy. Gawd, he drank a lot, always in fights. He was forever walking around with a busted fist or a blackened eye."

The Louden sheriff came forward. He wagged a finger in Rose's face. "Toby Shockton whacked off part of the old boy's ear once. Caught Wild Willy in bed with his wife. How about them apples?"

"You think Shockton could have killed him and the family?"

"Not likely. Toby got roarin' drunk and tried to stop a train. We buried what pieces we could find of him in the churchyard down at Friendship."

Rose leaned back. He threw one leg across his knee. "Anyone else you think might have killed Noland?"

"Not really, but I knew somebody was gonna do him some real damage if he continued to stay around here."

Briskey pulled a half-gallon crockery jug from beneath his desk. He uncorked the jug and held it out to Rose.

Rose waved it off, so Briskey poured a splash in his own cup. "Month ago, I had a heart-to-heart with Wild Willy. I told him if he didn't move on, I was gonna jail 'im." Briskey sipped the coffee/whiskey mix. "This is good stuff, Quill."

"He took you serious?"

"Yup. I heard he'd rented a farm over your way. I went out to the place where he and his family had been living, to check it out, and they was gone. Wasn't a stick there. I was happy to be shed of him, I'll tell ya that."

Briskey sipped again at his high-octane coffee. "I'll tell ya what I'll do. I'll nose around some. If one of our boys killed Wild Willy, he's gonna brag about it."

Rose rubbed the calf of his leg. "There's an odd thing about the murders."

"What's that?"

"Whoever did them, he cut the right hand off each person."

"Oh Jesus. What do ya think it was, anger? Maybe the killer didn't have a right hand of his own?"

ROSE SAILED HIS HAT across the office, ringing it over the top of the coat tree in the corner.

Tommy Jenks looked up. "How'd it go in big little city of Lenoir City?"

"Well, apparently everybody who knew our dead man hated him. Even Marcellus told him to get out of the county. That's how he came to move his family in on Pistol Creek."

Jenks shuffled reports from one pile on his desk to another. "You think somebody over there came over here and killed him?"

"It's the only thing that makes sense. Marcellus is going to shake the bushes for us. If it was someone from his county, he'll find him."

"Or her. I still think it could be a woman."

Rose paged through the notes by the telephone on the front counter. "Noland's wife was a good enough person, Marcellus said. Noland, he was a brawler, so it seems likely it was a man wanting to square an old score."

"Quill, I hate to be the one to tell you, but the fiscal court wants to see you."

A pained expression came across Rose's face, like he had a toothache. "What's got the squires' backs up now?"

"They wouldn't say. But they weren't too happy to find you weren't here."

"Meeting upstairs?"

"As usual."

Rose checked himself in the glass of the door. He straightened his necktie and suit coat before he proceeded out into the hallway.

County Clerk Grainger Murphy leaned out from his office. "You in trouble, Quill? The judges was breathin' fire when they come by."

"You sure?"

"Singed my deputy when she got in their track."

Rose scratched at his mustache, trying to think who he might have offended. On the stairs, he met the register of deeds.

Fred Mapes stared at Rose. "Quill, you got your gun?"

"Left it in my desk drawer. Why?"

"The court's fixing to have it out with you."

"What about?"

"Wouldn't say." Mapes hurried away.

Rose sighed and went on. He stopped at last at the door to the court's meeting room. There he rapped on the glass.

"Yeah?" came a voice from inside.

"It's the sheriff." Rose heard the scraping of chair legs on the wooden floor.

"Rose, get in here!"

He opened the door and stepped over the threshold.

Clarence McMahan–known to most as Mitch–waved from where he sat at the head of the table. "Come on, come on, Sheriff. Lollygagging at the door, you're only postponing the pain."

A distinguished man, some would say dapper–Clayton Johnson, the lieutenant governor of the state–pushed back from the table and got to his feet. He wore a tailored suit that appeared to have been freshly pressed. "Boys, you've got business, so I'll be on my way."

McMahan took out a tin of snuff and laid it on the table. "You come back, visit anytime, Clay."

"You know I'm going to run again, so I expect you all to say good words for me."

"Count on it."

Others around the table murmured their agreement.

Johnson came up to Rose, to shake hands, reaching out in that automatic way of a professional politician. He pulled Rose in close and spoke so no one at the table behind him could hear. "They're laying for you, Quill."

"So I heard."

"You can always quit this. You and Sis, you should come to Nashville. I can get you a state job."

"No thanks. This is home."

"Just a thought." Clayton Johnson, brother to Quill Rose's wife, Martha, a Blount County native son now living in Shelbyville, took two Panatellas from his breast pocket. He slipped them into Rose's breast pocket.

"You know I don't smoke," Rose said.

"Give them to somebody who does."

"All right. I need to know what brings you here."

"Business."

"You'll have supper with Martha and me, tell me all about it then?"

"Sorry, I've got to get on down to Chattanooga. You give my best to Sis and that new little boy you have."

"You know about that?"

Johnson gave a thumbs-up, then excused himself one more time from the fiscal court, called the county commission north of the Ohio River. He slipped out the door, leaving Rose to ease his way towards a chair.

McMahan glowered. "You two jabbered on a lot."

"Clayton and I, we're family."

"As well we know. Sheriff, don't bother to sit down 'cause we're about to burn your bee-hind."

"I take it you're feeling kinda nasty."

McMahan thumbed through a stack of papers. He pulled out one and thumped it on the table. "Gawddammit, Quill, you can't go around spending the county's money for clothes for strangers."

"Mitch, are you afraid you'll have to skip a meal at county expense if I go over budget?"

"Don't you go getting uppity with me."

Rose leaned a hand on the table. "Is this about the Noland family?"

"Gawddamn right it is."

"Mitch, they're poor. They deserve something better than rags to be buried in."

McMahan's eyebrows jammed together in a solid line of fury. "Then send the damn bill to Louden County. That's where they come from."

"Mitch, they lived here, maybe not long enough to vote in an election. But, by God, they lived here, and that makes them our responsibility."

"That's not the way we see it." McMahan hauled over his can of snuff. He stuffed a wad in his cheek and worked the wad like an angry bull. "You go on trying to commit us to expenses like this and we'll have you up for malfeasance."

"Can you spell the word?"

"Gawddammit, Quill, that's enough."

Rose went straight to the chairman. He snatched the bill from his hand. "I'll buy the clothes."

He stalked to the door, but came back before he got there. "Mitch, I'm like Clayton. I answer to the voters, not to you. I've been sent here six times by vote totals bigger than you've ever had. You and your miserly cohorts, you sicken me. Don't be surprised if the Tuckaleechee sends up a clean government candidate against you in the next go-round."

"You threatening me?"

"Mitch, you've known me, what now, twelve years? You know I never threaten." Rose stepped out through the doorway. He pulled the door closed, then stood there, waiting for what he knew was coming.

Something banged against the door and fell to the floor.

Rose smiled. He fairly danced down the stairs and on outside, trotting on the three blocks to Proffitts, a mammoth department store that filled half a city block, the building with its ornate front two-stories high. There he went upstairs to the offices, to the woman at the first desk. "J.C. here?"

"Inside."

"Anyone with him?"

"No, you can go in, Sheriff."

Rose rapped at the door, then leaned in.

J.C. Proffitts stood and waved to Rose. "Let me guess. You're here to pay a bill."

"How can you tell?"

"There's smoke rising from your suit. The fiscal court burned you bad, didn't they?"

"Those cheap—"

"Quill, cheap or no, they've kept this county afloat where other counties around us are flat busted."

"It doesn't make me like them any better."

"I know. Well, sit down. I told Roy I didn't want to send that bill to the courthouse, but he insisted. He said that's what you wanted."

"Yeah, is my check good?" Rose pulled a pad of checks from his inside pocket.

"You know it is."

"Well, I thank you for that." He scratched out the numbers from the bill, then handed the bill and the check to Proffitts.

After the store owner accepted them, he pressed a button on a box on his desk. "Tweets?"

"Yes," came a voice from the box.

"Would you come in for a moment?"

"Right now?"

"Tweets, did I ask you to come tomorrow? Yes, right now."

A man wearing a green eyeshade and black protectors on the sleeves of his white shirt opened a side door. Proffitts held the check and bill out to him. "Would you post this, Tweets?"

"Surely, Mister Proffitts." The store's bookkeeper took the two items and disappeared back into his office.

Proffitts settled back in his chair. "Quill, I don't know how it is around your shop, but here I have to beg people to do a little work."

"You know that's not true."

"Well, with Tweets it is, but he's such a good numbers man. We bring in auditors every year to go over our books and everything's perfect. They go out shaking their heads, just knowing that they had to have missed something. One time, one time they thought they caught Tweets until he pointed out a mistake in their own arithmetic."

"An honest man like that ought to be working for the county."

"Quill, I'll never let the boys down at the courthouse get him away from me." Proffitts came forward to his desk. He cupped his hand under his chin. "I understand your brother-in-law's in town. I also understand you've got a little child."

Rose chuckled. "You do have spies everywhere. Clayton? Now I didn't even know he was coming, and now he's on his way to Chattanooga."

"Must be nice having a high muckety-muck in the family."

"Gets Martha and me an invitation to the governor's inauguration–and two cigars." Rose pulled the Panetellas from his pocket. "You want them?"

"Ooo, now I thank you." Proffitts passed one of the cigars beneath his nose. He inhaled the aroma. "This is quality, my friend."

"Nothing but the best for Clayton. As to the child, on that one Martha insisted."

"Good for her. You two deserve children. Quill, I expect you'll be a good pap." Proffitts snipped the ends off the cigar. "How's your murder case coming?"

"Not a thing." Rose moved over to Proffitts's couch where he took up residence. On the wall above the couch was a framed map of Blount, Knox, and Sevier counties that showed the mountains separating the three county seats. Half of those mountains fell inside the Great Smoky Mountains National Park, a federal project Rose had initially opposed.

"Quill, did you know my granddaddy started this business?" Proffitts struck a match and held the flame to the end of his cigar. He puffed away until he had a good burn going. "He was a peddler, traipsing through the mountains on the map there, selling needles and thread out of a backpack. Did you know we still employ a few peddlers?"

"That I did not."

"Not everyone can come to Maryville or even to Townsend, to Grumble Jones's store."

"Why are you telling me this?"

"There's one I think you ought to see. Have you got the time?"

"Sure."

Proffitts pressed the button on his box. "Tweets?"

"Yes?"

"Sam Berry still with you?"

"I'm just balancing him out."

"Would you send him in, please?"

"Now?"

"Tweets."

"Mister Berry, Mister Proffitts wants to see you," Tweets said, the box in his office picking him up.

A second voice came from the box, more distant than the bookkeeper's. "I heard."

"He's on his way, Mister Proffitts."

"Thank you, Tweets." Proffitts took his thumb off the button.

The side door opened a second time. In stepped a stout, hard-muscled man only slightly taller than the bookkeeper, his face burned a deep brown from long days in the sun.

Rose stood and reached out to shake hands. But rather than a right, it was a left hand that latched onto

Rose's hand. Rose peered at it. "You wouldn't be the one they call 'One-Arm,' would you?"

"The same. Lost my arm at the Alcoa mill. Mister Proffitts here was good enough to give me a job after that."

"Quill, Sam is one of my best men, gets us a lot of business we wouldn't have if he weren't out there, driving the back roads and up into the hollows." Proffitts gestured for Berry to take the chair next to his desk.

Berry turned the chair slightly, the better to see Rose.

"Go ahead, Sam. Tell him what you told me."

"Sheriff, I hear things when I'm making my rounds."

"I expect you do, Mister Berry."

"And I get into areas of the county you don't get into, even in election years."

"Well, there are a few I skip because no one there votes." Rose leaned back into the deep comfort of the couch. "They won't even come out for the candidates who spread money around."

Proffitts shook his head. "Vote buying in our county? Shocking."

Rose raised an eyebrow.

Proffitts winked and blew a ring of smoke into the air.

Berry rested his one hand on his knee. "Word is down by Tallassee someone's pulling the shiners together to build a still to rival a factory. They intend to move supplies in on the river and hooch out on the same boats, upstream to where the river goes under the Four-Eleven bridge."

Rose scratched at his mustache. "Strange."

"Not really. If what I hear is right, they intend to load the hooch onto trucks and run it north and south."

"Oh?"

"A big bunch of that that's going north is to go on to Nashville." Berry bobbed his head, giving the impression he was sure of what he was saying.

"Hooking west on Seventy at Knoxville?"

"Uh-huh. Word is these people will be able to make the hooch so cheap and in such volume they expect to get most of the business in east and central Tennessee."

"Hmm. They'll have to be big and have a lot of money behind them. Do you have any names?"

"Nobody mentions names."

Rose parked his elbows on his knees, the fingers of his hands knitting together except for his index fingers. They touched one another at the tips. "Mister Berry, if I were to build an illegal still where people with badges would be reluctant to go, I'd put it up in one of those hollows under Shingle Mountain. There's a good two-lane road up in there that doesn't belong to the county. Buy off the right people and nobody would be the wiser."

"Word is that's where it's going."

"Have you been up there?"

"I've been warned off."

"You're smart to stay out."

"Are you going in, Sheriff?"

Rose straightened his jacket. "Oh, I'm like you, Mister Berry. I'm smart, too."

"Then they're going to get away with it?"

"Let's let them think so."

Chapter 5

Squirrel hunt

TOMMY JENKS OPENED THE DOOR of his decade-old pickup truck, a black Dodge his father had once owned, and whistled for his dog.

The hound came loping around the house. When the dog saw the open door, he charged for it and leaped, all four paws splayed out, hit down on the bench seat, and slid all the way across to the driver's side.

Jenks closed the door, but the hound scrambled back, to get his head out the window. He slobbered on the deputy's face.

Jenks jerked away, raking his sleeve across his cheek. "Ajax, you are one kissy dog."

He picked up the Twenty-Two rifle he had left leaning against the fender. Jenks pulled back the bolt to satisfy himself the chamber was empty, then pushed the bolt forward, and locked it down.

Rifle in hand, he strolled to the driver's side of the truck. Jenks chucked the gun under the seat, but when he attempted to get in, a shoving match ensued to determine who would sit behind the steering wheel, dog or man.

Jenks won, but not before Ajax sworped his tongue across the deputy's face a second time, crowding him still.

Jenks, with his rump, gave the dog one last mighty shove to get a little room for himself.

He pumped away at the accelerator, to push gas up into the carburetor.

Jenks's father swore by the Detroit Dodge brothers. Jenks swore at them. His father said those Dodge boys knew how to build trucks so they'd start every time. He was so confident of that he threw away the crank that had come with the truck.

Jenks stepped on the starter, and the motor burped.

He tried it again—the pumping the accelerator business, the stepping on the starter—and this time the motor burst to life, roaring like a caged animal trying to get out. Jenks bumped the truck up onto the pavement of State Four-Eleven and drove away with his elbow out the window, enjoying the spring air.

Ajax, at the other window, leaned far out into the breeze, riding that way for all the twelve miles to the Little Tennessee River.

A half-mile short, Jenks wheeled the pickup off the highway. He trundled the truck across a rough field and into a small grove of black oak trees well away from passing traffic. There he cut the motor and reached across Ajax to push the passenger door open. Jenks wasn't fast enough. The dog kissed him again before he bounded out of the truck.

Jenks got out with his the rifle. He chambered a shell as he let out a sharp whistle for his dog. Ajax came crashing out of the brush in answer, and Jenks slapped the brindle hound on the shoulders. "Come on, pooch, let's go get us a squirrel."

The dog's head snapped up at the word.

"That's right, boy—squirrel. Time to go to work."

They made their way out of the grove and into the scrubby brush, aiming for a patch of woods beyond. The squirrels had long been out of their winter nests, so Jenks intended to sharpen his marksmanship on the varmints and, in the process, bring down enough for a gem of a stew. And if he didn't get any squirrels, he told himself, at least he'd have given Ajax a good run.

In the hour they walked the fields and woods, Jenks knocked a red and a gray out the trees, hitting both in the head.

Jenks eventually came out on the marshy ground that bordered the Little Tennessee. He whistled for Ajax, and he and the dog worked their way south toward the highway. They'd gone less than a quarter of a mile when Jenks saw a dock jutting out into the river from the far shore.

Here, too, he came on a johnboat a fisherman had pulled up in the reeds and left for his next trip on the water.

Jenks decided to borrow the boat. He bent down, to put his rifle in, and stopped. A water moccasin laid coiled on the board seat, soaking up the morning sun. Jenks prodded the snake with the end of his rifle, but the moccasin, possessive of its place, struck at the rifle barrel.

Jenks worked the barrel under the snake, then whipped it into the air. He flung the snake as far out into the river as he could, the snake twisting and rolling before it splashed down.

"Ajax, into the boat. Where there's one snake, there's a pair. Let's get out of here before the other comes by."

The dog jumped across the gunwale.

Jenks threw his rifle and his squirrel sack in. He shoved the boat into the water and made his own leap into the boat. After he settled himself on the board seat that had been the moccasin's, he reached down for the oars, oars that weren't there.

Jenks searched around for something else he could use, but found nothing. However, the boat had two board seats, and Jenks needed only one, so he slammed his fist down on the end of the second seat. He slammed his fist down again, and the end came loose.

Jenks wrenched the seat free.

He dipped the board into the water as one would a paddle, jerking the boat left, then right as he alternated sides with his board. Jenks paddled until he figured he had the boat a safe distance north. He turned the boat into the current and paddled for all he was worth, to get across the river before the current carried the boat past the mystery dock.

Dip, pull, switch sides–dip, pull, switch sides–sweat soaking through his shirt as he worked.

Jenks broke the boat free of the current and slid it into an eddy that curled toward the western shore.

He rested, panting, puffing out his cheeks. After some moments, he nosed the johnboat into the reeds and paddled hard until the bow pushed up onto the river's muddy bank. Jenks tossed the board aside. He stepped over the bow and hauled the boat out of the water.

He raised a finger when the dog got to his feet. The dog whined, but settled back on his haunches.

Jenks got his rifle and worked his way west, out of the reeds, pushing to get to solid ground before he turned south. Twenty yards on, he came out into a brushy field, similar to the field on the other side of the river.

Jenks estimated he was three-quarters a mile from the highway when he moved south, and then he saw it, a corrugated-tin building near the edge of the reeds, partially masked by a grove of honey locust trees.

Jenks continued on. He angled through the brush toward the closest trees. When he stepped inside the first line of locusts, a click sounded behind him, and a voice.

"Set the rifle on the ground, feller. Do it now or I shoot ya dead afore you kin give it a second think."

Jenks leaned down. He was about to let go of the Twenty-Two when he heard a deep-throated growl.

"Ajax!"

The hound leaped from the brush. He slammed against the stranger.

Jenks spun around. As he did, he swung his rifle like a club, into the man's ribs. The blow threw the man back on the spikes growing from the bark of a honey locust tree, impaling him. The man screamed.

Jenks grabbed him by the front of the coat. He yanked him off the spikes and hammered his face until the man went limp. Jenks let go of him, and he crumpled to the ground.

Ajax, panting hard, bumped up against Jenks, and Jenks slap-patted him. "Buddy, you sure saved my hide. But where there's one, there's a pair. We gotta get outta here."

Jenks caught sight of the man's pistol a ways off in the brush. He scooped the gun up and stuffed it in his belt, then rolled the man onto his stomach to cuff his hands behind him. The man leaked red from a dozen punctures.

"Gawd, what a mess."

Jenks hefted the wounded man up onto his shoulder. He gathered in his rifle and, with Ajax at his heels, hurried away, back into the brush field, back north toward the boat.

JENKS SHOVED HIS WAY through Doc Stanley's outer office, giving a quick nod to the two women sitting at the side, reading Collier's magazines. "'Scuse me, Missus

Briggs, Missus James, but this old boy needs a mite of attention."

Jenks patted the fanny of the man he carried over his shoulder.

Disappointment etched deep into Minnie Briggs's face. "Deputy, I been waitin' a half hour."

Darcey James, though, took an intense interest in the stains on the man's jacket and pants. Then she saw the handcuffs. "Who you got there? Anyone we know?"

"Heck fire, Missus James, I don't know. All I know is he wanted to kill me."

"Ooooo."

"Now, Missus James, don't you go yakkin' that around town."

"Why not?"

"All right, I'll tell ya. This man is Muggs Olafson– 'Machine Gun' Muggs Olafson, the crazy Norwegian. You heard of him?"

Minnie Briggs's eyes widened.

"He's from Memphis. If word gets out we've got him, his gang's gonna shoot up Maryville to get him back."

"Ooooo."

Darcey James and Minnie Briggs peered at one another, then at Jenks and the handcuffed and bleeding prisoner. Darcey James put a finger beside her nose. "Trust me, Tommy. This will be just between the three of us."

"Got yer word on that?"

"Why?"

"Have I got yer word?"

"Tommy–"

"Yer word?"

"Oh, all right. Min and I won't tell a soul. Cross our hearts."

Jenks gave the two women the hairy eyeball, then pushed on into Stanley's inner office.

Stanley looked up from the boy in the chair in front of him. "Tommy, the body you got there, is it alive or dead?"

"Alive."

"Oh for shame. It means I'm not gonna get paid for working on him. Put him on the table." Stanley clamped a hand on his patient's shoulder. "All right, W.C., put your hand out."

The towheaded boy did, and Stanley dropped a steel bearing into it. "How'd you get this up your nose?"

The boy shrugged.

"We were lucky this time, W.C. Next time, I may not be able to fish it out. Now you go on outta here."

The boy hopped off the chair. "Ma says I should say thank you."

"And indeed you should."

The boy backed his way toward the door. "Well, thank you."

"W.C., stop right there."

"Yessir?"

"I don't want to see you again ever, unless you're dying."

"Yessir." The boy wheeled around. He dashed out, throwing the door closed behind him.

Jenks stared at the door, then at Stanley. "He really ram that thing up his nose?"

"His nose, his ears, in his mouth. W.C.'s swallowed the strangest things. I'm afraid of what I'll have to do if some kid gives him a baseball and dares him to stuff it where the sun don't shine."

Stanley scribbled a note before he came over to the table. "What've we got?"

"Someone who didn't take a liking to me."

"I see. Want to take the cuffs off him?"

Jenks unlocked the manacles and pocketed them.

Stanley lifted the man's coat. "What's all this blood from his back and butt?"

"Well, it's this way. He sorta fell into a honey locust tree."

"Ooo, I'll bet that hurt. Some of those stickers get to be four inches long. You help him into that tree?"

"A bit, yes, me and Ajax. The fella came up behind me with a gun."

"Anything else?"

"I may have stove in his ribs."

"Which side?"

"Left."

Stanley ran his fingers under the man's arm and around toward his chest. "Oh, yes, you did a fine job. I can feel three busted. How long's he been out?"

"Since I hit him, oh, couple hours ago."

"Well, give me a hand cutting his clothes away, and I'll clean him up. Doesn't look like he's leaking anymore."

Stanley got a scissors from a drawer in a side cabinet. He snipped up the back of the coat. "Know who he is?"

"Not an idea."

"Then why did you tell that cock-and-bull story to the women out there? I heard you through the door."

Jenks lowered his volume. "I've got an idea who he works for. If those two hens were to go talking it up, the word would get back, and we might never catch the ones we want."

"How much you want to bet they keep quiet?"

"Doc, makes no nevermind if they do blab it around. I gave 'em a hellacious lie."

"Does Quill know what you've got?"

"I'd better call him."

"Phone's on my desk." Stanley got a pan of hot water and a gauze pad. He washed the dried blood away from the edges of the wounds.

Jenks picked up the receiver. He clicked the line several times to get the local operator.

"May Ella, it's Tommy. Would you put me through to the sheriff's office?...Thank you, hon. How's Everett? You got him out digging in the garden yet?...Uh-huh...Yes, I hear it ringing.

"Quill? Hunting was better than I expected. I'm over at Doc's, showing him what I bagged. A real trophy. Maybe you'd like to come over and see for yourself."

ROSE STARED AT THE MAN lying on his stomach on Stanley's examining table. "For a squirrel, I'd say he's record size. Any idea who he is?"

"Nope. No wallet on him. Just this." Jenks held up a playing card.

"Jack of Spades?"

"Maybe it's left over from a poker game, but not this knife. I found this in his boot top."

Rose examined the weapon, a leather-wrapped handle, the blade six inches long. "This is some pig sticker."

"'Course, I got his gun." Jenks pulled that from his belt.

"Uh-huh, a Forty-Five. Very nice. I'd say this boy was expecting company, wouldn't you? How'd you come to catch him?"

Stanley stitched closed one of the more vicious of the puncture wounds. "Yes, that's what I'd like to know."

"Actually, Quill, he caught me. Ajax jumped him, and that gave me my chance. I banged him into a honey locust."

"That explains the holes Doc's working on."

Jenks leaned against a counter. "The building's right where we thought it'd be, only it's on the west bank. Door was open, and I could make out a tractor and what looked to be a tank trailer, gasoline markings I think. Ajax and me, we skedaddled before anybody else stumbled on us."

The man moaned.

Stanley snipped the thread free of the knot that held a stitch secure. "He's coming out of it. Good thing. I've got to tape his ribs, and I can't do that with him laying on his belly."

Rose leaned down to the man's face. "Can you talk?"

"Uhhhnnth, hurt—"

"I expect you do."

"Let's sit him up, Quill. Give me a hand."

Rose and Stanley got their hands under the man's arms and started to lifted, the man wincing, groaning.

"We're going to get you up on your butt, mister. Swing your legs over. That's it. You got some busted ribs, so I've got to tape you up." Stanley prodded Jenks into his place. "Get him out of his shirt and hold his arms up."

Stanley went to a cabinet drawer for a wide roll of adhesive tape. He pulled the end free and slapped it on the man's back, then whipped the tape around the man's rib cage.

"Uuuhhhhh, hurts."

"You've got a whole load of hurt, mister." Stanley whipped the tape around the man a second time.

Rose looked deep into the man's eyes. "What's your name, fella?"

"Who wants ta know?"

Rose flipped over the lapel of his suit coat, revealing a badge.

"I got nuthin' to say."

"Maybe you'd rather talk to my deputy here. He brought you in."

"Hell with him."

"What were you doing down by the river?"

"Fishin'."

"With a Forty-Five?"

"Don't need no bait with a gun."

Rose showed him the playing card. "What's this mean?"

"Don't know."

"And this knife?"

"Clean fish with it."

Stanley yanked down on the tape.

"Eeeyeah!"

"Mister, you have to forgive Doc. He doesn't like a smart mouth. Suppose you try answering my questions the right way."

The man jutted his jaw out. "Hell with you."

Stanley yanked the tape again.

"Ooohh!"

"Well?"

"You ain't gettin' nuthin' from me."

Stanley ripped the tape away from the roll. He slapped the end over the man's broken ribs.

"Heyy!"

"Maybe Tommy should have left you spiked to that locust tree."

"Doc, you about done with him?"

"Oh, I'm done. But I could do some more things to him, if you want, maybe poke up his bung hole for hemorrhoids."

"No, you've given him enough pain for the day. Come on, fella, we've got you a room over at our jail." Rose and Jenks helped the man to his feet.

"You gonna take me out with no shirt and my ass hangin' out?"

Rose glanced behind the man, at the great sections of his pants Stanley and Jenks had cut away. "Would be a bit breezy."

"Hell yes."

"Doc, you got a blanket we can wrap him in?"

"I'm thinking of calling Jens over at the Times, to get a picture from behind of you three walking up the street. That'd look great on the front page."

"Doc—"

"All right." Stanley pulled out another drawer. He took a blanket from it and tossed it to Rose.

Rose and Jenks proceeded to wrap the man up like a mummy.

Rose jabbed his thumb in the direction of the door to the waiting room. "Now are you going to give me a hard time out there?"

The man clamped his jaws tight.

"If you do, I'll shoot you with your own gun. Then I'll drag you back in here for Doc to patch you up, again."

"Keep that sumbitch away from me."

"Tommy, I think he's telling us he's going to behave."

Stanley opened the door to his outer office, and Rose and Jenks led the man out, but Darcey James stopped them.

"Oooo, Sheriff, can we see Mister Machine Gun's face?"

CHAPTER 6

Shakedown

ROSE KEPT THE MAN with no name until Stanley said
he was fit to travel. Then he made a telephone call, Rose
leaning close to his phone's mouthpiece. "Marcellus, I've
got a favor to ask. I've got a fella in my jail that I have to
get out of town. Can I put him in your lockup?"

WHILE JENKS DROVE the prisoner to Lenoir City,
Rose again had his telephone's receiver pressed to his ear.
    "Quill, I got something I think you oughtta see," said
the voice at the other end of the line.
    "What's that, Od?"
    "I stopped a gas tanker comin' through town, and I
don't think it is what it is. What's more, the driver's not
talkin'."
    "Where are you?"
    "Across the street from the Jiffy Market."
    "I'll walk on over."
    Od–J.D. Oddling–Maryville's town constable, was a
man not to be fooled with, yet people joked behind his
back because he had one eye that looked everywhere but
where a person stood when Oddling was talking to him.

He was a demon for enforcing the traffic laws. Oddling was forever pulling over old ladies for driving too slow or chasing down any of Maryville's several teenagers who had cars of their own, charging them with driving too fast. This driver had no brake lights, a sin against God and mankind in the eyes of the constable.

Oddling squared around to Rose. "I was behind him, not particularly interested in him. He stopped at the intersection—no brake lights. So I pulled around him, cut him off, ya see. I was gonna write him up a ticket and take him to the JP."

"So what's the problem?"

"Damn fool wanted to argue. So I stuck my gun in his face and cuffed him to his tanker. Well, I had him empty his pockets, an' I went through the cab of his truck, ya know. Guess what?"

"Are we playing Twenty Questions?"

"Quill, have you got no imagination? The man's got no driver's license—nuthin'—except this and a revolver."

Oddling handed Rose a playing card and a long-barreled Thirty-Eight.

Rose stuffed the gun in his belt, then turned the card face up. "Jack of Spades. Now you've got my attention. Let's take a look at this fella."

Oddling led Rose around to the back of the tanker where a man in faded bib overalls and a denim jacket sat on the bumper, his wrist handcuffed to one of the pipes that stuck out from the back of the rig.

Oddling jammed a finger under the man's jaw. "Mister, you give me a hard time, yer in trouble now. This is the sheriff." The constable's right eye studied the sign over the dentist's office across the sidewalk.

A sneer curled the man's lips. "I ain't talkin' to you, and I ain't talkin' to him."

Rose braced a foot against the bumper. "Well, friend, you're the second non-talker I've come on in the last several days."

"So?"

"Let's see how I can explain it. No driver's license, no brake lights, a concealed gun in your truck. If Od were to do some more poking around, I expect he could come up with three or four more charges, then take you to the justice of the peace."

"So?"

"Now I know old Abner, and he doesn't like drivers endangering the citizens of our town, particularly truck drivers. What do you say, Od, Abner'd fine him three hundred dollars?"

"Oh, at least. Maybe even four hunnerd."

"And, mister, since Od didn't find any money on you, Abner'd give you to me, and you'd become a resident in my jail. What're you hauling in this rig?"

"Gasoline."

"Where you going?"

"Nashville."

Rose took his foot down from the bumper. He stood there considering, then rapped on the metal of the tank. "Sounds full. What've you got in there, about four thousand gallons?"

"About that."

"Od could confiscate your load, sell it easy for ten cents a gallon. Get your fine that way."

The man glared at Oddling. "You wouldn't."

"Try me."

Rose aimed his pointer finger at a wet area on the pavement. "Did you know you've got a leak there?" He got down on one knee, to inspect the underside of the truck. Rose saw a plate bolted to the bottom of the tank.

He ran his hand along the edges and felt a liquid beading up.

Rose brought his hand out. He sniffed it. "Mister, this isn't gasoline."

Rose touched the tips of his fingers to his tongue. "Oh Lord, straight alcohol. Od, I think we've got us a tank of hooch."

Oddling rubbed his hands as if he were anticipating something excellent. "That's federal. That's prison time."

Rose wiped his hand dry with a handkerchief. "Suppose you tell us what's going on."

The man's gaze darted to the handcuffs, then to Rose's badge. "I'm just tryin' to make a livin', keep my family off the dole." His voice cracked.

"Aren't we all."

"Look, they hired me to drive this load to Nashville, that's all. Paid me top dollar."

"So you knew it wasn't gasoline."

"I had my suspicions. That's why I brought my revolver. But I wuddn't dumb enough to ask."

"Where'd you pick up the truck?"

"A building down by the Little Tennessee."

"Tell you what, mister, we're kind of interested in that building. You want to stay out of my jail?"

"Yeah, sure."

"Here's what you're going to do." Rose motioned for Oddling to unlock the handcuffs. "We're going over to the justice of the peace, and you're going to make a telephone call."

"I am?"

"Yessir, to the man who hired you. You're going to tell him he's got to come up here and bail you out or this wild-eyed constable is going to confiscate your truck."

"What if he won't?"

"Oh, you've got about three thousand dollars of alkie in that tanker. He'll come."

ROSE BRIEFED Abner Huskey, Maryville's justice of the peace who, every fifteen seconds, chased his children out of his front-parlor courtroom. When Huskey had had enough, he bellowed, "You kids come bustin' in here one more time and I'm gonna give you to the sheriff to take off to jail."

The children ducked away.

Huskey leaned hard against his cabinet of law books. "Now where were we, Quill?"

"I was telling you I want you to let this fella make a phone call, to his boss, to tell him there's a three-hundred-dollar fine that's got to be paid here or you and Od are going to confiscate his load of gasoline."

"But it's not gasoline."

"We know that, but we're not going to let on we know that."

"Ohhhh, I see. I see." Huskey swung about to the slope-shouldered man lounging next to Oddling. "Well, mister, go ahead. Make your call. Use the phone at my desk there in the corner."

"It's long distance."

"Well, damn, reverse the charges then. I'm not gonna pay for your call."

Rose raised a finger.

"Well, I'm not."

"Abner."

"All right, if I can get three hundred for the city, I guess maybe I can afford to pay it. Fella, you ask May Ella to put it through for you."

The man put the receiver to his ear. He clicked the phone several times to get the operator's attention, then turned his back to Rose and the others and spoke low to May Ella Wilson, co-owner and operator of the local telephone company. He turned back while he waited for the call to go through. The man tugged at the collar of his shirt.

"Hello," he said into the mouthpiece. "This is Clifford...Yeah, well, I'm in Maryville...The constable stopped me for no brake lights and no driver's license. I know I wasn't supposed to call, but he's got me at the JP's house, and the JP's fined me three hunnerd dollars–"

He put his hand over the mouthpiece. "He thinks I'm tryin' to jack him up."

Huskey ripped the receiver and phone from the driver's hands.

"Look you yahoo," he barked into the mouthpiece, "I don't give a diddly damn who you are. I got your driver, and I got your truck. You get your fanny up here with the money or I sell the gasoline to the Standard station...Yessir, Three Twenty-one Elm Street. You can't miss it. Your truck'll be parked out front."

Huskey clamped his hand over the mouthpiece. "You can bring the truck around, can't you, Quill?"

Rose winked.

Huskey again directed his voice into the telephone. "Forty-five minutes? I'll be here. Mister, you an' me, we're gonna get along just fine."

Rose shook his head, a smile tugging at the corner of his mouth. "Abner, you sure are convincing."

"It's easy when you know you're holdin' a full house and the other guy's only got a pair of duces. What else do you want, Quill?"

"Have you ever wanted to be a crooked judge?"

ODDLING STOOD peering out the front window of
Abner Huskey's house. "We got company."

A man in a black suit and slouch hat got out of the
driver's side of a mud-spattered Buick that had pulled up
on the far side of the street. He walked in front of the
tanker truck, eying it as he moved up onto the walk that
led to the justice of the peace's house. At the house, he
knocked on the front door.

Oddling opened it.

The man, big compared to the constable, glared at
him, then stepped around him. When he was inside, he
raised a fist to his driver. To Huskey, he pointed. "You the
JP?"

"Yup, Abner Huskey's the name. You gonna need a
receipt for the fine money?"

"Paper just clutters things up. Three hundred dollars?"

"Three hundred."

The man took out a roll of bills from his pants
pocket. He snapped off six fifties into Huskey's hand.
"That's it? We can go now?"

"Oh no, not just yet."

"Why not? We paid."

"That's just for today. Look, mister, just between you,
me, my constable, and the fence post, I know what you've
really got in that truck."

"Gasoline."

"Maybe in the top compartment. But in the belly
tank, you got booze, hooch, moonshine, white lightning,
corn whiskey."

The man's face did not change. "So what if we do?"

"Well, you and I know it's not legal or you wouldn't
have it in a gas truck." Huskey sat back on the edge of his
desk, his arms crossed. "My constable and I figure that's

not the only truck you're gonna want to run through our town. We got that right?"

"Maybe, maybe not."

"What's it worth to you not to be bothered?"

The man took out a cigar. He crammed the end in the corner of his mouth. "Mind if I smoke?"

"In my house, yessirree, Billy-boy. If my wife was to smell that stogie, she'd skin us both."

The man rolled the cigar in his lips. "I can chew it, can't I?"

"Chewin's fine, but no spittin'. I was asking, what's it worth to you to not be bothered?"

"And you're going to tell me?"

"My constable and me, we'd like to retire someday. Isn't that right, Od?"

Oddling grinned.

"We were thinkin' maybe you'd like to contribute to our retirement fund, say ten dollars each for each truck that comes through."

The man rolled his cigar again. "You want to ding me twenty bucks a truck."

"We're not greedy. You're in this thing for the long pull. We are, too."

The man rocked back on his heels. He eyed Huskey. "We could come through at night and avoid you both."

"Well, yessir, you could." Huskey picked up his fine book. He carried it across the room to a glass-front bookcase and shelved it with his ordinance and statute books. "But I got a night constable, and he's a sonuvabitch. If I have to tell him what we got going, he's gonna want to be cut in. And he'll tell you night work's expensive."

The man studied the end of his cigar, the end he had not yet lit. "So how're we going to work this?"

Huskey came around his desk. He hoisted a haunch up on the edge of it. "You give your drivers the money and tell them to give it to Od when they drive into town or come by my house if they don't see him. We'll trust you. You see, if we figure you're tryin' to run by us, we'll take one of your trucks and sell the damn thing." Huskey looked hard at the man. "Can you afford to lose four thousand dollars of booze and two thousand dollars of truck?"

The man rolled his cigar and rolled it again.

"I didn't figure you could. You got people to answer to, people who wouldn't be happy if you lost a load and a truck."

"Are we done here?"

"Almost." Huskey folded his arms across his chest. "I like to know who I'm doin' business with. Take out your wallet and hand it to my constable."

The man slipped his hand into his inside coat pocket. As he did, Oddling lifted his revolver from his holster.

Huskey rubbed his chin as he gazed at the man. "You'll have to forgive my constable. He's a little concerned about what might come outta your jacket. Just make sure it's your wallet an' nuthin' else."

The man brought out his hand, in it a well-worn leather billfold.

Oddling snatched the wallet away. He tossed it to Huskey.

Huskey opened the wallet to the man's driver's license. "Uh-huh, it's Mister Dumkin, I see." He closed the billfold and held it out. "Always a pleasure, Mister Dumkin. You come by soon, now, ya hear."

Dumkin pocketed the billfold, then aimed his unlit cigar at his driver and the door, and the two men strolled out.

Huskey laughed up his sleeve. "You can come out now, Quill."

Quill Rose opened a second door, one that separated the front parlor from the back parlor. He came in, laughing, too. "Abner, you should've been on the stage."

"Oh, I was in my younger days, as a student up at the University of Tennessee. And damn good, too, I don't mind sayin' it. His name's Robert J. Dumkin. Chattanooga address on his license." Huskey scribbled it on a scrap of paper and handed it to Rose.

"Can I use your phone?"

"Sure. Not long distance, is it?"

"Lenoir City."

Huskey sighed. He wagged his head. "Quill, you're gonna break me, but go ahead."

Rose picked up the candlestick telephone. He clicked the receiver several times. "May Ella, would you get me the Louden County sheriff?"

Huskey stared at Rose. "Now what're you doin'?"

"Setting up to take that truck again."

CHAPTER 7

The hijack

MARCELLUS BRISKEY and a deputy planted themselves in the middle of the westbound lane of U.S. Seventy, each man cradling a shotgun, a tanker truck rolling their way.

Briskey waved his shotgun over his head, and the big rig slowed. It jigged toward the side of the road where it came to stop on the graveled shoulder.

Briskey strolled up to the door.

The driver leaned an elbow out his window. "Trouble, Sheriff?"

"Yeah, son. You better climb on down here."

The driver, thin and worn from having missed more than a few meals, swung the door open and slid down off the high seat.

Briskey gestured back up in the truck. "You got all yer papers fer this rig?"

"Want me to get 'em for ya?"

"Naw, that's all right. Just come up front here with my deputy."

"What's this about, Sheriff?"

"Well, let's see how I can explain this to you. I'm takin' you to jail, and I'm keepin' yer truck." Briskey laughed, his belly jiggling.

"Hey, this is the second time today you John Law guys have stuck me up."

"You don't say. You must be one popular fella. Put out your hands." Briskey jabbed the twin barrels of his shotgun in the man's gut.

The driver, perplexed, brought his hands out, and the deputy snapped manacles on the man's wrists.

Briskey stepped aside. He swung the barrels of his gun up against his shoulder. "How about you go along with Ed there an' take a comfortable seat in my car? I'll be with you in a bit."

The deputy led the driver away toward a Model T top-down touring car. The vehicle was a dozen years old, but Briskey liked the old wreck because it permitted him to spread his bulk out in the back seat while one of his deputies drove him wherever he needed to go. He'd had a bar welded across the dashboard, the better to handcuff prisoners to.

The deputy set the spark and throttle, then cranked the engine. When it caught, he ran around to the driver's side, hopped in, and rolled the band transmission into first gear. He waved as he bounced the car up onto the pavement.

Tommy Jenks came up out of the bushes, toting a sawed-off shotgun of his own.

Briskey let off with a grin half the size of Tennessee. "Tommy, I'd say this was pretty slick, wouldn't ya?"

"You're the master."

"Well, when yer as fat as I am, ya make a helluva roadblock."

"What do we do now?"

"Quill says we wait fer him, but it shouldn't be long." Briskey peered off to the east, a hand at his forehead, shading his eyes from the morning sun. "I'm guessin' that's yer cruiser comin' over the hill."

Jenks squinted in the same direction. "Appears so. 'Course, all black Fords look alike."

"Well, whoever it is, he's slowin'."

The approaching Ford's wheels dropped off the pavement, and the car coasted up behind the tanker. Quill Rose, in tan pants and a tan shirt, got out. He reached back in the car and brought out a slouch hat and a pasteboard suitcase. Rose beat some shape into the hat as he came forward. "You've not been waiting long, have you?"

"Oh, a couple minutes."

"Any trouble?"

"Not a whisper."

Rose opened the door of the tanker's cab. He shoved his suitcase up on the seat.

Briskey came over, the barrels of his shotgun still leaning against his shoulder. "You want to tell me what this is about, Quill?"

Rose stepped back. He gazed at the truck. "Handsome rig, isn't it? Marcellus, if you were to climb up there on top and open one of the hatches and look in, you'd smell and see gasoline. And there is down to about here."

Rose put hand about a third of the way down from the top of the tank, then tapped the side. "This sucker's got a false bottom. From here on down, it's all alcohol."

"Damn."

"They didn't even cut the stuff before they shipped it. So I expect there's a bottling factory in Nashville where they'll do that."

"You thinkin' of delivering the stuff?"

Rose slapped the tank again. "We've got the drop spot from the driver you bagged, the Sunspot Petroleum yard. Like it says on the tanker, 'Sunspot, best gasoline under the sun.' Probably the best booze, too."

"This could be a mite dangerous. Can't say I'd wanna do it."

"You don't have Tommy." Rose waved Jenks over. "He'll look after me. I'm just curious what's involved in this operation."

"Quill, I'm beginnin' ta think yer a couple bricks shy of a full load."

"Look, nobody at that end is going to know who Tommy and me are. I don't have any identification. I left my badge back at the office. I even left my gun. And Tommy's going to give you his wallet, badge, and revolver for safekeeping. But that short two-barrel of his, that we keep. That's our hole card."

Jenks handed Briskey his stuff.

Rose pushed his hands in his pockets. "You take our cruiser, too. Key's in it. Drive it as much as you want until we get back."

"And that'll be when?"

"Maybe three days."

Briskey ambled over to admire Rose's Ford. "Looks new. I wouldn't want some damn culprit to scratch a fender, so I'll park it behind the courthouse. Oh, and about the two prisoners of yers I got, I won't let 'em see one another."

"Appreciate that, Marcellus." Rose started toward the cab and Jenks the passenger's side. "When we get this thing sorted out, whatever it is, Tommy and me, we intend to take you out for a steak dinner."

Briskey slapped his belly hanging over his belt. "You better bring all yer paycheck, Quill Rose, and I do mean all of it."

Rose waggled his fingers at Briskey as he and Jenks climbed up in the cab. Rose glanced over the floor shift. Satisfied with it, he started the engine and pumped the accelerator a couple times before he rammed the shift lever into first gear.

Rose slapped on the side of the door to get Briskey's attention. "You take care now."

"You, too, Quill Rose."

He let out the clutch, and the truck rolled. Rose wrenched the steering wheel to the left and brought the truck up onto the highway. He jigged it up to forty-five miles an hour, a comfortable speed as the highway wound its way toward Kingston and the bridge over the Clinch River. Then came the grind, the fifteen-hundred-foot climb up out of the Great Tennessee Valley along switchbacks on the face of the Cumberland Plateau. Rose pulled those miles in first gear when not in super low.

Jenks patted the suitcase between them. "Whatcha got in here?"

"Nothing."

"Empty? Really?"

"Yup."

"Then why'd you bring it?"

"It might be useful."

"Quill, do you have any idea what you're doin'?"

Rose glanced in the side mirror. "Not the damnedest."

CHAPTER 8

Night in Gassaway

JENKS ROLLED HIS WINDOW down, to let the cold air of the night wash over his face while Rose, slumped in the right-hand seat, dozed.

Jenks fought against a yawn. He opened his eyes wide and shook his head, then relaxed, but only for a moment because headlights flashed and flashed again, headlights in his lane.

Jenks slapped Rose's leg.

"Huh? What?"

"Those lights up ahead, think we better stop?"

Rose rubbed the sand from his eyes before he squinted through the windshield. "Could be somebody in trouble."

Jenks took his foot off the accelerator and racked down through the gears.

Rose doubled himself forward. He reached for Jenks's shotgun on the floor. When he found it, he rammed it up under the seat, into the springs. He also hauled a roll of bills out of his pants pocket and jammed that up into the springs as well.

Jenks glanced over. "What was that?"

"A little money I borrowed from Abner Huskey. Three large. It's a long story for some other time."

The lights continued flashing as Jenks hauled the tanker to a stop. Then they burned steady. When Jenks saw a silhouette coming his way, he stuck his head out his window. "Trouble up there, mister?"

"Not at all. You know how fast you was goin' back there?"

"Fifty. Been holding it steady for the last ten miles."

"You blew through a thirty-mile speed zone back there. Know that?"

"I didn't see a sign."

"Figured as much or you woulda slowed down." The man stopped near the truck's door. He aimed a flashlight up into Jenks's face.

Jenks brought his hand up as a shield against the harsh light. "You a cop?"

"Yessir, Deputy Charlie Green, Cannon County."

"I'm a deputy. From Blount County, Tommy Jenks."

"You are now? Got a badge?"

"No sir."

"License or a card provin' who you are?"

"'Fraid not."

Green held his light higher, to illuminate Rose. "Uh-huh. And I s'pose that feller sittin' up there next to you, he's the sheriff of Blount County."

"That's right."

"He wouldn't happen to have a badge or somethin'?"

Rose leaned across the seat. "I left it back at the office."

"Why am I not surprised." Green played his flashlight down along the side of the tanker, along the Sunspot sign and logo. "You boys just wheelin' around up here on the plateau in this big shiny tanker, a heckuva long way from home? Tell you what. You better follow me to the jail, and we'll get the sheriff to sort this out."

Green brought the light back to the door, then up to Jenks.

Jenks cast a glance at Rose. "What do we do?"

"The sheriff can't be unreasonable. I say follow the deputy."

AT LIBERTY, GREEN, DRIVING a dust-covered Plymouth coupe, turned south on State Fifty-Three.

Jenks slowed the big truck. He made the turnoff after Green and came onto a highway that neither he nor Rose had intended to travel when they left Maryville back in the morning.

Five miles on and they came on a sign at the edge of a town, a sign that read 'Gassaway, population 78'.

Beyond the sign appeared to be a courthouse. Rose could also make out several stores, a café with an Esso pump out front, and a handful of houses, no lights anywhere until the deputy and Jenks made the turn onto a side street behind the courthouse. Ahead a light burned at the jail.

Jenks slid the big rig to the side of the street. He slowed as Green slowed, stopped as Green stopped. He let out a great lung full of air, the air ballooning his cheeks, as he shut down the truck and pocketed the key. He and Rose exchanged glances, then both climbed down. They shoved the truck's doors shut and shambled after Green, followed him inside, into the glare of the jail's one light.

They found it a stark place, a cold place that smelled of baloney and bread–last night's supper for someone. There was a desk, two chairs that had seen more civilized days, three cells at the back, and on the wall by the desk a calendar from the Bank of Gassaway.

Rose rubbed with both hands at the whiskers on the sides of his face, to better wake himself up. "I didn't see a bank."

"We haven't had one since 'Twenty-Nine. Look at the year on the calendar."

Rose did.

Nineteen Twenty-eight.

Green went over to the wall phone next to the calendar. He took down the receiver and cranked the handle in two long bursts.

"Sheriff, did I wake ya?" Green said into the mouthpiece. "Well, I'm sorry about that...I know, but I got a couple a no-name speeders here who blew through Dowelltown...No, I don't think you should wait 'til morning. Think maybe you should come over here now. If nothing else, Sheriff, yer gonna get a mighty good laugh."

Green hung up the receiver. He eyed Rose and Jenks dawdling by the desk, Rose paging through a stack of wanted circulars. "Lookin' fer yerself?"

"No. Just habit." Rose dropped the circulars.

"Sheriff lives just up the street. Be here in a couple minutes. But I better warn ya, he won't be none too happy 'cause I woke him up."

"His name?"

"Amos Steadman. Unlike you, he's got a badge."

Steadman banged through the door, bleary eyed and three days of stubble on his chin. He recoiled at the bright light coming from the jail's sole bare bulb. "Dammit, that Sammy put that hunnerd 'n' fifty watter in there again? Charlie, get that sixty out an' put it in there afore I go blind."

Green gave a nod toward the sheriff's shirttail hanging over his belt in back.

"Oh yeah, thanks." Steadman tucked at the tail. As he did, Rose put his hand out. Steadman, still squinting, grabbed onto it and gave it a quick pump.

"I'm Quill Rose, sheriff of Blount County. This is my deputy, Tommy Jenks."

"Amos Steadman. Charlie told me on the phone he caught you racing hell-bent for Sunday through Dowelltown. I didn't see no cruiser out there. You doin' it in that oil truck?"

Jenks raised his hands. "I didn't see any speed sign, honest."

"That's what they all say."

Green interrupted. "Sheriff, they got no badges, no identification."

"What?" Steadman wheeled on Rose. "So we old country boys are supposed to believe who you two slicks say you are?"

"Would a sheriff lie?"

"Every gawddamn one of 'em around here does. Charlie, lock these who-dads up."

While Green got the cell keys from a desk drawer, Rose gazed at the telephone. He aimed his pointer finger at it. "Can I make a call?"

"What the hell for? I'm sure not gonna take the word of any yahoo talkin' on phone about who you are or who you may not are."

"Not even the sheriff of Louden County? We left him less than eight hours ago. How about you call him?"

Steadman snorted. "Hell, you two are probably in cahoots about somethin'. Wouldn't be the first time a crook had a sheriff in his pocket."

"How about the lieutenant governor of the state, then? He's my brother-in-law."

"Hah!"

Rose turned to Jenks, murmuring, "I think he wants money."

"What about—"

Rose raised his hand before Jenks could finish. He peered at Steadman. "Sheriff, I get the niggling feeling you want us to buy our way out of jail."

Steadman hitched up his pants. "Damn straight on that. I'm gonna take you before the county judge in the morning and, speedin' through Dowelltown in that deathtrap out there, that mean old man is gonna fine your butts off. Don't s'pose you got any money on you?"

Rose pulled out his pockets.

Jenks did the same.

"Boys, tell ya what's gonna happen. With no money, the judge is gonna give you to me to rent out on the chain gang for six months. And while yer sweatin' in the sun somewheres, I'll be selling that gawddamn truck of yers."

Rose pushed some of the circulars around with his finger. "Sheriff, wouldn't you rather have the cash money than have to go to all that trouble?"

Steadman slapped Rose's hand away from his papers. "Hell yes. Yer payday for us, boys, and the county's gawddamn broke."

"Then can I make my phone call? How much money are you going to need?"

Steadman scratched at his ribs. "Whatdaya think, Charlie, five hunnerd?"

"More like six, I'd say."

"That might be low. Seven-fifty'd be better."

"Why not make it eight?"

"Then, of course, that old judge is gonna want his cut." Steadman hitched at his pants again. "Strangers, make it an even thousand. That truck's worth a helluva lot more than that."

Rose made a pistol with his fingers and fired it at the wall telephone again.

"Go ahead. Three long rings to get the operator. You think I'm a hard nose. Wait 'til you get Mavis outta bed." Steadman sat in one of the chairs and parked his feet on the desk.

While Rose cranked the phone, Steadman yanked open a drawer. He found a package of Red Man and packed a wad in his mouth. Some shreds fell on his shirt front.

"This is Quill Rose down at the sheriff's office, the jail, actually," Rose said into the mouthpiece. "Would you connect me through to Knoxville, four-two-six-one?...Yes, he's here."

Rose held the receiver out to Steadman.

Steadman shifted the wad into his cheek. "Gawddammit, can't you even make a telephone call?"

"She wants to talk to you."

The sheriff pushed himself up. He grabbed the receiver and glared up at Rose, a head taller than he. "Yeah, Mavis...I know it's long distance...Go ahead and put the call through, dammit. What the judge is gonna fine this guy, the county can pay its telephone bill...Yeah, you and Howard, you'll get yer money...All right, then."

Steadman, still glowering, handed the receiver back to Rose.

Rose spoke into the phone. "Operator, let it ring as long as it takes for someone to answer. Thank you."

He looked over to Jenks. "She's through to Knoxville. There, I hear it ringing. Someone's picked it up...Will, is that you?...Quill Rose...Yes, I know it's late...Yes, I know my calling like this likely upset Faith, but what I've got for you is going to upset her a whole lot more, but it can't be helped...Uh-huh. Tommy and me, we're in jail up here in Cannon County, and I hate to ask you, but can you come up here and get us out?...No, they don't believe us. We left our badges and wallets at the office. I know that wasn't smart...Well, the sheriff says it's going to take a thousand dollars to spring us...Yes, it's a lot, but get up as much as you can. Remember, we've got this gas tanker...Uh-huh. Maybe you ought to call Marcellus...Yeah, Marcellus Briskey. After you talk to him, bring the paperwork along, too...I appreciate it, Will. And apologize to Faith for me for waking her up."

Rose hung the receiver back on the hook. "He says he'll get up here as quick as he can."

"He don't have to hurry none. You and your wide buddy here ain't goin' anywheres except to those cells Charlie's holding open for ya."

"I don't suppose we could get something to eat?"

"Mister, we don't feed prisoners. Not this time o' night."

"I've got five dollars in the top of my sock."

"I thought you said you didn't have no money."

"Well, I lied."

Steadman slapped the desk. "Hah! Maybe yer a sheriff, after all."

Rose put his foot on a chair. He rolled down the elastic on his sock until a five-dollar bill, folded several times, showed itself. He held it out to Steadman.

"For five bucks, we oughtta be able to get ya a couple weenies and a sody pop." Steadman took the bill and handed it to Green. "Charlie, take this and go over to the café. Bang on the door until somebody wakes up."

Green slipped the bill in his shirt pocket and left.

Steadman ushered Rose and Jenks back to the open cell doors. He shoved Rose in one cell and Jenks in a second.

ROSE AND JENKS HUDDLED against the bars far back in their cells, chewing on their hotdogs.

"Who'd you call, Quill?"

"Will Kaufmann." Rose waved his hotdog at Green watching them from the desk where he sat wolfing down his own plate of food. "Mighty good the way you got them to fix it, Deputy Green, with coleslaw, relish, chili an' onions and all. It's a meal."

"Well, that's the way Alice makes 'em."

"They're a wonder. You're lucky to have her in your town."

"We think so."

Jenks bumped Rose's elbow. "You called Trooper Will?"

"He's over to the lab now. I don't think we can call him Trooper anymore."

"You think he can get the money?"

"Doubt it."

"Lordy, we're gonna be stuck in here for sure."

Rose took a pull on his Royal Crown. "Tommy, have faith. Enjoy your hotdog and your RC and have faith."

Chapter 9

Savior in blue

STEADMAN STOOD OUTSIDE the bars, gandering at his slumbering residents, a billy club in his hand. Without warning, he raked the billy across the bars, back and forth, the rattling reverberating off the masonry walls. "Rise 'n' shine, boys. Time for all honest men to be up and about."

Rose forced open an eye, then the other. With an effort, he lifted his blanket back and sat up. "What time is it?"

"Hell, it's almost eight o'clock. As my dear old daddy would say, you boys've slept half the day away." Steadman drummed his billy on one of the bars. "Thought you might want to slap some water on yer faces, then pee in the little house out back. When yer ready, I'll take you over to the café for breakfast. Nine o'clock sharp, you stand up in front of the judge."

Steadman unlocked the doors. He stood there waiting, shaking his billy at the basin of water and towels on the desk.

Rose and Jenks shambled out. Rose clapped Jenks on the shoulder and pushed him on for the first wash. "Where's Deputy Green?"

"We're a two-man county. Charlie's nights, I'm days. By now, Charlie's home havin' a good time with his wife, if ya know what I mean. Then he'll get him some shut-eye."

"Nice fella."

"Not the brightest bulb in the barrel, but he's diligent."

Jenks dried his face and hands and passed the towel to Rose as he came over to Steadman. "The little house?"

"Outside and to yer right. Looks like all the other WPA outhouses they ever built in this state."

Rose took over the basin. He scrubbed at his face. "Are we going to get to shave?"

"Well, now I'll tell ya, I don't trust prisoners with guns nor sharp objects. No, yer not gonna get to shave. Shall we go by the little house?"

"I'm feeling the pressure."

The two walked outside. After Rose and Jenks had changed places and Rose had returned, the trio went kitty-corner across the graveled street to the Trail's End Café. They settled around a linoleum-topped table in the front window, the linoleum worn. Steadman gazed at Rose. "Coffee all around?"

"Sure."

"Chicory or regular?"

"Regular."

"We go fer chicory up here. We like our coffee with a bite." Steadman waved at the woman working behind the counter. He held up three fingers. "Two regular an' one chicory."

She acknowledged with a nod and went to the pots steaming on a hot plate.

Steadman parked his elbows on the table. He tapped the back of Rose's hand. "You didn't eat up all yer money, last night, so you've already paid fer breakfast. You can have anything you want, within reason, that is."

The woman appeared beside the table. She set a mug of coffee in front of each man. "These your nighttime guests, Amos?"

"Yup, real terrors o' the highway. It's amazin' they didn't kill somebody before Charlie stopped 'em. Alice, meet these, well, I don't know who they are. They don't have any ident."

Rose worked up a smile. "Call me Quill."

"I'm Tommy." Jenks picked up his mug and slurped at the coffee. "Good dogs, last night, thank you."

"Well, what will it be this mornin'?"

Rose cradled his coffee mug. "Grits, eggs over, and a short stack."

Jenks put his mug down. "Same for me, only double it. And throw some sausages on there and some soppin' gravy, maybe a little fried okra and a couple a biscuits."

Rose gazed up at the woman. "Can you get that in our money from last night?"

"Just barely. Amos, the usual?"

Steadman sighed.

The woman went back to the counter where she recited the order to a boy of about nine, standing on a milk crate in front of the grill.

Steadman gave a tilt of his head toward the boy. "That's J.T., Alice's boy. Damn good breakfast cook. His momma done taught him well."

The men chatted about the weather while they waited for their orders and about how soon the plateau's farmers might get into the fields.

Jenks shifted the subject. "Much coon hunting up here?"

"My gawd, we're overrun with coon hunters and their gawddamn scraggly hounds. Gimme a good blue tick any day, and I can run 'em all in the ground. Why I got this one—"

The woman set a bowl in front of Steadman. "Your hot mush, Amos. And you, Mister Quill, grits, eggs over, and a short stack." She placed a platter in front of him.

Jenks raised his hand.

"I'll be back with yours in a minute. It'll take both my boy and me to tote it all."

When she returned, she carried two platters, the second filled with okra, cathead biscuits, and a pile of sausage links. J.T., the breakfast cook, carried a platter of grits, eggs, and pancakes, plus, in a bowl, gravy.

They returned once more with pitchers of syrup and milk and a plate of butter.

The woman gazed at her son's handiwork, admiringly. "Anything else now?"

Steadman reached out for the boy. He pulled him in for a hug. "You're a big help to yer momma, J.T., and I appreciate you lookin' after her."

"Thank you, Granpa."

Rose raised an eyebrow.

"Yeah, J.T.'s my grandson. Helluva boy and handsome, too."

J.T. blushed.

The woman drew the boy back. "Now, Amos, you're going to spoil him with all your compliments."

"Daughter of mine, I only tell the truth." Steadman held up his hand as if he were swearing on a Bible.

The woman took his hand. She squeezed it, then she and the boy went back to the counter.

Rose again raised an eyebrow. "Family, huh?"

"Best thing there is for an old man like me. Alice says I can sit around here all day an' whittle an' spit and drink coffee, or sumpin' stronger, when I hang up my badge. You got family?"

"A boy my wife insisted we take in when his parents and sister were killed."

"Bad business, huh?"

"It was. But he's doing all right. Sure has latched onto my wife." Rose slathered butter on his grits and pancakes. "You mentioned hanging up your badge. Thinking of doing that soon?"

Steadman sweetened his mush with syrup before he poured on a splash of milk. "I figger I got about four more years in me, two more elections. I worry about Charlie. He's a good deputy, but I don't know as he can do the job of sheriff."

Steadman dipped his spoon in his mush. He worried a mouthful of it for some time before he swallowed it down. "You ain't really a sheriff, are you?"

"I really am." Rose forked some egg into his mouth.

"You know, I almost believe you." Steadman stirred at his mush, then stopped. "Gawddammit, why couldn't ya have had some proof, then I coulda cut ya loose?"

Rose shrugged. He cut a bite of pancake.

Steadman waved his spoon. "You know, Charlie and me got quite the little deal goin' here to keep the county afloat. About once a week, we haul over some outta-stater—some rich tourist—and occasionally a trucker like you 'cause yer load's worth somethin'. We throw 'em in jail and get 'em going real good, like we done with you, then the judge hits 'em with one helluva fine."

He stopped to take a mouthful of mush. "Last week, we had this couple from New York, ya know. We knew they was good for it 'cause they was driving a Cadillac. Within a day, they had two thousand dollars wired in here. Two thousand dollars. They was so happy to get out they thanked us when we left them at the county line."

"Sheriff, that's illegal."

"No, it's not. We caught 'em going at least sixty-five through Dowelltown. Just like you, they said they didn't see the speed sign." Steadman laughed, laughed so hard he nearly knocked over his coffee. "'Course, it waddn't up at the time, but it was up last night."

He stirred at his mush again, the laugh lines in his face turning down into a frown. "Wait a minute. You didn't steal that gawddamn truck, did you? We got a couple sheriffs up here who'll steal anything that's not chained to a telephone pole. They sell it and put the money in their own pockets."

"If I stole the truck?"

"Then you'd be in a helluva lot of trouble."

The conversation stopped. The men ate in silence for the rest of their time at the Trail's End. On the way toward the door, Rose and Jenks gave their thanks to the woman and her son for the breakfast. She looked to Steadman. "Be back for lunch, Amos?"

"I expect I will unless the judge has got some gawd-awful job for me."

"Your prisoners?"

"Somebody'll bring 'em back."

When they got outside, Rose bumped shoulders with Steadman. "She sure doesn't look like you."

"Thank God for small favors. Alice takes after her momma, a beautiful woman to marry an old coot like me." He flashed a toothy grin. "A man can carry an ugly puss like mine through life and get by fairly easy, but it'd be terrible if God put it on a woman."

They rounded the corner of the jail and Steadman stopped. He stared at a State Police cruiser parked by the door. "What the hell is that doin' here?"

"Don't know." Rose tugged at an earlobe.

Steadman went over to the car. He kicked the fender, then prodded his prisoners on into the jail.

There at the desk sat a state trooper in full regalia, his Sam Browne hat resting on Steadman's stack of wanted circulars. "Sheriff?"

"Yeah. Who you, darkie?" Steadman spit in a bucket by the door.

The officer pushed himself up to his full six-foot-three inches of height. With marked deliberation, he came over to Steadman and glowered down at him as he tapped the nameplate above his badge. "Corporal William C. Kaufmann, Knoxville post."

"Gawddamn—"

Kaufmann raised a finger, cutting Steadman off. "I hear you caught some bad boys."

"Might've."

"That them?" The trooper jerked his thumb at Rose and Jenks.

"Could be."

"The names Quill Rose and Tommy Jenks have a familiar ring?"

"Maybe."

"That tanker outside, Sheriff—Steadman, isn't it?"

"Yeah."

"We've been looking for that tanker."

"You have. Why?"

"It was hijacked yesterday, outside of Knoxville."

Steadman wheeled on Rose and Jenks. "Gawddammit, you bastards stole that truck. I knew it, I knew it, I knew it. Well, Trooper, I got first claim on these sonsabitches. I got 'em for speedin'."

Kaufmann handed Steadman a paper. "Sorry. State's attorney trumps you."

Steadman read the paper, at the bottom an official-looking seal. He studied the seal hard before he swung to Rose and Jenks. "Sorry, boys, this says yer goin' to Nashville. Some state judge wants to send yer bee-hinds to Brushyfork. Says here yer to take that gawddamn truck with ya. It's evidence. Gawddamn peculiar to me, though, they lettin' you drive it."

Kaufmann patted the revolver on his hip. "If they run, I get to shoot them."

"I s'pose."

Rose nudged Steadman. "You're not going to let him take us just like that? He could be a fake."

"Fake, my foot. You see the size of that gawddamn buck? You expect me to challenge him?" Steadman stepped over to Kaufmann. "Do I get any finder's fee or a cut of the fine?"

"Look, Sheriff, I know your county needs the money. If there's any left after the trial, I'll recommend the state's attorney send it here."

"Gawddammit, one more day, one more day and I coulda had that truck sold." Steadman kicked the bucket by the door the length of the jail, startling Rose and Jenks. "Gawddamn, the judge is gonna be mad."

Kaufmann took his paper back. "You want me to talk to him?"

"Hell, there's no point in you gettin' burned, although with your color, nobody'd notice. Take 'em and get ta hell outta here." Steadman threw a hand in the air.

"I appreciate your cooperation, Sheriff."

"Yeah, sure."

Kaufmann pocketed the paper as he pushed Rose and Jenks toward the door, outside, and to the truck, Rose chuckling all the way. "A warrant for our arrest?"

"Just be glad he thought so. If he'd made any calls, we'd all be in his jail."

"You're good, Will. You surely are. Sheriff Steadman's a good old boy, but I thought for certain he was gonna fill his pants when you stood over him."

"Yeah, well, are you going to tell me what this is all about?"

"Not here. Make a show of it, leading us out of town."

Rose climbed up into the driver's side of the cab while Jenks trotted around to the passenger's side.

Kaufmann watched them, then got in his cruiser. When he heard the diesel burble to life, he started his cruiser's engine and flipped up the switch for his flashing light. He wheeled into the street, the tanker behind. Kaufmann turned right at the first corner, then right again to get back to Fifty-Three.

At Gassaway's lone stop sign, he turned north, the tanker still behind him. As he passed the Trail's End Café, he saw a boy at the front window, waving.

CHAPTER 10

Pay day

KAUFMANN PULLED OFF the road just short of the intersection of State Fifty-Three and U.S. Seventy, the highway to Nashville.

Rose did the same. He and Jenks climbed down from the cab of the tanker and strolled forward to where Kaufmann stood waiting for them, resting his hand on the grip of his revolver. "What've you got to tell me?"

Rose took up a seat on the truck's front bumper. He pulled his hat off and ran his hand around the sweat band. "Will, Tommy and me, we stumbled on the distillery end of a moonshine operation."

"That's hardly unusual in your county."

"This sucker's bigger than anything you or I've ever seen."

"Really?"

Rose ran his hand around the sweat band a second time. "Story is it's so big the alkie pouring out of it will supply most of the liquor business in East and Central Tennessee."

Kaufmann let out a low whistle.

"It's a factory."

Kaufmann rubbed at the side of his face. "Well, it seems to me, if you want to put them out of business, the best way is to dynamite the still."

"Best, maybe, but not easy. That booze factory is back up in some pretty wild country. If we go in there, we're going to get shot up."

"Oh."

"I don't know about you, but I've never liked attending lawmen's funerals, and I sure don't want to be the guest of honor at my own. So we're not going in there."

Kaufmann pulled out a pack Camels. He took one for himself, then held the pack out to Rose and Jenks. Both declined the offer. Kaufmann scratched a match on the truck's bumper and brought the flame to his cigarette. "So instead you steal a truck. What's that got to do with anything?"

"You know what's in it?"

"Marcellus told me."

"By the taste, it's straight alcohol. They haven't even cut it with water yet." Rose leaned forward. "So I figure this truck is my ticket to the bottling plant at the other end. It's got to be in Nashville because that's where the driver was hired to take the truck. We might even learn who's running the big show."

"That could be interesting."

"Particularly if we should want to prosecute someday, really bust them up."

Kaufmann sucked on his cigarette. He blew out a lungful of smoke. "Quill, you should have brought the feds in, or at least the state police, instead of riding around up here like the Lone Ranger and Tonto."

"You listen to that program?"

"My boys insist. We dial it in on the big Stromberg-Carlson super het, and the whole family listens. Hi-yo, Silver."

"Yeah, I like it, too." Rose rubbed his hands on his trousers. "Will, the word is they're buying off people. I don't know who to trust. Right now it's Tommy, Doc, Abner Huskey, Od, and Marcellus."

"And me." Kaufmann touched his eyebrow in a salute.

"Yeah, and you. I figured now that you're in the crime lab, you're so far out of everything nobody gives a damn about you."

"That's pretty well true."

"It'd be a waste of somebody's good money to buy you off. But I do have to ask, why'd you ever take that job?"

"You never noticed I'm colored, did you, Quill? My captain did. He let me know he wasn't ever going to promote me off patrol. So my only chance was to get a specialty, and I've got that at the lab."

Kaufmann sucked again on his cigarette.

"Now, if the haul routes for the booze are Four-Eleven and Eleven north and south and Seventy east and west..." Kaufmann waved his cigarette in the general direction the three highways ran. "...you're right, they got to have protection. They could be buying off some post commanders, maybe a sergeant or two."

He flicked his cigarette on the ground. Kaufmann stepped on the butt and twisted it into the dirt. "Tell you what. I've got free rein as a lab man to drive about anywhere I want in the Eastern Kingdom. I'll do a little poking around for you."

"Will, be careful. I don't think these folks have got any qualms about killing. We're small potatoes out here.

Who's going to miss us other than our wives and a few friends?"

"You make it sound gawd-awful lonely."

"Well, look around. You could fire a cannon off in any direction, and all you'd hit is trees for two or three miles, well, maybe the post office over at Liberty, but that's about it. We've got a lot of territory like this in the Eastern Kingdom."

"True."

"We're exposed out here, my friend, so darn right, you be careful."

"You, too, Quill."

Rose slapped Tommy Jenks's leg. "As long as I've got Tommy with me, I'm just fine."

"Quill, that print I lifted for you down at Pistol Creek, did it do you any good?"

"Oh jeez, I was going to take it over to Marcellus to check it against any prints he's got. Right now, we're guessing the killer comes from his county. I got all involved in this hooch thing and forgot about it."

"Well, I've got a copy of the print at the lab. Do you want me to take it out to him?"

"Would you do that?"

"If it will help catch your man, that's my job." Kaufmann took out his pad and wrote a reminder note. "I'll stop by and see Marcellus on my way back to Knoxville. I've got to whump up some kind of story to tell my lieutenant about where I've been all day, and Marcellus may as well be the one to corroborate it. I sure can't use you, gallivanting around out here."

"I understand."

"I'm sure you do." Kaufmann pocketed his note and pad. "I'll mention the print to Marcellus and take it out in a day or two."

Rose and then Jenks shook hands with Kaufmann. They remained there in front of the tanker while the state policeman got into his cruiser. They watched him drive away, watched him turn east at the intersection, toward Knoxville.

"Well, this isn't getting the job done." Rose tossed the ignition key to his deputy. "Why don't you take us on into Green Hill for a bite of lunch?"

ROSE AND JENKS picked up a map of Nashville at the Green Hill Esso station and went next door to the Dinner Bell to study the map over a lunch of porkchops and sweet potatoes.

With his finger, Rose traced along Seventy as it entered the hilly area on the eastern side of Nashville, then down into the river district. He tapped the map. "See here. Here's where we cut off on First Avenue. That takes us to Woodland. We turn right there, see, up onto the bridge. Uh-huh, there it is, First Street South. Sunspot's depot has got to be right down in here someplace."

Jenks toyed with the last bites of his sweet potato. "So we're just going to drive into their yard bold as lightning?"

"That's what they're expecting their driver to do. But I think we ought to do something else, something that'll really get their attention."

"Like what?"

"Ransom that load of alcohol."

"You crazy?"

"Let me ask you, Tommy, who do crooks respect?"

"Certainly not us, or they'd all run to the jail and give up."

"Crooks respect crooks who are more crooked than they are." Rose speared a piece of porkchop. "Tommy boy, we're hijackers. What say we make us some real money?"

ROSE DROVE THE FINAL LEG into Nashville. After he brought the tanker across the Woodland Bridge, he downshifted for the turn onto First Street South. "There it is, up ahead on the left."

A rusting Sunspot Terminal sign hung from a post halfway down the block. When Rose and Jenks got closer, Rose saw a short gravel drive, then a wire gate, a check-in shack, and a tank farm beyond. He shifted back up to third. Rose stepped hard on the accelerator.

"You're not stopping?"

"Not here."

Rose leaned on the horn when he neared Sunspot's entrance. A man stepped out of the shack, and Rose waved to him. Two blocks on, Rose racked back into second and swung the tanker onto Fatherland. He ran to the end of the block and turned the rig onto Second Street.

Again he shifted up to third and sailed past the back fence of the Sunspot Terminal to brake for the stop sign at Woodland. Rose bounced his foot on the floorboard while he waited for a gap in the traffic. It came, and he hauled out onto the street that would take him back across the Cumberland River.

Rose relaxed when he rolled the tanker out onto the bridge. Maybe it was the rumbling of the tires on the bridge's steel ribbing or just having some distance between himself and the terminal.

Jenks, too, relaxed. He laid his arm across the seatback. "What's next?"

"Think I saw a Sunspot station on the other side of First Avenue, in the District. If you want to hide something, best place is in plain sight, right? You think they'd think to look for this tanker at one of their stations?"

Jenks roared with laughter.

Rose stopped at the foot of the bridge. Again he waited for a break in traffic. When it came, he drove on, waving to a policeman writing a ticket for someone who had parked a delivery truck across the entrance to an alley.

One block on and Rose turned onto Second Avenue.

He trundled the tanker along four blocks to Broadway, crossed that main artery for city traffic, and saw at the far end of the block the Sunspot station he was looking for. Rose wheeled in and around and into a slot beside the station, out of the way of cars that pulled in for gasoline.

After he killed the engine, he reached under the seat for his wad of bills. "Tommy, anything behind the seat we can wrap the shotgun in?"

Jenks looked. "Yeah, we got us a blanket here."

"You take care of that while I see if I can get us a car. And bring the suitcase."

Rose pulled the key from the ignition. A man came walking toward him as he climbed down from the cab, the man working a tired rag over his oil-stained hands. "Kin I hep ya?"

"Yeah, be all right if I left my truck here for a bit?"

"Company truck, no problem, mister."

"I've got to run up to the state motor vehicle department. Trooper stopped me, told me I've got something wrong with my driver's license. You wouldn't happen to have a car I could use?"

"I didn't know the department was open on Saturdays."

"Trooper said there's a skeleton crew there to take care of little things like this."

"Well, if you won't be gone long, I guess ya could take my car. I was just changin' the oil in it. It's a real nice one. How about you come this way?"

Rose motioned for Jenks to follow as he stepped out with the garage man. They went around to the front of the station, to a service bay.

"There it is. Whaddaya think?" The man held out his hand toward the car there, a Studebaker. "Bought it used. Do you think I got me a good buy?"

Rose grinned as he tilted his head at a yellow roadster, the top and the windshield down.

The man noticed a grease smear on the sleeve of his coveralls. He went to rubbing at it. "Just two years old, a President's model. My little wife thinks it's one sweet ride."

"Pretty fancy for just running uptown."

"Oh, don't you worry about it none." He turned his rag and rubbed some more. "Sunspot's done right by me. I'd back it out for ya, but I guess I've got some grease on me. You go ahead and get on in it."

Rose opened the driver's door. He slid behind the wheel and admired the gauges on the dash. "Friend, the best I've ever driven is a Ford. This is gonna be a treat."

Jenks came into the bay. He laid the wrapped shotgun and the suitcase in the back seat, and got in on the passenger's side.

The man leaned over Rose's door. "It can be a little tricky to start. Go ahead and try it."

Rose pushed the clutch in and turned the ignition key.

Nothing.

"Jigger the key there."

Rose wiggled the key in the ignition switch, then turned it, and engine came to life.

"I haven't had time to fix that yet. Probably nothin' major, but it kin be a nuisance. I'll go outside and direct ya back, keep ya away from the pumps."

"Well, thank you. Thank you very much." Rose stepped on the gas pedal and let up, then did it again. Rose flicked his eyebrows each time the Straight-Eight roared and burbled back down. He found reverse and twisted around to catch the hand signals from the garage man. Rose, following the signals, rolled the roadster back out of the garage.

The man gave a thumbs-up. "Yer all right now!"

Rose waved and drove away.

The car gleamed in the afternoon sun, the engine in a low rumble as again Rose made his way across the Woodland Bridge, steering with one hand. "Tommy, this criminal life is something. A car like this, I could come to like it."

Jenks patted the dashboard. "A car like this makes me wonder what the station man's got going on the side that he can afford it."

"Yes, what could it be?"

Rose took the long way around to the Sunspot terminal, letting himself come into First Street South from the southeast.

He slowed at the Sunspot block, switched off the engine, and allowed the car coast to a stop at the edge of the gravel drive. "Tommy, I'm going up to talk to the man in the shack. If I raise my hand, you unwrap the two-barrel and hold it up where he can see it."

"That's it? That's all you want me to do?"

"Look, I don't expect trouble, but if there is, you've got my permission to shoot whoever you want. Just don't shoot me."

Rose reached into the back seat for the suitcase, Jenks for the blanket that hid the shotgun. Rose got out and strolled up the drive, whistling a melody he'd heard a country band play on the radio, 'The Wabash Cannonball.'

A man stepped out of the shack. "Can I help ya?"

"Yessir, I reckon you can."

"What's that?"

"I want to see your boss."

The man laughed. "He don't see nobody."

Rose loosened a stone in the drive with the toe of his shoe. He kicked the stone away. "I think he'll see me. I've got something he wants." He took the playing card from his pocket and held it up.

"Holy hell. Don't you go nowhere or, gawddammit, we'll hunt you down and kill ya."

The man dashed away, into the terminal yard, toward a building near the first of three mammoth steel tanks.

He went inside and, in less than a minute, came back out, hustling to keep up with another man, a man in suspenders, barrel chested, his shirt sleeves jammed above his elbows. They marched up to Rose.

The new man, the stump of a cigar gripped in his teeth, glared at Rose. "What's this about, mister?"

"You know. Your man told you."

"Where's my truck?"

"I hid it."

"Why? You got paid on the other end."

"Well, it wasn't quite enough. You see, I know what's in the belly tank."

"Ralph, this gawddamn guy's a hijacker. Kill the bastard."

When the gateman reached behind his back, Rose raised his hand. "I don't think you want to do that."

"Why the hell not?"

"See that fella behind me, by the car?"

Jenks waved his shotgun, then brought it down level.

"I jump out of the way, the spread of that blast, he's going to wipe you both out. Then with all the gasoline you've got around here, he's going to put the second shell into something that'll go boom."

"Gawddammit." The man spit at the gravel. He looked hard at Rose. "All right, what's it going to take to get my gawddamn truck back?"

"Oh, I figure a dollar a gallon for the booze is fair, say three-thousand dollars."

"Are you crazy?"

"Not a bit."

"I ain't got that kinda money around here."

"Come on, a bootlegger like you? When you're bringing it in by the tanker load, you've got the money."

"Gawddamn you." The cigar smoker tilted his head. He again glared at Rose from beneath his bushy eyebrows. "All right. You bring that truck in here, and I'll give you the gawddamn money."

"Aw, come on now, it doesn't work that way. You give me the money, and I'll tell you where the truck is. To show you my good faith, here's the key."

Rose flipped the ignition key to the cigar man who made a grab for it but missed. He retrieved the key from the gravel, then studied Rose for a long moment while jiggling the key in his hand. "All right. Ralph, let's get him what he wants."

"No, you stay with me. Ralph, he gets the money. Anything goes wrong, I want somebody we can shoot, and you're it."

"He don't know the combination to the safe."

"So tell him."

The two men huddled, then the one called Ralph hurried away toward the office.

The cigar man gazed around as he puffed on his stogie. When he couldn't get any smoke from it, he slapped his pockets for a match. He found one and flicked the sulfur end with his thumbnail.

The match flared, and he sucked the flame into the cigar again and again, until a half-inch of the end glowed red. "Am I gonna be rid of you after this is over?"

"You never know. Three thousand dollars for a couple days' work, my partner and me, we could be back again. Of course, you could put us on the payroll."

"Gawddamn bandits, it'll be a cold day in hell. Where's my driver?"

"Oh, you don't need to know that. It'd just upset you. But you are going to have to get someone to drive in his place."

Ralph came out of the office, clutching fistfuls of bills. He trotted on up.

The cigar man snorted smoke out of his nostrils. "You want to count it?"

"No. You trust me, I trust you." Rose brought his suitcase up. He opened it. "Just put it in here."

Ralph looked at his employer. When he got a nod, the henchman tossed the cash in the suitcase.

"All right, where's my truck?"

"If I tell you now, my value to you has ended. You might be tempted to shoot me, even with old Tommy sighting down the barrels of his shotgun at you." Rose edged away. "No, you stay by your telephone. I'll call you in a couple minutes."

He ran for the car.

He and Jenks flung the doors of the Studebaker open and leaped in.

Rose turned the ignition key, but nothing happened.

He turned the key again.

"Oh, jeez—" Rose jiggled the key and twisted it a third time.

The cigar man sent Ralph running in the opposite direction.

"Come on, come on—" Rose jiggled the key in the ignition switch and twisted the key again.

A Buick roared around a fuel tank, slowing for the cigar man.

"Quill, now!" Jenks yelled.

"I'm tryin'." He turned when he heard the Buick spin in the gravel. "Shoot the tires out!"

Jenks whipped his shotgun over the door. He jerked the trigger.

Headlights shattered, and a tire exploded.

The Buick swerved and plowed into the terminal's fence. The cigar man rolled out with Ralph's pistol in his hand. He came around the far side of the car, blazing away.

Rose twisted the key one more time. The ignition caught, and he tromped the accelerator to the floor. At the end of the block, Rose skidded the heavy car onto Woodland. Again he sped up, the super structure of the Woodland Bridge a blur as the Studebaker raced across the deck.

Jenks kept a hand on his hat. "No traffic on First. Goose it!"

Rose shot the car through the intersection on the far side of the bridge, braking for the turnoff to the Sunspot station's street.

Five blocks on and he turned again, casually now, this time into the station, as if he and Jenks were coming home from a leisurely fishing trip. His hand, though, shook as he guided the car into the garage.

The station man came out of the office. "How'd she run fer you boys?"

Rose squeezed his fist to stop the tremor. "Oh, sweet, really sweet. You've got yourself a mighty fine vehicle."

"Didn't give ya no problems?"

"Other than you're right about that ignition switch, no." Rose handed the key to the station man. "You're probably going to have to change the switch out."

Rose and Jenks got out of the car, Jenks with the rolled-up blanket and the suitcase. They went out to the pump area, the station man at Rose's elbow. Rose motioned at the tanker. "Another driver's going to pick it up. My partner and me, we're heading for home. Thank you for the loan of your car."

"For the company, anytime. You all come back now."

Rose and Jenks continued on to the street. At Broadway, they hailed a city bus.

"You wouldn't happen to be going by the Hillsboro Theater?" Rose asked the driver.

"I can drop you within a block. You boys intend to take in the Grand Ole Opry?"

"No visit to Nashville would be complete without it."

The driver beckoned Rose up the steps. "It'll be crowded. They pack twenty-four hundred people in there."

"I think we can hold our own."

The driver peered at Jenks. "I expect you can. You got tickets?"

Rose stopped at the top of the steps. "Figure to get them at the door."

"Sorry, you got to get 'em from a National Life agent. Didn't know that, didja?"

"Surely not."

"Well, there's always this one fella hawkin' a few tickets on the street. But it'll cost ya."

Rose stood there with his hand on the bus's fare box. "Money's not a problem."

"Good. Then just each of you fellas drop a nickel in the box, and we'll get this bus a-goin'."

"Can you break a bill?"

"Probably. Whatcha got?"

Rose pulled out his wad, on top a five. He peeled it off and handed it to the driver.

The driver took some bills from his jacket pocket. He counted out five ones to Rose, then reached in the fare box for a fistful of nickels for the ninety cents in change. "Buck in the fare box now."

Rose stuffed a bill in, then put the rest of the money in his pocket.

"Go on back and get you a seat. Remember, the back's for the niggers, so you sit forward of there." The driver gave a knowing jerk of his head.

Rose returned a shrug. He and Jenks worked their way along the aisle, nodding to the other riders. Halfway back, they found an empty bench seat and took it.

Rose placed the suitcase on his lap.

Jenks let the butt of his wrapped shotgun rest on the floor. "What's this about the Grand Ole Opry?"

"Think about it. Where better to get lost than in a crowd? And tell me, haven't you ever wanted to see Uncle Dave Macon play that banjo of his, and Cousin Wilbur?"

Jenks shook his head. "It's an adventure working for you, Quill."

"Isn't it, though?"

"But let me ask, how are we gonna get home?"

"We could take the Knoxville bus, but it's a long a ride and awful cramped. What say we instead take the morning train?"

"Good by me. Train's got a dining car. I always like that."

Rose and Jenks became engrossed in the buildings that passed beyond the windows of the city bus, the State Capitol on Cedar Street, the War Memorial, the massive National Life & Accident Insurance Building.

At one stop, the driver looked up in his mirror. "You boys still want the Hillsboro?"

"Yeah."

"Then this is where you get off."

Rose and Jenks abandoned their bench seat and worked their way toward the front of the bus.

The driver tapped his thumbs on the bus's steering wheel while he waited. "Theater, you'll find it one block on your left. First thing you do is track down that hawker. You get your tickets, then you find yourself something to eat."

"We'll surely do that." Rose, with Jenks behind him, clambered down the steps to the sidewalk.

The driver gave a wave as he pulled the door closed and drove off.

Rose and Jenks pushed on toward the Hillsboro where they came on a small mousey man working the crowd clustered around the lobby doors.

"Got to have a ticket to get in!" The man waved a fistful of tickets over his head. "Got to have a ticket to get in!"

"Two," Rose called out.

The man elbowed his way over. "That'll be fifty cents."

Rose counted it out in nickels to the hawker. "Where might we get supper?"

"The Chicken Shack." He pointed across the street before he pulled two tickets from his wad.

Rose took the tickets, and he and Jenks went across to where they faced another crowd, this one milling around in front of a hole-in-the-wall restaurant. They muscled their way inside to two stools at the counter and ordered a platter of Southern fried chicken.

Hardly a minute passed before the waitress came hustling out of the kitchen with the platter, bowls of potatoes and gravy and baked beans, and a plate of biscuits and butter.

Jenks prodded at the biscuits. "Wouldn't happen to have some honey, wouldja?"

"Sure, sweetie." She left and as quickly returned with a pitcher and with coffee. She filled the cups for the men, then left again.

Jenks examined a chicken leg before ripping into it. "When do you plan to call Sunspot?"

"Not just yet. Let's let the cigar man stew a while."

Chapter 11

The Opry

BY THE TIME Rose and Jenks laid down the last chicken bone, the crowd on the street between the Chicken Shack and the Hillsboro looked like that on a state fair midway at peak time. Cars, pickup trucks of all ages and descriptions, and buses and cattle trucks as well, had pulled in everywhere, some even on the sidewalk.

Rose wedged into the crowd, holding his ticket over his head as he pushed toward the theater's doors and an usher standing guard. Rose thumbed back at Jenks. "He's got a ticket, too. Got a payphone in there, haven't you?"

The usher gestured toward the auditorium doors inside as he hauled open the lobby door. "Inside and to the right."

Rose moved on. When he got to the phone, he took a scrap of paper and a nickel from his pocket. He picked up the receiver, listened, then dropped the nickel in the slot. Rose squinted at the paper. "Operator, Franklin four-three-five."

Jenks worried his ticket. "Quill, people are startin' to go in."

"This'll only take a minute."

The people now crowding in from the street kicked up their volume, to make themselves heard over the

others, as they gabbed about everything from the health
of their relatives to who was on the bill this night. The
name of Uncle Dave Macon bounced from lobby wall to
lobby wall.

"Yeah," Rose said into the mouthpiece. "This the
cigar man?...Ralph? No, Ralph, gimme your boss...Cigar
man?...Yeah, your truck's at the Sunspot station on
Second Avenue...Why didn't we call earlier? We were
hungry. Wanted to get a bite to eat. Knew you weren't
going anywhere...Now you know you don't have to use
language like that. After all, we're fellow businessmen.
And, yes, your money bought us an excellent dinner. We
appreciate that."

Rose slipped the receiver back on the hook before he
picked up his suitcase. "Can you believe it? He wasn't
none too happy with us."

Rose, with Jenks at his side, worked his way into the
flowing crowd. It swept them both into the auditorium
and forward to where ushers were wagging hands toward
empty seats.

Rose and Jenks grabbed two. They shoved the
suitcase and the wrapped shotgun beneath—on the floor—
doffed their hats, and settled in.

The bill featured Little Rachel, the Weaver Brothers,
Elviry, and Uncle Dave Macon, the man from
Murphreesboro, Tennessee. The audience went wild
when Macon picked out 'Rock Along Saro Jane' on his
clawhammer banjo, his plug hat bouncing, his gates-ajar
collar flapping. They applauded more loudly when he
flashed his gold-teeth smile.

Four encores, then George Hay, the Opry's Solemn
Old Judge, stepped to the radio microphone. "That's
might fine, Uncle Dave, mighty fine, but we've got to
move along now. David Stone?"

An announcer with brilliantined hair came to a second microphone. "Thank you, Judge. This next portion of the Grand Ole Opry, heard all across the country on fifty-thousand-watt WSM Radio in Nashville, Tennessee, is brought to you by the makers of Prince Albert Tobacco, the cool-smoking tobacco. Listeners, Prince Albert and thirty other tobaccos were recently tested on a smoking machine, and Prince Albert won the test hands down. With its crimp cut and premium tobacco, it's the easiest to roll into a fine cigarette. Prince Albert. Buy it wherever fine tobaccos are sold."

Hay leaned in close to his microphone, his hand on the stand. "Thank you, David Stone, for that commercial message. Now you in the audience here in the theater and you at home in front of your radios, welcome a new act to the Opry, all the way from Knoxville, Tennessee, Roy Acuff and the Crazy Tennesseans."

A train whistle sounded–Wooooo-Whoo-Ooooo!

I stood on the Atlantic Ocean / The wide Pacific shore–

Acuff, at a center-stage microphone, sang, his fiddle and bow in his hand, hanging loosely at his side.

Rose punched Jenks. He raised a thumb.

Acuff brought his fiddle up under his chin when the band went into the bridge. A second fiddler stepped in next to him, and the two went on a tear through the chorus.

Rose elbowed Jenks. "Know who that other guy is?"

"No."

"That's Frankie Seabolt, from up at Fish Camp. Man, I didn't know he was such a good fiddler. We've gotta see him after the show."

Acuff rolled into the third verse and then the final chorus–

Hear the mighty rush of engines / Hear the lonesome hobos' call / We're traveling through jungles / On the Wabash Cannonball.

Rose shot to his feet, pounding his hands together, Jenks whistling.

Everyone in the auditorium came up.

When the applause reached its peak, Acuff and Seabolt came back to the microphone and dueled through one more chorus, finishing with their bows thrust high in the air.

The applause, like thunder, shook the theater.

George Hay pulled his microphone in. "They love you, Roy. Really fine. You can tell by the applause, we're going to have you back."

The show went on for another hour before the ON AIR sign above the stage winked out.

Rose, followed by Jenks, pushed up the aisle.

"Mister Hay. Mister Hay!" Rose called out.

"Yeah?"

"Quill Rose from Maryville. One of the boys in Roy Acuff's band is from up our way. Can we see him? Say howdy?"

"They're packing to leave, but, sure, come on back. Watch your step. Don't trip on the cables."

Rose caught his toe and fell into Jenks.

Jenks, stumbling, gripped his wrapped shotgun hard to keep from losing it.

Hay got hold of both men and hauled them through the curtains and into the wings. "Roy?" he called.

"Yeah, George?"

"These fellows know one of your boys. Want to say hello."

"Sure." Acuff held out his hand to Rose. "I'm Roy Acuff. Where you boys from?"

"Maryville."

"Well, I claim Maynardville as home, but I went to high school right up the road from you in Fountain City. Who'd you want to see?"

"Frankie Seabolt."

"Oh yeah, Frankie, he's the best, isn't he? Frankie?"

"Yeah?"

"You got company."

Seabolt broke away from other performers who also were packing to leave. He came over, a slender man carrying a violin case. "Well, Quill Rose, it is good to see you."

The two men fell together. They hugged and slapped one another on the back until Seabolt leaned away, the better to see Rose. "How long's it been?"

"Couple years, maybe three."

"Yeah, since I started playing with Roy."

"Frankie, this is my deputy, Tommy Jenks. Tommy, this is Frankie. I told you about him."

They shook hands, then Seabolt put his forearm on Rose's shoulder. "Quill, you're one long way from home."

"Tommy and me, we had business in Nashville, so I said we ought to take in the Opry. But I never guessed you'd be here."

"We didn't know we'd be here, either, until just the other day. Harry Stone, the station manager, called us and said he'd like to try us out."

Rose poked the fiddler in the ribs. "Oh, you and Roy and the band, you were good."

"I hate to cut this short, my friend, but we're loadin' out. We got to drive to Kingsport tonight. Show there tomorrow afternoon. Then Monday we're back at KROL in Knoxville, playing on the radio. Roy keeps us hoppin'.'"

"Well, you keep playing like you did tonight, won't be long, as they say, and you'll be in the tall cotton. You got to go, Frankie, we got to go, too. Good to see you."

They hugged again. Then both swung away, Seabolt toward the Acuff band and the equipment they were hauling out the stage door, Rose and Jenks toward the lobby and the front doors.

In the lobby, Rose stopped dead. He grabbed Jenks and pulled him back into the auditorium. "The cigar man, he's on the street, and he's not alone."

"Uh-oh."

"I'll say uh-oh. Let's go out the back."

Jenks glanced toward the lobby doors. "How'd he know we were here?"

"Maybe something in the chatter around the telephone tipped him." Rose made his way back up onto the stage. He tripped over microphone cables a second time yet continued on to the stage door. Rose stepped out and, just as quickly, stepped back in. "It's Ralph. And he's got two goons with him."

Seabolt came over. "I thought you were leaving. There a problem?"

"We've got some bootleggers mad at us this afternoon, and they're out there, front and back. We can't risk a shoot-out with all these people around."

"Quill, I've got me an idea." Seabolt went over to Acuff. "Have we got room in the cars for these two?" He thumbed at Rose and Jenks.

"They needin' a ride?"

"Quill's a sheriff and Tommy's his deputy. There are some bad men out front and in back that want to kill 'em."

"Well, we can't let that happen to a couple of East Tennessee boys. It'll be a squeeze, but sure, we can shoehorn 'em in."

Seabolt came back to Rose. "Quill, we've got to change you." He called to another musician. "Hey, Slim, would you bring one of your suits over here this fella can wear and your extra cowboy hat, yeah, that would be good. Quill, while you change, I'll get something more for you."

Jenks tapped his thumb on his chest.

"Tommy, I know just the thing. Jess plays bass fiddle for us, and we've not taken his fiddle out yet. You can carry it. You keep it between you and whoever you don't want to see you, and it'll hide you pretty good."

Seabolt led Jenks over to a tall case that contained the standup bass, a small box on the floor beside it. Seabolt opened the box. He took out a small bottle and a hideous, oversized, droopy black mustache. He made his way back to Rose, Rose working at the front of his shirt. "A couple more buttons and I'm ready to go."

"For now, just stop. I want you to look at me."

"Something wrong?"

Seabolt pulled a brush from the bottle and smeared a smelly substance over Rose's mustache.

Rose grimaced. "It stinks."

"It's supposed to. It's spirit gum. Hold still." Seabolt slapped the fake mustache on the stickum and held it there. "It's one of our Crazy Tennessean mustaches. Where's Slim's hat?"

Rose motioned to his suitcase.

Seabolt positioned Rose's finger on the mustache, then swept up the hat and planted it on Rose's head. He pulled the brim low. Rose's own clothes he stuffed in the suitcase, but the money stopped him. "Quill, what's this?"

"That's what they really want."

Seabolt took a deep breath. He snapped the suitcase shut and passed the suitcase and his violin case to Rose. "You put them in the trunk, then you get in the car."

Seabolt turned to Jenks. "Tommy, I'll get the door."

Jenks wrestled the bass fiddle toward the door, the wrapped shotgun getting away from him, falling.

Seabolt caught it. "What is this, anyway?"

"My shotgun."

"Oh Christ." Seabolt pulled over another musician. "Jess, Tommy's gonna give you a hand with your bass. You two get it up on the roof and tie it down."

Jess Easterday, Acuff's bass player, opened the stage door for Jenks and followed him out.

Seabolt grabbed the door, but stopped Rose. "Your mustache."

"What about it?"

"It's slipped, looks like a horseshoe worn sideways." Seabolt righted the mustache and pushed Rose out. "Fast, now, before it falls off."

Ralph stood looking over the musicians. Rose ducked as he clattered down the steps, hustling to catch up with Jenks and the bass, but Ralph seized him by the arm. "Don't I know you?"

"Maybe. You see the show tonight?"

"I was out here."

"Too bad."

Ralph squinted at Rose. "You've got the damnedest mustache I've ever seen. Is that real?" He reached out to touch it. As he did, another musician, toting an equipment case, plowed into him, crowding him out of the way.

Rose saw his break and slipped off to the car. He threw the two cases into the trunk and dashed around to the passenger's side. As he hunkered down to get in the front seat, his mustache fell to the ground. He grabbed it up and slapped it back in place as he slid into the center.

Seabolt handed the shotgun in, then slid in beside Rose. "You have a problem back there?"

"Almost."

"I saw that guy stop you, so I sent a buddy in to run interference."

"Sure worked, thanks."

Acuff came in from the other side. He settled himself behind the steering wheel. When he glanced at Rose, he broke out laughing. "Frankie, is that what we look like when we wear those damn things?"

He stuck his elbow out the window and called to the others, "Ready to go?"

Easterday shoved Tommy Jenks in the back seat of the second Packard. "Let's git!"

Acuff started the engine, then laid on the horn.

Ralph, in front of the car, jumped.

Acuff leaned out the window. "Get outta the way or you'll be a hood ornament!"

Ralph hopped to the side, and Acuff started the car moving, but stopped when he came up beside the moonshine muscle. He leaned out again. "Good show tonight, wasn't it?"

"I told another guy I didn't see it."

"Oh, too bad. I'm Roy Acuff. You all come back another night."

Acuff again started out of the alley. At the end, he turned onto the street, glancing in the mirror to make sure the second Packard was with him. "Mister Rose, there was a gun bulging in that feller's jacket pocket, no question. What'd you do to get him mad at you?"

Rose peeled the mustache off. He rubbed at the spirit gum. "Guess I can tell you now."

CHAPTER 12

Home again

IN THE TWILIGHT that preceded dawn, the twilight that shimmered through the window in Martha Rose's kitchen, Quill Rose unharnessed himself from his shoulder holster and the long-barreled Colt it held secure. As silently as he could, he laid them both on a shelf in the closet.

Rose sniffed at the aroma drifting about the room. Cookies. His nose told him they likely were oatmeal raisin, that Martha must have been baking yesterday.

When he swung around to go in search of the cookie jar, he leaped for he didn't expect someone to be standing behind him. Rose clutched at his chest. "You tryin' to give me a heart attack?"

Martha Rose hugged her house wrap to herself, her hair a mess from a night of restless sleep. "Where've you been?"

The words had a cut to them.

"Nashville," Rose forced out.

"Two days? Two nights? What was it this time you couldn't call me about before you went or while you were there? And why'd you take our suitcase?"

"You noticed?"

"It wasn't in the attic when I went up there to put some things away."

Rose, bushed, flopped on a chair. "Well, it's like this..." He ran a hand back through his hair. "...Tommy and me, we were on the track of a whiskey ring."

"And?"

"And it led to Nashville." He raised his hands in apology. "I'm sorry we had to go so quickly. We just didn't have time—"

"Quill, you never have time. You get so wrapped up in what you're doing."

"That's not true."

"You left me here with a two-year-old, you know that? He cried, Quill, when you weren't here to read to him the night before last and last night again."

"Yes, well, what can I say?"

"I don't know." She went to her Home Comfort stove and stuck kindling and a fistful of newspaper in the firebox. She struck a match and put the flame to the paper. "Quill, this little boy that we've got, he's getting curious about his world. He's opening drawers and cabinets and closets when I turn my back to do something." She whipped around after she had a good fire going and jammed a finger in front of Rose's face. "If you want to keep on keeping your guns in my broom closet, you've got to put a lock on that door he can't open. I won't have him shooting himself."

"I won't, either."

From the sideboard, Martha Rose scooped up a handful of hardware and thrust it at Rose.

He stared at her and the hardware, perplexed. "What's this?"

"I went to Anderson's. Jake said this is what I need for that door, an eye hook. He says you put it up where the boy can't reach it but you and I can—five feet, better five and a half feet. I want you to do it right now."

"I was hoping to get a little sleep before we went to church."

"You can sleep after church." She rapped on the table. "I want this done, no excuses, do you understand me?"

Rose shrugged. He forced himself up, got his box of tools out of the closet and pawed through until he found an awl and a hammer. He went back to the closet door and proceeded to tap in starter holes in the door frame and the door for the eye screws five feet three inches up from the floor, splitting the difference in Martha Rose's directive. He measured it twice to get it exact, then twisted the first screw in.

Toenails clacked into the kitchen on the linoleum, Rose's dog with a small boy in a nightshirt shuffling along beside him, the boy's fist clutched tight to the hair on the dog's shoulders.

Rose glanced down at the boy. "How you doin', little feller?"

The boy gave a sleepy-eyed grin.

Rose twisted at the second eye screw, talking over his shoulder. "You do like that dog, don'tcha? And I can see he sure likes you."

The dog—Fletch—licked the boy's face, the boy scrunching up at the raking given him by the dog's wet tongue. He shuffled forward to the closet, wiping his sleeve at his face as he went, and reached in for something, a shotgun that leaned in the corner next to Martha Rose's mop.

Rose put a hand down in front of the boy. "Whoa there, partner. The lady of the house doesn't want you touching that."

Martha Rose swooped in. She swept the boy up in her arms. "See what I've been telling you about, Quill?"

"You're right as you usually are." Rose closed the closet door. He dropped the hook from the eye screw in the door frame into the eye screw in the door. He did it a second time and a third, then pulled on the doorknob, the eye hook stopping the door from opening sufficiently that a child could squeeze his fingers in.

CHAPTER 13

Tax auction

THE DAY STARTED for Rose with breakfast with the Kiwanis club and a shave at the barbershop on the way to the courthouse—leisurely, no worries. He would have whistled 'When the Morning Glories Bloom' if his whistling was good for anything other than calling his dog.

He strolled into his office, up to his secretary's desk. "Morning, Hezzy."

"Mornin', Sheriff. Have a good time Friday?"

"Pardon?"

"Friday, you have a good time?"

"Oh, I surely did."

"What'd you do? You and Martha take that little boy you're looking after out to buy new shoes?"

Rose twisted a letter on his secretary's desk to himself. He glanced down the page. "Why this interest?"

"You usually tell me where you're going before you disappear."

"I usually do, don't I? You remember Tommy had to haul that prisoner over to Marcellus's jail? I ended up over there, too. We just gassed the afternoon away."

"You want coffee?"

"I can help myself." Rose hung his hat on the coat tree on his way to the hotplate and the coffeepot. "Is there anything I have to do today?"

"Tax auction in ten minutes."

"Oh, I hate that. A fella works a lifetime to pay for his place, then times get hard and he can't pay his taxes. And it comes to me to be the bad man and sell his place out from under him." Rose poured coffee into a well-stained cup. He sipped at it. "By God, Hezzy, today it's gonna be different."

She held out a handful of papers and a hammer. "Tommy's already outside on the steps, setting up a table for you."

Rose stuck the papers under his arm. He took the hammer and his hat in one hand and his coffee cup in the other and started for the door.

The secretary hurried ahead to open it.

"Thank you, Hezz. This place would be nothing but a pile of bricks without you."

At the next door—the door to the outside—all Rose could do, still with his hands full, was kick at it until someone heard him and opened it, the someone Tommy Jenks.

Rose made his way to the table on the courthouse steps. "Everybody here?"

"We've got Avery Moore from the bank and Newt Owenby."

"That old miser? Jeez."

Jenks tilted his head toward the side where a half-dozen people huddled together. "Those are the families."

Rose went over to them.

"Mornin', Sheriff," one of the men said.

"Mornin', Samuel, Ada, Bent, Irene." Rose extended his hand to the third man and the woman next to him. "I don't believe I know you two."

"I'm Axel Dunn. My wife, Lytha."

Rose shook hands with them, then drew the three couples into a huddle. "Did you bring your deeds?"

Bent Thatcher shifted his weight. "We're going to lose our places, aren't we, Sheriff?"

"That's the bad part of these tax auctions. Of course, if you can pay the back taxes, the places are yours to keep."

The men shoved their hands in their overalls pockets and studied the cracks in their leather shoes.

"Well, don't give up. Let's see how the bidding goes. If the bank buys them, Avery will likely rent your places back to you. He has in the past. If Newt buys them, well, he usually moves the families off."

Samuel Rayfield reached for his wife's hand. "Either way we end up with nothin'."

"Maybe, but let's see what happens." Rose moved over to the table. He spread out the tax liens and took one last sip of coffee. "Avery, Newt, you boys know how this works. Minimum bid is the tax bill, so let's get this done."

Rose picked up the first paper. He read from it. "First is the Rayfield place at Binfield. If you've been out there, you know it's a sweet little farm. Three years back taxes owed—ninety-seven dollars and a quarter."

Rose banged the table with the hammer. "All right now, do I have an opening bid?"

Moore nodded.

"Thank you, Avery. Now I'll take a hundred-dollar bill. Do I have a hundred-dollar bill?"

Owenby touched his nose.

"A hundred-dollar bill, now one twenty-five, one twenty-five, one twenty-five? Avery?"

Moore shook his head.

"Well, then one-fifteen, one-fifteen, one-fifteen. No? One-ten. One-ten? I've got one-ten."

Owenby swivelled around, searching for the new bidder. "Whose bid is that?"

Rose polished the head of his hammer. "I don't have to tell you, but it's mine."

Owenby glared over the tops of his glasses. "You can't do that."

"Why not? I've got money. That makes me a qualified bidder as far as the county's concerned. I've always wanted a little farm, and this is my chance. So I repeat, I've got the bid at one-ten. You want to go one and a quarter, Newt?"

"One-twenty."

"All right, now we're moving. You're in at one-twenty, and I've got the bid at one twenty-five. You want to go one-thirty? One-thirty? One-thirty? You in or you out, Newt? One-thirty? One-thirty?"

Owenby waved a hand in frustration.

"I take that as a no. Seeing no other bids, Quill Rose is the buyer at one twenty-five. Next property is Bent and Irene Thatcher's place up at Wildwood. What is it, Bent, ten acres?"

"Twelve."

"Snug little house, some outbuildings, twelve acres. Bent and Irene raised a nice family there. Taxes due the past three years, twenty-eight dollars. Do I have an opening bid? Avery? Newt?"

Moore scratched at the corner of his jaw while he considered it. "No, bank's not interested."

Owenby shook his head.

"All right then. The third property is the Axel and Lytha Dunn place on Pistol Creek, south of Rockford. I've driven by it. Seems to be a decent farm. Back taxes of one hundred twelve dollars and twenty-five cents owed."

Owenby raised a finger. "Hunnerd and thirty."

"Thank you, Newt. We've got interest here. Are you in on this, Avery, for one-fifty? I'm looking for one-fifty. One-fifty? One-fifty? One-fifty? One-forty then."

Moore shook his head.

"All right, let's try one thirty-five."

"Sorry, Quill, the bank officers only want bargains. They won't let me go that." Moore walked off.

"Well, Newt, it's you and me. How high do you want to go?"

Owenby haruumphed. "I'm in at one-thirty."

"I'll go you one-forty."

"One forty-five."

"One-fifty. Are you going up again, Newt?"

"One fifty-seven fifty."

"One-sixty."

"One sixty-one twenty-five."

"One sixty-two."

Owenby hesitated.

"You've got to go better than one sixty-two, Newt. What're you doing, counting the pennies in your pocket?"

Owenby crumpled the auction notice. He threw it on the steps. "It's yours. And I hope to hell you choke on it."

"I'll try not to." Rose banged the hammer on the table. "I declare the auction closed."

The three couples came over. Samuel Rayfield and Axel Dunn held out the deeds to their farms.

Rose bunched together his tax liens. "You keep your deeds."

Rayfield still held his out. "You bought our places fair."

"There's nothing fair about a tax auction. Here's what I want you to do. I want you to stay on your farms. You work them and take care of them like they're your own, because they are. Someday, you pay me back."

Rayfield gazed at his wife, relief in his eyes, as he slipped the deed back in his inside coat pocket. "I don't know what to say."

"Don't say a thing. You're nice people. You've got some money coming. Rules of the auction, the county gets its taxes, and you get the balance of the bid price. Mister Dunn, that means you've got forty-nine dollars and seventy-five cents coming. Let's not bother with quarters. Let's just call it fifty dollars."

Rose pulled a roll of bills from his pocket. He counted out the money and put it in Missus Dunn's hand.

"Samuel, you're due twenty-seven dollars and seventy-five cents. Call it twenty-eight." He peeled off two tens, a five, and three ones and gave them to Ada Rayfield. "Now what I'd do is go in and see the county treasurer. Pay that money down on next year's taxes. Then, when the bills come out next spring, Mister Dunn, you'll be paid up and, Samuel, you'll owe just a couple dollars."

Rayfield shook Rose's hand. "We'll just do that."

"One more thing, if you ever decide to sell, you come see me. Let me make an offer."

"Surely, Sheriff, and thank you." Dunn bobbed his head.

Rose took the Thatchers aside. "Bent, Irene, you're on the books to the county for twenty-eight dollars. You two have supported me in every election, and I don't want to see some yahoo coming by the courthouse and putting you out by buying up the tax lien. So I'm going to pay your taxes, then you'll be clear with the county."

Thatcher, staring down, moved the toe of his work shoe around on the step. "You don't need to do that."

"You're right, I don't need to. But I want to."

"That's awful kind. I'm old, you know, an' me and Irene, we're both a bit lame, but you can count on us to go a-callin' and turn out the vote for you long as you want to keep on bein' sheriff."

"I'll take you up on that. Now the two of you, you go along home."

Missus Thatcher reached for Rose's hand. "You come by and see us."

"You know I will."

After the Thatchers left, Jenks picked up the table, to take it back inside. "Where's all this money coming from that you're paying people's taxes with?"

"The booze money. I don't see much point in letting all of it sit in the bank for two-percent interest. And speaking of the bank, after I pay the taxes on these parcels, you and I, we'd better take what's left and go see Avery."

AVERY MOORE proved to be more than pleased to open a new account for the sheriff's department. After he counted the money in the suitcase, he wrote a receipt for two thousand, six hundred forty-six dollars and thirty-two cents. "And the source?"

"Moonshine money we confiscated."

ROSE HANDED the tax liens to his secretary to stamp and return to the county treasurer. That chore done, he went to his desk to check through the morning mail. After he settled himself, he hoisting his feet up on his desk. Rose peered at the first envelope and flipped it toward the secretary's wastebasket halfway across the room. "Trash."

"Trash–trash–trash." More envelopes sailed toward the wastebasket. "Oh, here's one from Will's office. Let's see what he didn't tell us Saturday."

Jenks looked over from his job of thumbing through an envelope of circulars that had come down from the State Police headquarters.

Rose tore off the end of the envelope. He shook out a letter. "Ah-ha, Will's inviting us up to the lab to learn about the science of ballistics. Wonder what that is?" He read down the letter. "Oh, that's matching a bullet that's been fired to the gun it's been fired from. That could be interesting. You want to go, Tommy?"

"When is it?"

"Next week, ahh, Wednesday."

"What I'd really like to learn is how to read fingerprints."

"Now that I can teach you." Rose swung his feet down. He opened his desk drawer and hummed while he rooted among the contents. "Ahh-ha, here we are. Sherlock Holmes's magnifying glass. Now where'd I put that print Will sent us?"

Rose dug through a clutter of envelopes on the corner of his desk.

"Uh-hmm, here is it." He held it up for Jenks to see. "Now bring our file box over here, and let's do some checking."

Jenks went over to a cabinet for the recipe box in which they kept fingerprint cards for all the prisoners who had passed through the county jail in the past two years. He brought the box to Rose's desk.

Rose huffed specks of dust from his magnifying glass. "Get you out a handful of cards, and let's do some comparing."

Jenks pulled out five. He spread them in an array on Rose's desk.

Rose took the print card from Kaufmann's envelope and held the magnifying glass over the card. "See there in the center of the print, where the pattern is the tightest? That's called the whorl. I study that. I memorize that pattern before I start looking at other prints I want to compare it to."

Rose took Jenks's index finger and turned it up. He put the glass over it. "See the pattern of your whorl? It's totally different, particularly on the right side."

"I don't see it."

"Here, you take the glass. You study your finger, then you study the print card. Remember the print on your finger is backwards to the print on the card. Go back and forth, back and forth, and you'll start to see differences."

Jenks peered at his finger, then at the card, his finger and the card again. A smile came to the corners of his mouth. "I see it now, yeah. I can't be the fingerprint on that card."

"That was lesson number one. Now lesson number two. Give me the glass. Now I go back to the print I'm trying to match, and I look for anything strange, unusual, odd, different." Rose gazed through the glass. "Ah-ha-ha-ha-haaa."

"What is it?"

"See there on the left side, there's a break there across ten, maybe fifteen lines or ridges. Not a ragged break like you get if you catch your finger on a barbwire fence. Smooth and straight like a cut you get when you're scaling fish and your knife slips. This boy cut himself."

Rose handed the glass to Jenks. "Now you look over these cards. See if you can see anything like that on one of them. I'm going upstairs to the judge's office."

ROSE FOUND Judge Enos Limke in his shirt sleeves. "Quill, what can I do for you on this fine morning?"

"Tommy and me, we're starting to line up things we need to be doing. Before we got too far, I thought I'd better check with you on the court calendar, see when you'll be needing us."

Limke had been on the bench as long as Rose had been sheriff. They had developed a comfortable alliance over the years, so much so that in the last four elections they had driven together around the county, campaigning for votes at every post office, country store, and barbershop where people gathered on weekends, the days when the courthouse was closed.

Rose drove because Limke refused to wear his glasses anywhere other than in the privacy of his office or at home. The lenses were as thick as the bottoms of Royal Crown Cola bottles. As a consequence, Limke was always bumping into chairs or catching the toe of one shoe or the other on door sills. His constituents thought he was clumsy.

Limke pulled over his calendar book. "Well, this is an easy week. We've got that burglar and that little weasel, Jesse Tubbs. He sold an old lady stock in a phony aluminum mine he told her was down in the south end of the county. The old gal never got out much, so that idiot thought she'd never go down to check up on it. What say we put them both on Friday?"

"Fine. And next week?"

"Nothing criminal right now. Why do you ask?"

Rose settled in the chair next to Limke's desk. "Well, the State Police lab in Knoxville is doing a session on the new science of ballistics. Tommy and me, we're thinking of going up for it."

"Bull-what?"

"Not bull, Enos. Ball—ballistics. They now can match a bullet to the gun that fired it."

"And that's helpful?"

"It is if we've got a shooter, and he won't confess."

"So when's this session?"

Rose brought out Kaufmann's letter. He scanned down the page. "Wednesday next."

"I won't schedule any trial work that day. Might even take off and go along with you."

"I'm sure you'd be welcome."

A rapid knocking came at the door.

"Yes?" Limke called out.

Tommy Jenks pushed in. "Excuse me, Judge, I don't mean to interrupt."

"But you have. What is it?"

Jenks handed Rose the glass and two cards. "Quill, I think you better see this."

"What is it?"

"Look close at the card from our file box."

Rose did, concentrating on the print from the index finger. Then he went back to the print Kaufmann had sent. He stared up at Jenks. "That's our boy."

Limke gave a tuck to his spectacles, pushing them up on the bridge of his nose. "Who's that?"

"The boy who killed those three people up on Pistol Creek. Tommy caught him when he was poking around a booze operation. We never made the connection because the fella refused to talk to us. Judge, can I use your phone?"

Limke pushed his telephone to Rose.

Rose put the receiver to his ear, then clicked the receiver hook three times. "May Ella, it's the sheriff," he said into the mouthpiece. "Would you get me the sheriff over in Lenoir City? Try him at his office."

"What's Marcellus got to do with this?"

Rose put a hand over the mouthpiece. "Long story, but we put the man in Marcellus's jail because we didn't want anybody around here knowing we had him."

He took his hand from the mouthpiece. "Marcellus?...Quill Rose. Our anonymous man, I want him back. Tommy matched his fingerprint. He killed the family on Pistol Creek...He what?...When?...Aww jeez, Marcellus, why didn't you call me?...I know, I know. Do what you can."

Rose edged the receiver back on the hook.

Limke tilted his head. "You look like you've just been told your favorite hunting dog died. What is it?"

"He posted leg bail."

"Escaped? When?"

"Last night."

"Can Marcellus catch him again?"

"He figures he's skiddaddled from the county. Somebody stole his police car."

CHAPTER 14

Bullet class

WILL KAUFMANN spread his fingers on the lectern. "So there you have it, gentlemen. You saw me shoot Deputy Jenks's gun, recover the bullet, then match the striations against three other bullets of the same caliber to determine which one of the three had also been fired from his gun."

Kaufmann held up the matching bullets. "It used to be that all I had was my microscope. I had to remember what the bullet looked like when I looked at the next bullet." He moved over to a table on which rested a camera. "Now with this I can take a picture through the microscope. Then I can hold the pictures of two bullets side by side and really compare them, go over them with a magnifying glass if I have to, to be absolutely sure."

Kaufmann held up the matching photos. "We've got one judge here. Judge Limke, do you think these pictures would convince a jury?"

"May I look at them?"

"Sure. Here."

Kaufmann handed the photos and the magnifying glass to the judge.

Limke held the glass against his face as he studied the bullets in the two pictures. "By God, it'd sure convince me."

"Thank you. There you have it, gentlemen, evidence you can take into the courtroom."

The baker's dozen of local police officers applauded, then pushed back from their tables. Several came over to talk with Kaufmann while others prepared to leave.

Limke waved the pictures. "Quill, I didn't know we had all this stuff available to us. I'm glad you brought me along."

"Enos, this science is amazing stuff. What do you think, Tommy, this can help us?"

"Can't wait to try it in a real case."

Rose gathered up copies of Kaufmann's handouts. "What do you say we get on down the road?"

Kaufmann beckoned to Rose. "Can I have a moment?"

"Sure."

Kaufmann put his hand on the shoulder of the Anderson County sheriff as he walked him to the door. "Edgar, you've got that bank robbery. Anything I can do to help you, you call me."

After the Anderson sheriff had gone out, Kaufmann closed the door. He came back to the table where Rose, Jenks, and Limke lingered. "Can I talk with the judge here?"

"Enos? He likes a nip of corn whiskey now and then, and he doesn't think I know where he gets it."

Limke's mouth gaped open.

"Aw, come on, now, Enos, you've been getting it from my shirttail cousin for fifteen years. Will, other than that, the judge is as straight as they come."

"All right, then. I told you I'd do some checking around. I'm going to give you an envelope. In it are the names of a dozen troopers in the Eastern Kingdom who are as straight as your judge if not more so. We can call on them anytime, day or night, and they'll help."

Kaufmann opened a folder. He took a plain white envelope from it and handed it to Rose.

"There's another envelope just like this one locked in my evidence safe. In it are the names of six who've been bought off. This is State Police business, Quill, so you don't need to know those names."

"If you say so."

"They're bad. I'll make sure you're steered clear of them."

"Do I know any of them?"

"Two. And one of them's here in the Knoxville post."

"Figures."

"Yes, it does." Kaufmann closed his folder.

"I'd like you to make a trip into Nashville with Tommy and me."

"Anytime."

Rose gazed at his fistful of handouts. "This was a good day, my friend. We learned a lot."

"I'm thinking of holding sessions like these quarterly. What do you think?"

"We'll be here."

OUTSIDE, ON THE STREET as the three men from Blount County made their way to Rose's cruiser, Limke turned the conversation to the cryptic talk of Rose and Kaufmann. "Are you going to share what that was about?"

"You're going to find out sometime, so I'll give you the quick summary. Tommy and I have stumbled on the biggest moonshine operation. They're making it up under Shingle Mountain and shipping it out by the tanker load. And before you ask, Luther Click's too honest to be involved in this, so your supplier's safe."

A weak smile lifted Limke's face.

"This thing's big, so big that they're out buying protection. You heard it. Will's found six in the State Police on the take."

"Think any sheriffs are in on this?"

"Indeed. I don't know who yet. What I really want to know is who the money men are, who put this together. If we're to blow this thing, Tommy and I, we intend to blow it open wide."

"Any leads?"

Rose slowed to rub an itch at the front of his shoulder. "We know where there's one stop in

Nashville. We also know there's another, and it's about time we found out where it is."

"Any of this going to end up in my courtroom?"

"It's possible." Rose put his arm around the judge's shoulders as they walked on. "But I think most of it's going to go to state court."

"Any way I can help you?"

"By not talking about it, not to anyone, particularly not your wife. Nettie's a sweet person, but she can't keep a secret to save her soul."

CHAPTER 15

Job offer

QUILL ROSE WANDERED into the Tennessee Valley Authority building in Knoxville, his hands pushed deep in the pockets of his rumpled suit. He glanced around, looking for someone to whom he could ask a question. Ahead and to the right he saw a switchboard, two operators working it, pushing pins at the ends of cords into holes and pulling other pins out, all the while talking into tubes that rested on their chests.

At the counter in front of the switchboard sat the person he needed, a beauty next to an information sign.

Rose took off his slouch hat as he ambled over. There was something about this person that puzzled him. "You're Nadine Willis, aren't you?"

"Mister Rose." The young woman gave off with a smile that was electric, and her hand came out.

The two took shook hands, but still Rose was puzzled. "I didn't know you were here. Of course, I've not seen your family in an age."

"Oh, I've been working here for six months."

"Really?"

"Yes. You remember I graduated high school last year."

"Uh-huh."

"Then I did a little secretarial school here in Knoxville, and the TVA hired me."

Rose parked his elbow on the counter. "How's your momma?"

"Fine."

"Your pa?"

"Not good."

"Oh? Why's that?"

"You know we lost our farm to the TVA. It's all going to go underwater when the Fort Louden dam's finished. Daddy's just can't get used to town life."

"I should go over and see him."

"He'd like that. But how can I help you?"

Rose glanced at the sign-in log next to the information sign. "Nadine, the lieutenant governor asked me to meet him here."

"Mister Johnson?"

"Yes."

"He's upstairs with Mister Morgan." She touched the arm of the closest operator. "Mae, would you please call Mister Morgan's office and tell his secretary that Mister Quill Rose from Maryville is here to see Mister Johnson?"

The woman, not much older than Willis, plugged a pin into her board. She waited a moment, then spoke into the tube that carried her voice to a telephone microphone.

Willis swept a hand out at the immense lobby. "Isn't this some place, Mister Rose? I've never seen so many people working in one place and on so many things."

"Well, from what I read, this federal thing is a mighty big project."

"Oh, it is." She leaned into Rose. "They tell me it's going to change our state and our neighboring states in ways we can't even comprehend."

"As long as it's for the good."

The operator interrupted. "Missus Minshall asks that you bring Mister Rose up."

Nadine Willis smiled that electric smile again. "Mister Rose, if you'd come with me."

She came out from behind the counter and guided him toward the stairwell. Together, they trotted up three flights of stairs to the fourth floor where the stairwell opened into a room almost the size of the entire floor. Rose couldn't be sure how many people were there, but his gaze took in coveys of engineers and draftsmen hunched over tables, drawing, conversing, studying charts, and going over materials specifications. Nadine waved to one of the younger men, and he waved back.

"A friend?"

"Uh-huh."

"More than a friend?"

"I hope so."

"Oh, to be young and in love."

"Are you teasing me?" she asked as the two made their way through the maze of tables to an office suite against the far wall.

"Do your parents know?"

"Not yet."

Willis opened the door to the first office and led Rose in.

"This is Mister Rose," she said to the matron at the desk before her.

The woman stood up. She extended her hand. "Mister Rose, Mister Morgan has asked me to take you right in."

"Mister Morgan?"

"Mister Arthur Morgan, chairman of the TVA Commission."

Rose glanced at Willis, his eyes widening. She nodded.

Missus Minshall pointed Rose's escort to the outer door. "Miss Willis, you may return to your post now."

Willis smiled at Rose and departed the office.

Minshall, wearing a gray suit dress with an ivory and gold broach on the lapel, stepped away from her desk. "So you know the lieutenant governor."

"He's my brother-in-law."

"Really? Right this way." Minshall took Rose to a side door where she rapped. She waited a beat, then opened the door and led Rose on into an inner office dominated by a side table cluttered with engineering drawings and the chairman's polished walnut desk, the top bare except for a model steam shovel that a child of monied parents might have. There was not even a nameplate on the desk.

The chairman and Johnson, sitting on a leather couch, conversing, came to their feet.

Clayton Johnson's hand came out, his face wreathed in its ever-ready politician's smile. "Quill, I'd like you to meet the head of the TVA, Arthur Morgan. He was just telling me about the city he's building up by the Norris dam."

Morgan's hand also came out. "Mister Rose, Clayton's told me all about you. You really ought to be working for us." Morgan matched Rose for height, but he was broad shouldered while Rose was slim. The chairman's face projected authority—square jaw, gray hair brushed back, round, black-rimmed glasses.

Rose did his aw-shucks, I'm-just-a-poor-country-sheriff shtick.

"Now, really, Clayton says you're an honest man, that you care for the people of your county. I respect that."

"Well, I'd suggest you take what Clayton says with a smidgen of salt. We're kin."

Morgan took Johnson by the elbow. "Clay, I've got to get out on one of my jobs. You use my office for as long as you want." He shook hands with Rose one more time, then left with his secretary, she closing the office door.

Johnson tugged at the front of his tailored suit coat. "Have you ever been up here before?"

"Never had the occasion."

"Come over here." Johnson lead the way to one of the office's long walls on which hung a five-state map. "See all these areas marked out in blue?"

"Uh-huh."

"That's the Tennessee River and all its tributaries, six hundred fifty-two miles of river in the Tennessee itself. We're in the process of building thirty-five dams on the river system for navigation, flood control, and the generation of electricity, biggest damn federal project there is, and most of it's right here in our state." Johnson swept his hand along the breadth of Tennessee. "Quill, it's going to change everything, the end of springtime flooding, the end of malaria that every year knocks down a third of our population, jobs by the tens of thousands, good-paying jobs. Can you see why I want to be governor? There are exciting times ahead for us."

Rose massaged his chin while he admired the map and its details. "Exciting times for you. I'm happy where I am."

"Martha isn't."

Rose glimpsed Johnson from the corner of his eye.

Johnson went to Morgan's desk. There he opened a side drawer and took out two glasses and a bottle of Jack Daniels sipping whiskey. "Care for a drink?"

Rose didn't turn away from the map. "You know I don't."

"Mind if I have one?"

He shrugged.

Johnson took the cap from the bottle and poured three fingers in one of the glasses. He sipped down a swallow. "Damn, we make good whiskey in our state." Rose swung around to Johnson, Johnson raising his glass. "Come to work for me, Quill. Get Martha into a fine house in Nashville."

"On a state salary?"

"If it's the right state salary." Johnson motioned Rose toward one of the side chairs while he settled in Morgan's high-backed leather chair. "Quill, do you know our state attorney general?"

"I've never met him." Rose rotated his hat in his hands.

"Just as well. Gawddamn Republican. How we let him in office, I'll never know, but word is he's about to go on a tear of investigations that will get him so many headlines he could be elected our next governor."

"What's this got to do with me?"

"I've talked to the Old Man. He's given me the authority to put together my own investigations unit, beat old Randall to the punch and knock him out of the box. I need you to head it up. Pay's damn good." Johnson tossed back the rest of his whiskey, baring his teeth when the liquor hit his stomach. "Come on, Quill, you're family. We look out for family."

"You going to hire Edgar, too?"

"My other sister's husband?"

Rose gave a weak smile.

"Hell, Edgar can't find his fanny with a map. He can't do anything for me, but you can. You're an investigator, Quill. You're a lawman. That's what I need."

Rose set his hat on the corner of Morgan's desk. "If I were to say yes, and I'm not saying I am, where would I be working?"

Johnson poured himself another splash of whiskey, then swung his feet up on the desk. He leaned back in the comfort of Morgan's chair. "Memphis, most times. Quill,

we've got the damnedest corruption over there. It's time
we bring it down. We clean up Memphis—and we can do
that, Quill—we can pick any target in the state that we
want to go after. What do you say?"

Rose leaned back in his chair. He folded his arms
across his chest. "Give me a couple weeks?"

Johnson sipped from his glass before he set it aside.
He stared at Rose over the toes of his well-polished shoes.
"I can't wait long. I've got to beat Randall or all us
Democrats are going to be sitting out on the back porch
steps waiting for scraps."

CHAPTER 16

The set-up

QUILL ROSE SWUNG his feet out of bed.

He rubbed his whiskered face with both hands, to bring himself awake, then stumbled down the stairs, a ringing telephone insisting he hurry. Rose knocked the receiver from its hook when he got to the hallway phone. He gave the receiver a weary look as it dangled on the end of its cord, grabbed for the receiver, and brought it up to his ear.

"Sheriff here," he mumbled at the mouthpiece. "This better be gawd-awful good."

"Quill?" a voice asked from the other end of the line.

"Od?"

"Quill, I got what you want."

"Got what?"

"Two tankers. They just went through town. I talked to the drivers. They're on their way to Nashville."

"Good. That's good, Od."

"Quill, you need to know ever since you grabbed that tanker, they been sending them through with two men in the cab. I couldn't see in this mornin', but I'm willing to bet the second man's got a shotgun."

"Oh, now that makes for more interest. Appreciate the call, Od."

Rose did not hang up. He instead clicked the receiver's hook. "May Ella, get Tommy for me at his house, please."

Rose raked his fingers through his hair while he waited. A click came on the line. "Tommy?"

Rose heard a yawning and a mumbled "yeah."

"Tommy, we're on. Two tankers. Give me a chance to shave, then pick me up, say, half an hour."

"Sure." Jenks hung up.

Rose clicked the receiver hook again. "May Ella, I need Marcellus Briskey in Lenoir City. Don't know the number...at his house, yes."

He leaned to the side to peer in the hall mirror. "Lord, if I don't look like some squinty-eyed old possum."

"Sheriff here," came Briskey's voice from the receiver.

Rose turned back to the mouthpiece. "It's Quill. Sorry to call you so early."

"It idn't early. I was at the breakfast table, enjoyin' sausages an' johnny cakes an' eggs."

"Took a world of effort for you to step away from that, didn't it?"

"Uh-huh."

"Marcellus, I need your help on the highway again."

"Whatcha got?"

"Two Sunspot tankers coming your way in about an hour. I want 'em both."

The sound of chewing answered.

"Marcellus?"

"Yeah?"

"What are you doing?"

"Eatin'. I brought my plate with me from the table."

"Did you hear what I want?"

"For me to stop two tankers for ya. I s'pose you want me to keep the drivers in my jail along with the other I got."

"If you would, Marcellus, but you're gonna get four men today. Od tells me there's a gunner riding passenger in each truck."

"Hm. Always like a little challenge. The boys and me, we'll take care of it for ya."

Briskey hung up.

Again Rose clicked the receiver hook. "May Ella, Knoxville this time, four-two-six-one."

He picked up the newspaper from the hall table and opened it to the editorial page. "Wonder what old Wallace is ranting about this week? Anything, so long's it not me. Will?" he said into the mouthpiece.

"Yes."

"Quill Rose. Want to go to Nashville for a couple days?"

"Leaving when?"

"In an hour."

"What do you have going on?"

"We're hijacking two tankers. Tommy and I'll drive, but we need someone to make sure no one sneaks up behind us."

"I can do that. You want me in uniform or civilian?"

"I'm glad you asked. You couldn't by chance lay your hands on a chauffeur's rig?"

"By chance I can."

"Then get it. Tommy and I, we'll be by your house to pick you up."

Kaufmann hung up.

Again Rose stayed on the line, clicking the receiver hook. "One more call, May Ella...Avery Moore. Thank you...Avery? Quill Rose."

"Quill, awful early for you to be calling. How can I help you?"

"You still have your daddy's car, don't you?"

"The Bradford, yes. But I don't drive it. Kind of embarrassing. It looks so rich, you know."

"But it runs?"

"Oh yes, runs fine. I keep the battery up, and almost every Saturday I'm out in the barn, waxing the car or tinkering with the motor. It's a beautiful car."

"Could I borrow it for a couple days?"

"Sure. Mind me asking why?"

"Tommy and I, we're going to confiscate some more moonshine money. We've got to build up that bank account, you know."

"When do you want to get it?"

"About half an hour."

CHAPTER 17

Hijack times two

MARCELLUS BRISKEY reached over from the backseat and put a hand on his driver's shoulder. "Pull off here, Jacob."

The deputy let the Model T touring car coast to a stop at the side of the highway.

Another open touring car stopped behind Briskey and Jacob Miller.

Five men got out, Briskey and Miller from their car and Deputies Charlie Davis, Henry Thornton, and Buck Deeds from the second.

Briskey motioned for his men to circle in. "I expect we got us a couple minutes before those tankers get here. Jacob, Henry, you jack up the rear end of my car and pull off the left wheel. Make it look like we're broke down. Charlie, you take your car on up ahead, pull off in the borrow ditch and hide it off in the brush somewheres. And all of you, get your shotguns and make sure they're loaded. Hurry now, boys."

Thornton and Deeds went back for their weapons while Miller pulled a jack and tire tools from beneath the seat of Briskey's car.

When the deputies returned, they scrounged along the roadside for rocks with which to block the Ford's wheels. They found several of good size.

Miller had the jack positioned under the rear axle when he heard Thornton and Deeds jam the rocks in front of and behind the wheels, so he pumped away on the jack handle.

Thornton picked up the tire wrench. He broke the lug nuts free and spun each off before the wheel lifted from the ground. When the wheel did clear the ground, he yanked the wheel off and let it flop on the pavement.

"That's good, boys." Briskey aimed his trigger finger off to the side of the road. "Charlie, Henry, Buck, you go down in the weeds and stay outta sight."

Davis started away, but turned back. "What about stoppin' those tankers?"

"Don't you worry none, I'll get 'em stopped. When I do, Charlie, you and Henry come up from behind on either side of the second truck. You take the driver and his gunner. Buck, you get the gunner on the lead truck, and I'll get the driver."

Miller noodled the gravel with the toe of his shoe. "What about me?"

"Jacob, my boy, I want you on yer knees, pretendin' to study the tire. You keep yer shotgun where you can get it."

"Knees and shotgun, right."

The three deputies, two in denim overalls and the third in a black suit like Briskey's, trotted off.

Briskey leaned against the back of his car, talking with Miller now crouched down on the pavement. Every few moments, Briskey glanced up the highway. "Here they come. Stay there with the tire."

The Louden sheriff stepped out into the road. He waved his arms over his head, grinning when the lead truck slowed.

Briskey continued to wave, and the driver downshifted and downshifted again, the first truck rolling to a stop a dozen feet short of Briskey.

The driver leaned out his window. "Trouble, mister?"

"Yup." Briskey ambled toward the truck. "Busted a tire."

"So?"

"Don't have any inner tube patches. Got everything else to fix the damn thing, but no patches." Briskey, now beside the cab, looked up at the driver. "You wouldn't happen to have any, would ya?"

"I'll look in my toolbox."

The driver, after he opened his door, slid down to the pavement, then reached back inside, under the seat. He brought out a metal case and set it on the running board. He jiggled the latch to make the top open. "Wrenches, screwdrivers, hammer. Ahh, here's my patch kit."

Briskey pressed the muzzle of his revolver against the back of the driver's neck.

The man froze.

DAVIS, THORNTON, AND DEEDS crept out of the ditch near the back of the second truck, Davis ducking under the tank to get to the driver's side.

They moved on their toes until they were just short of the cab, then Davis and Thornton brought their shotguns up.

Davis tapped the driver's door.

The driver turned.

Davis settled his finger on the trigger. "Don't move, mister. Don't say a thing and sure don't touch that horn button."

The passenger ducked down. Thornton saw the movement and jumped on the running board. He jammed the barrel of his pump shotgun through the window. "Don't do it!"

Deeds raced forward. He swung out to the side of the cab of the first truck, his shotgun against his shoulder. "Hands up!"

The passenger in the second truck inched his way up. When Thornton's gaze flicked away for an instant, toward the lead truck, the passenger slammed his door open, flinging Thornton from the running board. Thornton's shotgun discharged.

Davis grabbed his pistol from his belt. He leaped to the driver's running board. With one hand he jammed his pistol in the driver's neck, with the other he trained his shotgun on the passenger. "No more, mister!"

Deeds glanced back when Thornton's shotgun exploded.

The man, who a moment before had been Deeds's prisoner, threw open the door, catching Deeds in the shoulder, spinning him away. The deputy fell.

The man flung himself from the truck, shotgun in hand. He came down on the ditch bank, slid to the bottom, and raced for the brush.

Jacob Miller, at the rear of the car, fired once in the air, but the gunner didn't stop, only kicked up his speed.

Miller bolted to Deeds on the ground, Deeds clutching at his shoulder.

"Don't stop for me! Get him, Jake!"

Miller vaulted across the ditch and disappeared into the brush. Three shotgun blasts followed in rapid succession and a scream.

Then silence.

Briskey continued to press the barrel of his revolver into the first driver's neck. "Buck, what happened?" he called out.

"Don't know. Jake went after the other man."

"Can you go out there? See?"

Deeds rolled up on his knees. "Yeah, guess I can."

He got to his feet and recovered his shotgun from where it had fallen in the gravel. Deeds slapped the dust away from his trousers as he started down into the ditch, moving in the direction of thrashing sounds in the brush coming his way. He brought his shotgun up.

The gunner stumbled out, his hand clamped tight to his arm, blood leaking between his fingers.

Miller came out next, carrying his and the gunner's shotguns.

"Jake, Sheriff wants to know if yer all right?"

"I am, only 'cause this damn yahoo's got terrible aim, an' I got better. Here." Miller pitched the gunner's shotgun to Deeds.

"Winged him, huh?"

"Gonna be a month of Sundays afore he works a gun again." Miller prodded the man forward.

The man slipped as he climbed up the side of the ditch. Deeds grabbed the gunner's good arm and pulled him along.

Briskey shoved his man, in handcuffs, around the front of the truck, the driver's face red with anger. "You know who your dealin' with here? You're in big gawddamn trouble."

Briskey kicked the driver's legs out from under him, dropping him to the gravel, then stepped down on the man's shoulder. "Sonny boy, I don't give a good gawddamn who you and yer buddies are. You just remember who's got the guns and who owns the jail where yer gonna be livin'."

"But—"

"Don't say another word. I ain't above a little pistol whippin'. Jacob, y'all right?"

"Yeah."

Deeds pointed his shotgun at Miller's pant leg.

Miller looked down. "Aw, Jesus, he put some birdshot through my pant leg, didn't he, and these are new britches." He pulled his trousers up to his knee. Miller ran a hand over the skin and muscles of his lower leg. "Well, least he didn't put no holes in me. But damn, he ruint my pants. Two seventy-five out of the Monkey Ward catalogue. My wife's gonna kill me."

Briskey hauled his man to his feet. "Charlie? Henry? You got yer men?"

"We got 'em, Sheriff!"

Davis and Thornton pushed their two ahead of them, also handcuffed. The deputies carried their own guns and the guns they had taken from the driver and the driver's passenger.

"Looks like we're all accounted for, boys. Charlie, go get yer car and take these who-dads to the jail. Then call the doc to come over and pick the birdshot out of this idiot." He turned on the wounded man. "Fella, you better wrap your arm in your coat. If you bleed on Charlie's car, he's gonna whup up on ya."

CHAPTER 18

Traveling in style

WILL KAUFMANN STEPPED OUT on his porch and threw his arms out wide. "How do I look?"

Quill Rose gave him a once-over. "Every inch the part."

Tommy Jenks, though, cast a more critical eye. "Funny looking' britches, seems to me."

"They're jodhpurs. These, the knee-high boots, the little cap, Tommy, it's the uniform the best chauffeurs wear."

Rose marveled at Kaufmann. "Where'd you get the togs?"

"From my neighbor. He drives for Mister Myerson."

Faith Kaufmann, her hair wrapped in a scarf, came out the door. She held the hand of her younger son beside her while her older boy, Samuel, lagged behind. "Don't my man look handsome, Quill?"

"That he does. Maybe you'd like to see the car he's going to drive." Rose stepped aside so the Kaufmanns could see past him to the street.

"Oh my, my, my, my, my."

"Sweet Jesus." Kaufmann slipped an arm around his wife's waist. He reached back for Samuel, and the foursome hurried down to the street.

"Is this what I think it is?" Kaufmann let go of his son's hand and caressed the long, wide, gleaming hood of the limousine. He picked up his younger son, John Mark, and swung him over the door, down onto the leather seat. The boy giggled as he gazed back up at his father.

Kaufmann tweaked the boy's nose. "It's a Bradford, John Mark. Someday it'll be important to you. Quill, what vintage?"

"Nineteen Twenty-Eight."

"And I get to sit up here in the open air and drive while you two white boys sit back there in the closed car and look important. Have I got that right?"

Rose laughed. "Did you bring your gun and badge?"

"They're in my bag. Sammy, would you go back in the house and get my bag for me?"

The older boy, who had been studying his image in the limousine's side mirror, broke away. He ran back to the porch and inside, the door banging shut, only to be thrown open again as the boy ran back out, swinging a carpet bag.

Kaufmann set it inside the driver's compartment, on the floor. He and Samuel then strolled around to the driver's side of the car, admiring its clean lines as they went. The boy stopped. He wiped his hand over a headlamp the size of a dishpan. Kaufmann, though, opened the door and slid in behind the steering wheel.

"Will, when you be back?" Faith Kaufmann asked.

He threw the question to Rose, and Rose scratched at his earlobe. "There's a chance maybe tomorrow. More likely, the next day."

"Well, you take care of my man for me."

"I brought Tommy to do that."

She reached over the door for her younger son. She caught the boy under the arms and lifted him from the car, but not before Kaufmann tousled the boy's hair. "You listen to your momma. You do what she says, son."

She smiled at Rose. "He's daddy's boy."

"And not real big on goodbyes." Kaufmann waved to the boy before he got down to the business of studying the dash panel and the controls.

"Sammy." Faith Kaufmann beckoned for her other son to join her.

The older boy shagged himself away from the front of the car as Rose opened the back door for Jenks. For himself, he slipped into the front passenger seat.

Kaufmann started the car. He listened to the engine rumble. "Oh, isn't that sweet?"

"A Straight-Eight."

"Powerful."

"Eats cars like my cruiser for breakfast. We better go."

Kaufmann found first gear and let the clutch out. He waved to his family as he steered the Bradford out onto Vine Street and down the hill. At Gay Street, he turned south. Kaufmann gazed over the polished walnut instrument panel as he drove. "They didn't spare any expense when they made this one, did they?"

"No. Back there where the rich folks sit, where Tommy is—Will, it's silk plush, arm rests, a vanity case, a cigar lighter—and neither Tommy or I smoke." He laughed as he slapped Kaufmann's leg.

At Cumberland, Kaufmann aimed the car west on Cumberland Avenue, a street that would go through two name changes as the miles rolled on, becoming Kingston Pike, then U.S. Seventy.

At Bearden, just beyond the Knoxville city limits, Kaufmann could no longer restrain his curiosity. "Where'd you get this? You can't afford it and neither can I, not even if we put our paychecks together."

"The banker. It's another one of those proverbial long stories."

"Quill, we're going to be driving all day."

"All right, here's the short of it. Avery's pap financed the Knoxville Jitney Company back in Nineteen-and-Twenty-Eight. They ordered three Bradfords for a new taxi service and did good business that first year. But 'Twenty-Nine came—"

"And they went under, have I got that right?"

"Old Mister Moore had to call in the note. KJC didn't have any cash, so Mister Moore sold two of the cars and wrote off the rest of the loan, keeping this car for himself."

"He have a chauffeur?"

"For a year." Rose glanced to the side, at a stretch of farmland. "Then his bank came close to going under, so he had to let the man go. He put the car up on blocks."

"It's a beautiful thing."

The Bradford continued rolling westward, through Farragut and on toward Eaton Crossroads. Just before the Crossroads, Rose put his hand on Kaufmann's arm, to get his attention. He pointed ahead.

Kaufmann nodded and let the big car slow as they came up on two gasoline tankers parked at the side of the highway. He herded the car over onto the shoulder.

There, on the back bumper of the near tanker, sat Marcellus Briskey, working at a cud in his cheek and bobbing his foot from side to side.

Rose got out of the limousine. "Marcellus, have you been waiting long?"

"'Bout half an hour. Kinda wished I'd brought along my mandolin this mornin'. Coulda played a little to pass the time."

The Louden sheriff pushed himself up. He stopped when he saw Kaufmann get out of the driver's side of the Bradford. "Good gawd, lookit you."

Kaufmann came around to Briskey. He parked a gleaming boot up on the tanker's bumper and, with extreme deliberation, flicked a speck of dust from the shine. "Marcellus, if this thing goes sour and the State Police toss me out on the sidewalk, I'm thinking I could have me a new profession here. You couldn't happen to use a chauffeur, could you?"

"Heh, in my Model T?"

Rose parked his shoe on the bumper, too. "So you got your car back."

"Yup, Knoxville police found it at the Southern Depot. It'd been there a couple days when they got curious and called me."

"Ah-ha, our bad boy took the train."

"Appears that way. The L&N agent remembered him and remembered selling him three tickets, to Bristol, Chattanooga, and Nashville. But no one saw which train he got on."

Rose stared off across the brush beyond the ditch. "I know which one."

"Ya do now."

"The Chattanooga, only he didn't go to the end of the line. Tommy caught him in the south end of the county."

"Meaning—"

"If he's run anywhere, he's run up under Shingle Mountain. That fella's going to be hard to catch. You have any trouble stopping the tankers?"

Briskey rubbed his fanny. "Got a little numb sittin' here. No, Quill, no trouble. We put four men in the bag for ya."

"Thank you as always." Rose beckoned to his partners. "Tommy, Will, we better be going. We've got a lot of miles to travel."

Briskey sidled up alongside Rose. "I'll walk up front with you. My Tin Lizzy's beyond the first truck."

Tommy Jenks opened the cab door of the tail-end tanker. He pushed his shotgun and bag up on the high seat, then climbed in.

Rose and Briskey continued on. "You know, Quill, if you bring me any more of these Sunspot fellas, my jail's gonna get kinda crowded."

"Maybe you could transfer some of them to Brushyfork."

"That'd take a judge's order, and my judge is none too happy with me right now."

"Maybe I can get my judge to do it." Rose opened the door of the cab of the lead truck. He tossed his bag up on the seat. "I've been meaning to ask, how'd our bad boy get out of your jail?"

"Trick so old it's got hair on it."

"Oh?"

"He fell down on the floor of his cell, moanin' and clutchin' at his gut. My night man made the mistake of going in to check on him and got the tar whaled out of him for his trouble."

"You fire him?"

"Oh, hell no. He's got a couple little kids. He needs the job." Briskey spit a stream of tobacco juice to the side. "I figure now he's gonna be the toughest damn jailer I got. He's not gonna let anybody get away with anything."

"You've got a good heart, Marcellus. You take care now." Rose climbed up in the cab. After he got comfortable, he pulled the door closed.

Briskey held up two playing cards. "You'll be wantin' these."

"Well, Jacks of Spades. Isn't that nice?" Rose slipped them in his shirt pocket.

"Found 'em on the drivers. Didn't figure they'd need 'em anymore. You be safe now, Quill Rose."

ROSE WHEELED OFF at Lebanon long after the sun had set. He took the big tanker into a dirt parking lot in front of Mazie's Copper Kettle. Jenks stopped his tanker next to him, and Kaufmann headed the Bradford into a spot near the end of the diner.

Rose climbed down. He shook out the kinks before he started for the front door.

Jenks hot-footed it to catch up. "You as hungry as I am? It's been a long day since lunch, and it was a kinda puny one at that."

"Looks like a good place here. This ought to make up for it."

Kaufmann sidled in beside Jenks as Rose pushed open the door to the Copper Kettle. The trio headed for a back booth. Rose and Jenks slid onto opposite bench seats.

Kaufmann removed his cap. He loosened his collar while he gazed around the diner. Conversations at other tables and booths stopped.

Rose slapped the bench. "Come on, sit."

Kaufmann did.

In the moments that followed, conversations around the room resumed, slowly and subdued as first. Then the volume built back to what it had been.

A waitress came over with three glasses of water. She put one in front of each man and spoke to Rose. "We're not used to seeing black men in here, not coming in by the front door, least ways."

"Oh, well, this man's our friend. We go everywhere together. It's all right for you to speak directly to him. He's amazingly good with language."

"Sorry."

"Apology accepted. Now we've been on the road a long time. What would you recommend for supper?"

"How about the mountain oysters?"

"They fresh?"

"Came in today."

"Tommy?"

Jenks raised a thumb.

"Will?"

"Pigs' nuts?"

"Pigs' nuts." Rose massaged the creases in his brow. "What's the matter, you didn't grow up on the farm like us?"

"I grew up on chittlin's which you white folks sure didn't, but not pigs' nuts. We fed those to the dog."

"Will, my boy, you're in for a treat." Rose looked up at the waitress. "Mountain oysters, a big platter, please. Fried potatoes, green beans, and have you got any of that pickled corn?"

"We make our own. It's awful good."

"Pickled corn. A loaf of home-baked bread and lots of butter."

"Coffee all around?"

"Coffee all around. Where's your toilet?"

"Through that door there." She motioned toward the hallway behind Rose and Kaufmann. "I'll get your coffee, then start bringing your food."

Rose hunched forward on his elbows. "Will, you want to try out the little room first?"

"Sure." He slid out of the booth and left.

A moment later, a burly man in a checkered flannel shirt got up from a stool at the counter. He made his way toward the door that led to the toilet, but when he got abreast of the booth, Rose put his hand out. "We're next."

"Hey, man, I gotta go."

"That's all right. But there's someone in there, and my friend and I, we're next."

The man slapped the back of the booth. "What if it ain't all right?"

Jenks grabbed the man's wrist. He yanked down hard until he had the side of the man's face squashed against the tabletop.

Rose peered at him from beneath his eyebrows. "What can I say to help you understand we're next?"

"Gawddamn nigger lovers."

Jenks let up on the man's wrist for the length of time it took a mosquito to siphon a splat of blood from a horse's rump. Then he hauled down with both hands. He slammed the man's face into the table.

Rose peered at him a second time. "Maybe you'd like to leave."

The man grimaced. "I might at that."

"Don't worry about your bill. I'll pay it for you." Rose pulled a long-barreled revolver from his shoulder holster and laid it on the table.

The man's eyes widened. "Yeah, yeah, I'll leave."

"Good."

Rose gave a tilt of his head to Jenks, and Jenks released the man.

The man rubbed at the side of his face as he backed away. He turned and, stumbling, blundered his way toward the front door.

Rose exhaled. He stuffed his gun back in his holster and pulled his jacket closed over it.

The waitress came out of the kitchen with three cups of coffee. "What was that all about?"

"A little misunderstanding."

She set the cups on the table. "With Russcob? That's easy to happen."

"Give me his bill."

"You don't have to pay for him. He only had pie and coffee."

"Oh, I told him I would. A dollar cover it?"

"With change back."

Rose handed a dollar to the waitress. "Keep the change. When you see Mister Russcob, you thank him for the tip."

The waitress pocketed the money and went on to another table.

ROSE AND JENKS were stirring at the steaming black liquid in their cups when Kaufmann returned. "Ah, good, coffee's here. Man, I'm ready to fill up now."

The mountain oysters surprised Kaufmann. He licked his fork clean, preparatory to attacking the dessert of Dutch apple pie. It went down fast, with Kaufmann going over his plate with his index finger, getting up the last drops of sugar-sweet sauce. He sucked them from his finger. When there was no more, Kaufmann slapped his belly. "Boys, I'm going to sleep tonight."

"Yeah, we better find us a place to stay." Rose nudged him out of the booth, then went to the counter to pay the bill. As the waitress counted out his change, Rose braced his hand on the counter top. "Know a place where we could get a room for the night?"

"We got tourist cabins out back."

"That'd be fine."

"I'll get my pa. He takes care of that." The waitress disappeared into the kitchen.

In a moment, a man, his hair poking out from beneath a paper cap, pushed through the swinging door, wiping his hands on a soiled apron. "My daughter says you'd like one of our cabins for the night."

"Big enough for the three of us."

The man looked from Rose to Jenks to Kaufmann. "Him, too?"

"He makes three."

"I'm sorry, mister. He can't stay."

"Why not?"

"I hate to be the one to tell you, but he's a coon. I don't allow coons in my cabins."

"What would it take to change your mind?" Rose pulled a roll of bills from his pocket. He peeled off a five and laid it on the counter.

The man eyed the money, but didn't respond.

Rose peeled off another five. He laid it on the first bill.

The man's eyebrows knitted together.

Rose put a third five on the counter.

The man picked up the bills. "I like the color of your money, mister."

"Thought you would."

"It's number four, just out back. Oh, and it's another five-spot for you and your white friend."

CHAPTER 19

War memorial

ROSE, JENKS, AND KAUFMANN skipped breakfast the next morning. They instead cleaned up and drove on to Green Hill. There Rose guided his tanker into a graveled lot in front of the Dinner Bell.

It was there that the men put down a leisurely meal.

The waitress brought over a pot of coffee for refills. "You been in here before?"

Rose put his hand over his cup. "A couple weeks ago. You were so good to us that Tommy and I had to stop back."

The waitress primped her hair and laughed.

"This fella's Will Kaufmann."

She brushed a curl back behind her ear. "He sure don't look like a truck driver."

Kaufmann motioned out the window at the Bradford. "That car, that's what I drive."

"Oooo, work for rich people, do you now?"

"They've got all the money in Tennessee."

She laughed again. "So where you going?"

"Nashville."

"If you weren't black, I'd ask to ride along."

"If you weren't white, I'd let you. I'd even let you ride up front."

That brought a blush from the waitress. As she went back to the counter, she still managed to give the back of her hair a smart flip.

The men finished their coffee and drove on to Nashville where Rose began looking for a truck stop. He spotted one, the Ace High, with other trucks pulling into it.

Rose slid his tanker in at the end of the line. He drove around to the back of the lot, to the farthest row of trucks. There he found a space open large enough for his tanker and Jenks's. He backed his tanker in and cut the engine.

Jenks backed his tanker in beside Rose's.

Kaufmann stopped in front of the two trucks.

Rose and Jenks got their bags from the cabs, and Jenks his shotgun. They came over to the Bradford and tossed their gear in the back.

Kaufmann looked in his mirror. "What's the plan now?"

"Time to arrange a ransom." Rose held out his hand to Jenks, and Jenks put his truck's ignition key in it. "Will, I'm going inside to use the telephone. Meet you and Tommy around front."

"I've got to fill up with gas. The needle's on the big E."

Rose pulled a ten-dollar bill from his pocket. He snapped it and handed it to Kaufmann. Then he worked his way through the forest of cargo trucks to the back door of the Ace High, jingling the trucks' keys as he went.

Inside he found a telephone booth. Rose picked up the receiver. He listened for a moment before he dropped a nickel in the slot. "Franklin four thirty-five, please."

Rose glanced around. "It's ringing, boys. Come on, pick it up...Hello, this the boss man?...It isn't?...Oh, Ralph, what's it been since we talked, ten days or so?...Ralph, I've got two of your tankers. If you want them back, put the cigar man on the telephone...Now you don't need to use language like that." Rose hummed while he waited. "Well, good morning, cigar man, guess what I've got of yours?...Times two...That's right. It's going to cost you six thousand dollars to buy them back...Yes, I figured you didn't have that much in your safe, but you know I know where you can get it...What say the War Memorial in a half hour. I'll be by the columns on the front porch. Follow me inside, and we'll find us a quiet place to make the transaction. Of course, if I see Ralph or anybody else with you, it's over. I'll sell your alcohol to someone else and your trucks, too."

ROSE PLACED HIS BACK against the second of the six Doric columns that made up the portico of Nashville's War Memorial Building. The portico, three stories high, dwarfed him and the others who came and went.

He glanced toward Union Street. As he did, he took a railroad watch from his pocket and pressed a button on the side that let the cover spring open. Rose checked the time, then closed the cover. He looked up, and this time he saw the man he was waiting for, hurrying up the sidewalk from the southeast, alone and with a satchel in his hand, the man chewing on a cigar.

Rose watched him stop short of the portico and peer around. He let him stew for a long moment before he stepped into the open.

The cigar man saw him, and Rose swung around and went inside. He hurried across the central court whose granite walls bore the names of thirty-four hundred Tennesseans who had died during The Great War. Rose took no notice of them, although a half dozen of the names were those of friends, men with whom he had grown up, men who would be forever young because death in a distant war had frozen them in time.

Rose had his focus on reaching a staircase. At the top, he snatched a glance back, to make sure the cigar man was coming, then took the steps down two at a time. The marble stairs brought him out into a cavernous gray room of unfinished concrete, unfinished except for the tile floor. The air had that damp feel and stale smell of a long neglected basement.

Rose heard shoes clipping down the stairs from above. He swivelled around, taking in the few details that existed as he moved into the center of room. A lonely place, he thought, but he liked it, particularly the way a single light fixture on the far wall illuminated the room.

The shoes he had heard touched the tile behind him. They stopped.

Rose turned to the cigar man standing at the bottom of the steps. "Glad you could make it."

The cigar man leaned to the side, trying to make out the features of the man who had spoken to him, a man silhouetted by that single light on the far wall.

"Money in the bag?" Rose asked.

"Yeah. How do I know you really got my trucks?"

Rose took two playing cards from his shirt pocket. He held them up. "Jack of Spades, twice."

"Bastard."

"I'd speak kindly. Set the bag on the floor and kick it across to me."

"Not 'til I know where my trucks are. I'm not goin' for that telephone crap again."

"Didn't think you would. The place is on the cards." Rose let them fall. They spiraled to the floor.

"Where are the keys?"

"I've got them. But before I give them to you, I'd like to know who I'm working with. Well?"

"Matthew. Matthew Shutts."

"Matthew. That's a good Bible name. I'll tell
you what, Matthew, I trust you." Rose jingled two
keys in his hand. He tossed them toward Shutts, but
tossed them short so he couldn't catch them. The
keys clittered on the tile. "The money now."

Shutts set the satchel on the tile. He kicked the
satchel to Rose.

Rose bent down for the bag, but spotted
Shutts's hand going behind him. "Matthew, if your
hand comes out with a gun in it, there's someone
behind you, and he's going to blow a hole in your
spine."

"Bluffs don't work with me."

A sound came from behind Shutts, the click of a
hammer being drawn back.

Tommy Jenks stepped out from behind the
staircase, his shotgun leveled at Shutts.

"Tommy, he's got a pistol."

Jenks jabbed the twin barrels into man's back.
"I'd stick my hands out where I can see 'em, Mister
Shutts."

When Shutts's hands inched away, Jenks
yanked the man's coat up and relieved him of his
gun.

"Matthew, if you would, please," Rose said,
"kindly back up to the stairs."

Shutts put one foot back, then the other until his
heel struck the bottom step.

Rose came around beside him. He snapped a
handcuff on Shutts's wrist.

"Hey, you can't do that."

"I just did." Rose snapped the other cuff to the stair railing.

Rose and Jenks departed for the door beneath the light fixture but turned back when they heard Shutts jerk against the handcuffs.

"Oh, Matthew, you'll need the strength of another Bible man to break those manacles. You remember Sampson, but I'll make it easy for you." Rose dropped something. It, too, clittered on the tile with Rose and Jenks backing out the door.

SHUTTS SWORE. He pulled as far from the stair railing as he could, stretching a foot toward where he had heard fall what he hoped was the handcuff key.

He raked his shoe back, but nothing came with it.

Shutts stretched again. Still nothing.

He tried a third time, then ran up the steps for help, but a handcuff hit a support pipe and yanked him back.

He was about to holler for help when footsteps came from above. "Ralph, that you?"

"Matt?"

"Ralph, where the hell have you been?"

"You got inside before I saw where you got to. Been lookin' for ya."

Ralph, Shutts's foreman, clattered down the stairs.

"The bastard handcuffed me to the rail. There's a key out there on the floor. Find it."

The foreman scurried on into the room. He bent low, squinting. "Got one."

"Bring it here."

He hurried over, but couldn't make the key go in the lock.

Shutts punched his henchman. "Gawddammit, that's a truck key. The handcuff key's still out there."

The foreman picked up the search from where he had found the first key. He saw a second and brought it back to Shutts.

Shutts slapped him, sending the foreman's hat flying. "Dammit, that's another truck key."

The foreman went after his hat. "I didn't know. Hey, there's a couple cards here–"

"I want 'em, gawddammit."

"–and another key."

"That's got to be it. Hurry up."

The foreman came back. He put the key in the lock of the cuff on Shutts's wrist and twisted the key.

The cuff opened and fell away.

Shutts snatched the key from his foreman and unlocked the other cuff. He jammed the handcuffs and the key in his coat pocket, then held his hand out with a gimme motion. "Your gun."

"My gun?"

"Gimme your gun. They got mine."

The foreman took a pistol from his belt holster.

Shutts grabbed the gun and ran for the far door, a door that took him into a second stairwell. He stared up, then sprinted up the double flight of steps before him, his foreman following. At the top, Shutts threw open a door and dashed out onto a city sidewalk, into the blinding light of the mid-day sun. Shutts shaded his eyes as he scoured around, spying a man in a chauffeur's uniform, polishing the hood of a limousine. "Hey, you. See two guys come out here?"

"Pardon, sah?"

"You stupid or something? You see two guys come out that door?"

"Yassah."

"Well, which way'd they go?"

The chauffeur fluttered his fingers down the street, in the direction of the river district. "Got in a car that way."

"What kinda car?"

"Black car. All them Fords is black, mistah."

"Aww, Jesus. Come on, Ralph." Shutts ran up the sidewalk, with his foreman beside him. They swung off onto another sidewalk, one that carried them past the front of the War Memorial.

THE CHAUFFEUR wiped his hands on the polishing cloth as he watched the two disappear around the corner before he pounded on the side of the car. "You can come out now."

Jenks, on the floor in the back seat, threw off the blanket that had covered him.

Rose rolled out from under the Bradford, on the street side.

Kaufmann tossed his cloth on front seat. "Couldn't have worked better. We follow them now?"

"No, we know where they're going." Rose slapped the dust off his trousers. "Take us to the truck stop. We'll follow them from there. It's time we found the bottling plant." He climbed into the back seat with Jenks while Kaufmann got in the front and started the Bradford.

Kaufmann drove out of the city center as rapidly as traffic permitted, out Cedar to Eighth Avenue. He stayed with that street until Edde, then turned northeast to stop where Edde teed into Lebanon Pike. He parked there, across from the Ace High.

Rose rolled down the window that separated the closed compartment from Kaufmann. "Shouldn't have to wait long."

"Not long at all." Kaufmann gestured across the road to two Sunspot tankers coming out of the Ace High lot. The tankers stopped. When a break in street traffic came, the first tanker turned west and the second followed.

Kaufmann waited for two cars to pass before he pulled out onto Lebanon. Despite the building traffic, he saw the tankers turn onto First Avenue.

Rose pulled himself up to the open window. "Where the heck can they be going?"

"My guess the River district. Maybe they're bottling the stuff in the basement of the Capitol."

"Oh, that's a good one."

"They're turning again."

The tankers pulled onto Shelby and a bridge that took them northeast over the Cumberland River.

Kaufmann fell back. He let a third car come in between him and the tail-end tanker.

At the end of Shelby, the trucks turned onto South Tenth, and Kaufmann followed. He followed them onto Gallatin Pike, Eastland, and Porter, but when they turned onto Rosebank and stopped at a set of railroad tracks, Kaufmann slid to the side the street to watch.

The tankers moved. Not far beyond the tracks, they rumbled over a culvert and into a warehouse parking lot.

A horn sounded, answered by double doors swinging open.

The tankers rolled inside the warehouse.

Kaufmann stared at the building. "Could that be where they bottle the booze?"

"Got to be, but I'd like to be sure. Drive on by."

Kaufmann turned the big car onto Rosebank. He bucked across the railroad tracks and continued down the street. "I don't see any windows not boarded over that we can peek through."

Rose stuck his elbow out the open window that separated the chauffeur's seat from the passengers' compartment. "Can you make out the sign above the door?"

"Pretty washed out. It looks like Old Hickory something. Old Hickory Cartage, that's what it says."

"I wonder who owns it."

"We can find that out quick enough." Kaufmann slowed the big car and turned it around at the end of the block. "Doors are opening again."

"Well, look what's coming out."

"A one-ton."

"And he's got a tarp over his load."

"Who wants to guess what's under the tarp?"

"Let's follow and find out."

Kaufmann waited for the truck to turn onto Porter, then started the limousine moving. When he turned onto Porter, the truck, well ahead, turned west onto Eastland.

Kaufmann stepped down on the accelerator. At the end of the block, he ignored the stop sign and swung out onto Eastland.

"Still got him, Will? He's a block ahead. See him?"

"I got him. He's turning again." Kaufmann pressed the accelerator to the floor and held it there until he had to brake for an intersection thick with cross-street traffic.

An opening came and Kaufmann rammed the big car onto Gallatin. "Can't see him."

Rose climbed through the window to the front seat. He stood up, bracing himself against the roof behind, one hand on his hat to keep the wind from blowing it away. "I got him!"

"Where?"

"Six, seven cars and a bus between us. My gawd, he's going back downtown!"

Kaufmann made a try at passing the car ahead, but pulled back in the face of an approaching truck.

The southbound traffic flowed onto Woodland and the Woodland Street Bridge.

"He's turning!"

"Which way?"

"Left! Ohmigawd, he's stopping."

"We'll go past him." Kaufman yanked on Rose's trouser leg. "Sit down."

Rose slid down onto the passenger's seat as Kaufmann wheeled the Bradford onto Fifth Avenue. "There he is."

"Yeah, go on. Go on."

"Space open at the end of the block. I can park there."

Rose bolted from the car before Kaufmann had stopped. He yanked the back door open. "Come on, Tommy!"

Rose peered down the block. "He's got something on his shoulder. He's going in that place."

Rose took off on the run, Jenks working to keep pace beside him. They slowed when they got near the end of the block, forcing themselves to walk as if they had no cares, as if they were tourists here to see the Capitol. Rose nodded toward a window, the lettering on the glass proclaiming 'Backroom Diner.'

Jenks went over. He shaded his eyes as he peered in while Rose sidled up to the truck. He lifted a part of the tarpaulin.

Jenks broke away from the window to Rose and hauled him around the corner.

"What's your hurry, man?"

"He was comin' out. What'd you see?"

"Cases of whiskey. No labels on the bottles."

"Gutsy. What are we, two blocks from the Capitol?"

"Lawmakers get thirsty, too, my friend." Rose peeked around the corner. "Hey, he's got another case. He's going inside again. Come on."

Rose and Jenks slipped in among the people moving along the sidewalk. They stole a glance at the Backroom as they passed by, then continued on to where Kaufmann paced beside the Bradford.

"Well?" Kaufmann asked.

"Cases of whiskey. All the bottles full."

"Perfect. The county clerk's office is two blocks from here. We can leave the car and walk."

The trio hiked southeast along the sidewalk until they got to Church Street. There, around the corner and across the street, stood the Fifth National Bank building. Kaufmann, followed by Rose and Jenks, dashed through the street traffic to the lobby doors.

"The county clerk's here," Rose asked, "not in the courthouse?"

"Didn't you see when we came past Public Square? The courthouse is gone. The county fathers tore it down two years ago so they could build a new one on the site."

"Now that you mention it, I did see some construction."

Kaufmann glanced around for a directory board. He found one and scanned down it. "Fourth floor."

Elevator doors opened, and a half-dozen people spilled out.

Kaufmann led the way into the now empty elevator car, empty except for a uniformed black man who had his hand on the control handle.

Kaufmann pointed up. "Fourth floor, please."

"Yassah." The operator closed the doors and engaged the lift motor. "You got biddness wid da county clerk?"

"How'd you know?"

"Clerk's got all the space up theah, 'cept for the bank's supply room. That all changes next ye-ah."

"How's that?"

"The new courthouse will be done, an' the clerk an' his peoples get ta move back." The operator talked while gazing up at a pointer over the door, the pointer edging its way toward Four. He slowed the motor, then put the control lever in stop to open the doors. "You watch yo step now."

Kaufmann, Rose, and Jenks left the elevator.

"On yo right, down at the en' of da hall," the operator called out.

"Thank you."

A buzzer sounded, and the elevator operator closed the doors.

The three worked their way through the cluster of people between them and a sign that read 'Clerk's Office.' They went through the door, Kaufmann raising his hand to get the attention of one of the secretaries.

A middle-aged woman of some heft looked up from her desk. "No niggers allowed in here."

Kaufmann took his badge from his pocket and held it up.

The woman shot to her feet. She glowered at Kaufmann as if he were something that disgusted her. "That badge don't make no never mind. You still have to leave."

Rose held up his badge. "I'm a sheriff. My deputy's here, and this man you just insulted is a state policeman. Get your boss out here."

The woman huffed, then disappeared into a side office. A moment later, a man came out, rubbing at his eyes. He put on his spectacles. "Ethel tells me we've got a little problem."

"Not at all." Rose laid his badge on the counter. Jenks and Kaufmann did the same. "We need to see your property ledgers."

"Is he really a state policeman?"

"Look at the badge."

The man picked it up. He turned it over as he examined it. "Gawddamn. All right, follow me."

The man directed Rose, Jenks, and Kaufmann around the end of the counter where he led them back to a vault and inside.

"I'm Nathan Ferguson, the county clerk, so I know pretty well where everything is. What are these properties you want to look at?"

"One-Twelve South First Street and Twenty-Six Rosebank."

Ferguson gazed down the racks of leatherbound ledgers. He pulled one down from a high shelf and handed it to Rose.

"First Street will be in that one, and..." Ferguson went back to the racks. "...Rosebank, Rosebank, Rosebank."

He pulled out a second volume. "Rosebank is in this one."

Kaufmann took that ledger.

"You can work at the table in here. Any way I can be of more help to you, all you need do is ask." The county clerk left but returned a few moments later with a file of papers he stuffed into various cabinet drawers.

Rose caught him peering Kaufmann's way as he and Kaufmann pulled out chairs. They opened their ledgers and paged their way in.

Rose touched a line on his page. "I found mine, One-Twelve South First. Sunspot Petroleum Inc."

The county clerk glanced up from his filing. "Well, I could have told you that. What's the other one?"

Kaufmann continued paging into his ledger. "Twenty-Six Rosebank."

Ferguson came over, still with a fistful of papers. "Rosebank, that's out by the Cornelia Airport. How close to the railroad tracks?"

"Just the other side."

"Hmm." He leaned over Kaufmann's shoulder. "A couple more pages, I think. Ah, there it is." He pointed to an entry.

"Says J&W Properties." Kaufmann planted his elbow on the table. "The sign on the building said Old Hickory Cartage."

"Old Hickory went bust in 'Twenty-nine."

"Who's J&W Properties?"

"As long as they pay their taxes, I have no reason to ask." The county clerk went to another rack of ledgers and pulled one down. He opened it to the middle, then paged back. He adjusted his glasses. "Here it is. J&W acquired the property in 'Thirty. Paid their taxes promptly every year since."

He showed the page to Rose. "Want to know anything more, you'll have to go up to the Capitol, the Secretary of State's Office, look through the corporation records."

Kaufmann closed his property book. "What say, Quill?"

"Sounds like a good place to root around." Rose handed his ledger to Ferguson who returned it to the rack.

Ferguson then collected Kaufmann's ledger and put it up as well.

On the way out of the vault, Rose put his arm around the county clerk's shoulders. "It's about lunchtime, Mister Ferguson. Would you come with us? I'm buying."

"Oh, that's inviting, but I don't take lunch until one o'clock."

"Well, I understand your need to keep the office open. The Backroom, is that any good?"

"It's a black joint, but old Micah makes a mean barbecue sandwich. If you go there, you'll want to have a near beer with it."

"Can we get a whiskey?"

"Don't think so, but I shouldn't have to tell you lawmen it's illegal to serve anything stronger than three-point-two beer in the State of Tennessee, although whiskey, I'm told we make a lot of it. Law just says we can't serve it."

Chapter 20

First answers

OUTSIDE, ROSE, JENKS, and Kaufmann walked back to Fifth Avenue and the Backroom. Rose opened the door. He held it while four hefty black men pushed their way out.

Kaufmann put a hand on Rose's arm. "If you really want to eat here, you better let me go in first. I know this joint. The counterman would throw you white boys out on your fannies."

Rose considered himself cautioned and let Kaufmann pass. "So where do you want to sit?"

"How about that back table?"

They worked their way past a half-dozen men standing at the cash register. The men, all black, eyed the strangers.

Kaufmann, Rose, and Jenks had hardly gotten seated when a big-gutted fellow came over, an apron tied up under his arms. "What'll it be?"

Kaufmann tapped the table. "You Micah?"

"Yeah. 'Scuse me." He mopped his face with his apron, then raked his fingers back through his thinning hair. "Hot workin' the barbecue pit."

"The county clerk says you make a good barbecue sandwich."

"You know Nate?"

"We were just at his office."

"I turn out the vote for him in the ward every two years."

"So you're in politics."

"A little. But mostly I sell barbecue, and I don't mind braggin' a little. I do make a good sandwich." Micah placed his meaty hands on the table. "So you and your white buddies heah, you each want one?"

"And a beer."

"Near beer. Market Street do ya?"

"Market Street?"

"Best in the city." Micah straightened up. "Brewed three blocks from heah."

Rose brushed shoulders with Kaufmann. "Anything stronger?"

The man studied the white interloper before he shook his head.

"Near beer's weak as pee, but if you've got nothing better, I guess I'll have it."

Jenks waved an okay.

"Back in a minute." Micah held up three fingers to his counterman and pointed to the table before he went out the door to the kitchen.

The counterman came over with three bottles of Market Street. He took an opener from his pocket and opened a bottle. He put it in front of Kaufmann, then opened another. "First time heah?"

"Been here once before, about a year ago in mid-afternoon." Kaufmann took a swallow. "Didn't realize this was such a popular place."

"Noon hour. Sometimes folks have to wait thirty minutes just to get in the door." The counterman set the second bottle in front of Rose and opened the third. He

cast his eye at Kaufmann as he set the last bottle in front
of Jenks. "You a chauffeur?"

"Yes."

"What kinda car they let you drive?"

"A Bradford."

The counterman wobbled his hand. "Hoity-toity."

"Yes, the people I drive for are."

"These wouldn't be them people, would they?" The
counterman waved the opener in the direction of Rose
and Jenks.

"Not hardly. Truck drivers, friends of mine."

Micah came through the door, carrying a platter.
"Heah ya go."

He dealt out three plates, each piled with home fries,
a giant dill pickle, and a man-sized bun fat with
barbecued pork. "If I can getcha more, you stop me when
I come by."

Jenks bit into his sandwich. "Will, this is really good.
Mister Micah, can I get another?"

"Now? You certain? Most of my customers consider
one sammich a meal. Some cain't even eat it all."

"I'm certain."

"All right." Micah mopped his face again as he went
back to the kitchen.

Kaufmann tried his sandwich. "This is good. But my
daddy, and I'm not bragging now, my daddy was a
masterful barbecue man."

Rose sipped his beer. "How so?"

"He'd get up in the middle of the night to start the
fire, and nothing would do but hickory wood which we
boys had to gather for him. Daddy'd get that fire going,
then put his hog meat in there with the sauce. He'd never
tell anybody how he made his sauce."

"Not even you?"

Kaufmann wiped his mouth. "Not even me. He brought that meat out about mid-day just dripping. Oh, the eating was gooooood."

Kaufmann chewed a moment, then took a swallow of beer. "Every time we had big doings at the church, Preacher would insist Daddy bring barbecue, and it was gone first thing. Those who weren't fast enough getting into the line had to settle for Aunt Mape's fried chicken."

Rose bit off the end of his dill pickle. "And you'd had so much of your pap's barbecue, I bet you took the chicken."

"Every time. You know, sometimes I wake up at night, wishing I had Daddy's recipe. I miss him." Kaufmann picked up his Market Street. He stared at the bottle for a long time before he took a pull on it.

When they had put away the barbecue, the fries, the pickles, and the near beer—and Jenks a second barbecue— the three sat in silence. Jenks burped and let his belt out a notch.

Rose fished under his chair for his hat. When he found it, he brushed the dust from it. "Boys, this isn't getting our work done. We better stagger up to the Capitol." He thumped Tommy Jenks on the shoulder.

Jenks moaned. "Too much food."

"Hear that, Will? Remember this day. Mark it on your calendar. Today we filled Tommy Jenks up to capacity and then some."

They pushed back from the table and made their way toward the front door. At the cash register, Rose slipped a ten to Kaufmann who then held it out to the counterman.

The counterman made change. "How'd you like Micah's barbecue?"

"Good. We'll be back next trip in."

The counterman gave Kaufmann several bills and a handful of coins. "You hurry back now."

"Oh, I couldn't buy a number, could I?"

"A number? Sure." The counterman reached down for a cigar box. He opened it and brought out two slips of paper. "What number you want?"

"Three digits?"

"You can have four if you want."

"Let's see. I met my wife on the Twenty-first of October. That's ten twenty-one. Ten twenty-one is it."

The counterman scribbled one-zero-two-one on each slip of paper and initialed them. He tossed one in the box and handed the other to Kaufmann. "That'll be a quarter."

"What's the payoff if I've got the winning number?" Kaufmann put a coin on the counter.

The counterman swept the coin into the box. "Last week, thirty-seven dollars."

"That's good. Say, what's your name?"

"They call me Eazy. Short for Ezekiel."

"Will Kaufmann. Good to meet you, Eazy." He waved and followed Rose and Jenks out to the street.

Rose stopped and looked around. "Will, you sure you should have given him your name?"

"He doesn't know me from the fire plug over there."

"All right, then."

They crossed Dedderick and continued up Fifth.

Rose pushed on, his hands in his pockets. "Either of you see anyone order liquor?"

Kaufmann did a hop-step over a crack in the sidewalk. "Not order, but I saw a lot of it served."

"You did?"

"Those cups coming from the behind the counter, they didn't all have coffee in them, my friend. Some of those men were tossing it back far too fast for it to be hot coffee."

"That's the last time I sit with my back to the action."

They crossed Cedar and turned southwest, going on for a block and a half, and there it was, crowning a long, grassy hill—the Tennessee Capitol building.

Rose glanced at Jenks. "Ever see such a fine looking place?"

"Sure beats our little courthouse in Maryville."

They started up the hill. The closer they got to the building, the more it appeared to tower over them. They moved on, on now up the steps.

Before Rose got to the massive oak doors, he removed his hat, feeling it wasn't right to wear it in so grand a building, a place of such monumental importance to Tennesseans.

Kaufmann pointed ahead when they were inside. "Secretary of State's at the far end of the hall."

"We'll follow you."

The three sauntered past the governor's office, the lieutenant governor's office. Rose stopped. "Why don't you two go on? I'm going to step in and say howdy to Clayton."

Kaufmann raised an eyebrow.

Jenks bumped Kaufmann's elbow. "Clayton Johnson, the lieutenant governor. He's Quill's brother-in-law."

"Oh."

ROSE RAPPED on the glass of the door.

"Come in."

Rose did and found Clayton Johnson reviewing a letter with his secretary.

Johnson, in shirt sleeves, the cuffs turned up twice, and his necktie loose before his open collar, looked up. He gave off with a stunner of a smile and hurried around to Rose. He grabbed Rose by the arm and dragged him in.

"Evelyn, you've heard me talk about my brother-in-law. This is Quill Rose, the man from the Smokies."

The lieutenant governor's secretary stood up. She extended her hand. "You're a sheriff, Mister Rose. Mister Johnson is so proud of you."

"Well, I thank you. I help get him a vote or two so he can be here."

"We're thinking he could be the next governor."

Johnson waggled a finger. "The boss has got to retire first. Evelyn, you finish that letter. I'm going to take Quill inside to see my office. He's never been here, although he's let my sister come up for the inaugurations."

Johnson guided Rose into an inner office stuffed with stuff—the Great Seal of Tennessee above the entrance door, stacks of papers on side tables and in bookcases, photographs on the walls of Johnson with state and national dignitaries, a fish that appeared to be three feet long, maybe more, mounted on a plaque over a fireplace filled with state law books. Most striking, a black bear reared up on its hind legs, either guarding or threatening Johnson's desk.

Johnson stroked the fur of the beast. "Remember when I got him? You led the hunting trip that time up on the back side of Chilhowee Mountain."

"Sure do. He was big in the outdoors, but he looks a heck of a lot bigger in here. Where'd you get the fish?"

"Wisconsin. That's a muskellunge. The governor sent me up there to represent him at a meeting. I caught that critter in one of their big lakes. Anybody here asks, I tell 'em I caught it in the Little Tennessee, and their eyes just bug out."

Johnson slapped a leather chair beside his desk. Rose took that as his cue to sit. Johnson settled on the edge of his desk. "Well, you make a decision?"

"About what?"

"Coming to work for me."

"Oh, Clay, I'm sorry. I'm into something right now, and it's got me all bollixed up. I really hadn't thought about your offer."

"Well, I told you I can't wait long." Johnson jigged a thumb at a side table. "All that stuff over there, I and a couple handpicked men, we pulled that together, but I really need a chief. I really need you."

"Can I call you tomorrow on that?"

Johnson gave Rose a playful slap on the knee. "Sure. So tell me what really brings you by?"

"I can't go into much detail yet, Clay. You see, I've stumbled on a moonshine ring, and I'm trying to find out who's behind it. I thought maybe the state corporation records could tell me something."

"That big?"

"It's that big."

"Well, I'll help you. Let's go down to the Secretary of State's office."

"Oh, you don't have to do that. I know you've got more important things to do. Besides, I already have a deputy and a state trooper down there, going through the records."

"You could at least let me walk you down. One of the things of working here is I know everybody."

Rose pulled himself up out of the leather chair. He straightened his jacket as Johnson slipped his arm through his.

The two started for the door.

"I DIDN'T KNOW Quill had family here," Kaufmann said as he and Jenks walked on.

"Clayton grew up in Maryville. After he got his law degree at UT, he set up a practice over in Shelbyville.

Quill married Clayton's sister 'cause she was still at home. A short time later, Clayton and Quill went into politics, Quill running for sheriff in our county and Clayton for county attorney in Bedford. Quill says his interest has never gone beyond the county line, but Clayton, well, he's in a whole bigger world."

"I expect so."

The two moved on past the grand staircase that went up to the legislative chambers, then past the treasurer's office. Ahead, the gold-leaf lettering on the glass of a set of double doors told them they had arrived at their destination. 'Office of the Secretary of State.'

Kaufmann pushed one of the doors open. When he didn't see anyone in the outer office, he made his way to an open doorway and looked into a large room filled with desks and filing cabinets and a covey of secretaries and clerks at work.

He motioned to one. "Ruthie?"

A clerk turned away from her work. Her smile lit up the room as she popped up from her desk and hurried to Kaufmann. "Will, what you doin' out of uniform?"

He put a finger to his lips. "Quiet now. It's an investigation. No one's supposed to know."

"I can keep a secret."

"I know you can. Ruthie, I'd like you to meet Tommy Jenks, deputy sheriff from Blount County." He waved Jenks into the room.

"Ma'am," Jenks said.

"Ruthie's my cousin."

"I'm pleased to meet you, Deputy. Will, is there something I can help you with, or you just come by to catch me up on Momma?"

"We need to look at some corporation records."

"You're in luck. They're over here in these filing cabinets." Ruthie McCoy, a snippet of a black woman at four-foot-nine, led the men to a corner of the room. "Which ones you need?"

"Sunspot Petroleum and J&W Properties."

"Sunspot, that's going to be right here." Ruthie McCoy pulled open a drawer. She dug back through file folders, glancing at the names on the tabs. She pulled out one and handed it to Kaufmann. She pulled open another drawer. "J&W is gonna be in this cabinet. J&W–J&W– here we are." She handed that folder to Kaufmann as well.

"Got a desk or a table where I can work, out of the way of everybody?"

"Take the one over by the window."

"You're a sweetheart, Ruthie."

She slid the file drawer closed. "I keep reminding my husband of that. He doesn't always listen."

"Well, he ought to. Oh." Kaufmann reached into his pocket for a slip of paper. He held it out to Ruthie McCoy. "I bought a number for you at the Backroom."

"That's a den of sin."

"Maybe, but they serve up a good barbecue. You go by there next week. Maybe you'll have won some money."

"If I do, it all goes in the church collection plate." She took the paper and went back to her desk.

"Good place to invest your gains from gambling." Kaufmann let off with a wicked laugh and swaggered toward the window table where he and Jenks found chairs and settled in.

Kaufmann winked at Jenks as he opened the Sunspot file. "Let's see what we've got here. Incorporator, Harmond Watson and a Nashville address. He appears to own all the stock. Corporation secretary is Velma Watson, same address."

He opened the J&W file. "Incorporator– incorporator–New Century? Who can New Century be?"

Kaufmann slid the open file in front of Jenks. "The address is the same as J&W, so that doesn't tell us anything. No officers listed."

"Uh-huh, and it says here New Century owns all the stock."

"Right. Excuse me." Kaufmann picked up the file and strolled over to his cousin's desk.

There they talked for a moment, then went to the bank of filing cabinets. Ruthie McCoy pulled out a file and handed it to Kaufmann. He pointed to something in the file, and she opened another cabinet and handed a second folder to Kaufmann.

He read down the first sheet, Ruthie McCoy reading along with Kaufman. He again pointed to something, and she crossed the room to another bank of cabinets. Ruthie McCoy dug in one of the drawers for some minutes. When she returned, she held up a folder.

Kaufmann opened the new folder. He touched the woman's arm and came back to Jenks. As he sat down, a smile spread across his face. "It pays to have a relative who knows where things are. We've turned up trumps."

Jenks hopped up. "Clayton," he called in greeting to Johnson and Rose coming his way.

The lieutenant governor gave a wave of his hand in response.

Kaufmann, too, stood. As he did, he turned the folders face down.

Rose pushed Johnson forward to Kaufmann. "Will, I'd like you to meet my brother-in-law. Clayton, this is Will Kaufmann. Will works in the State Police crime lab in Knoxville."

Johnson pumped Kaufmann's hand. "You boys finding what you need?"

"Pretty much, sir."

"Glad to hear it. There are good people in this office, but if I can be of any help, I hang my hat just down the hall."

"That's good to know, sir."

Johnson put his hand on Rose's shoulder. "Well, I'll be getting back to my office. In about ten minutes, I've got to go upstairs and preside over a session of the Senate. You ought to look in before you go."

"Clayton, we just might do that."

Johnson wandered away. He stopped to visit with several clerks and secretaries on his way out.

Kaufmann and Jenks resumed their seats, Kaufmann motioning to an empty chair for Rose. "I was telling Tommy before you came in that we've turned up trumps, but you may not like it."

"Why's that?"

"Let me show you." Kaufmann turned the Sunspot file over. He opened it. "Sunspot is owned by Harmond Watson of Nashville."

He turned over the J&W file and opened it. "J&W is owned by New Century. Tommy and I knew that."

He opened a third file and laid it on the J&W folder. "New Century is owned by Indelmo Corporation."

He opened a fourth file and laid it on the New Century folder. "Indelmo is owned by Raines Vendors Inc. And Raines Vendors is owned by–"

He opened a fifth file and laid it on the table. "Harmond Watson of Nashville and Clayton Johnson of Shelbyville"

Rose leaned back. "Oh damn."

"Yes, the lieutenant governor, and listed as an officer is a Marion Johnson, also of Shelbyville. Would that be his wife?"

"It is."

"Are you going to tell your brother-in-law we're on to him?"

Rose stared at the floor. He shook his head. "But the sad truth is I may have let it slip. He asked me what I was doing at the Capitol, and I mentioned a few things."

"Enough that he knows?"

"I hope not."

"This is going to create a problem at home, isn't it?"

"Huge. Martha loves Clayton. He's her big brother, nigh onto perfect."

Kaufmann took a notebook and pencil from his pocket. He made notes on the chain of ownership, closing each folder and setting it aside as he finished with it.

Ruthie McCoy came over. "Find everything you need?"

"More than we wanted. Oh, there is one thing. The owner of Sunspot, one Harmond Watson, do you have anything that'd tell us who he is?"

She peered at Kaufmann, perplexed. "You don't know him? Will, I'm surprised at you. Well, of course, you wouldn't know him. You don't live here."

"So who is he?"

"Harmond Watson—Big Harm—he's head of the Democratic machine in our county. Nobody doesn't get elected who doesn't first visit him with a bag full of money."

"Statewide offices, too?"

"Particularly statewide offices. Big Harm and his cousin in Memphis can turn out the vote and put you in or, if he doesn't like you or you wouldn't pay enough, put your opponent in."

Kaufmann handed the files back to his cousin.

"You going to thank me?" she asked.

"Of course. Thank you, Ruthie."

"Anytime."

"And, Ruthie, if anybody asks, you don't know what files we looked at."

"If that's important to you."

"It's important."

Ruthie McCoy whisked away, back to the cabinets to return the files to their rightful places.

Kaufmann sat in silence, rubbing his face and forehead. "Quill, what are we going to do with this?"

Chapter 21

Home once more

ROSE SAT AT THE KITCHEN TABLE, his attention buried in the newspaper open before him, while the boy, sitting on a stack of catalogs on the chair beside Rose, spooned oatmeal out of his bowl and onto the floor.

Martha glanced over from where she worked at the stove, scrambling eggs in a cast-iron skillet. "Quill, you're supposed to be watching him."

"Watching who?"

"The boy. He's throwing his breakfast on the floor."

Rose peered at the grinning child. "Little feller, now you've got us both in trouble. Come here." He laid his paper aside and pulled the boy over onto his knee. Rose commenced to bouncing him, cooing to him, "Giddyap, giddyap, giddyap."

The boy giggled and reached out for Rose's mustache, the boy's hand jiggling with the bouncing, Rose pulling his head away.

Martha raked the eggs onto two plates, one piled with fried potatoes and sausages–for Rose. "Quill."

"Yeah."

"Have you decided on that job Clayton's holding for you? We could move to Nashville, that's not a problem."

"The job? I don't think I can take it."

"Why not?"

"I've just got a bad feeling about it."

"It would be more money, and if we're going to have to raise this little boy—"

"We can get by here, Martha. This is home. I'm not Clayton. This is where I belong. Besides, we're about to—"

"About to what?"

"Oh, it's nothing."

She slid Rose's plate onto the table before him and her plate at her place. After Martha sat down, she hauled the boy over onto her lap. "We've got to name this child. We can't go on calling him little feller forever."

"Martha, how many times have I said it? We've gone through the family's Bible. The girl's listed there, birth date and a name. And the boy's there with a birth date but no name. The parents must've never got 'round to it." Rose cut into a sausage. He held up a chunk before he put it into his mouth and chewed. "If we find family for him, the naming business, it's up to them, not us."

The boy reached for the eggs on Martha's plate, but she pulled his hand back. "For now, we're his family. I've decided. His name's Nathaniel, after my father."

"I don't know."

"You have a problem with that name? It's my father's name, remember."

"I guess that would make your dad Big Nate and the boy Little Nate. Hmm, come to think of it, that's not too bad." Quill tickled the boy under his chin. "Little Nate, you like that?"

The boy, grinning, clapped his hands together.

Rose winked at him. "Then Little Nate it is. Little Nate Noland."

"Little Nate Rose," Martha said as she picked up her fork.

Rose stared at her.

CHAPTER 22

The killing

IT WAS SOMETIME after midnight when the telephone rang.

Quill Rose pried open an eye.

After the second jangle, Martha Rose mumbled.

"What?" he asked, straining to hear what she said.

"Phone, ignore it."

"Can't."

She rolled away from him. "Whoever can call back in the mornin'."

"I 'spose." Still Rose laid there listening to the rings. Five more and he gave it up. He roused himself from the bed and padded out and downstairs to the telephone mounted on the wall in the front hallway.

He came back more slowly.

"I've gotta go," he said.

Quill Rose fumbled in the dark for the clothes he had left on the back of a chair. He put them on without lighting the lamp. Done, he went to the closet for a coat and his hat. He found his caulk boots there as well and pulled them on.

Rose kissed Martha, she pretending to be asleep, then did his best to make the steps that creaked creak as little as possible as he went down the stairs and out the front door.

It was Rose's habit to bring the Ford cruiser home in the evening. He rarely needed it, twice that he could recall in what, eight years that the fiscal court had supplied him with one? This, he decided as he drove away, would be the third time.

He stopped at Tommy Jenks's house. There he pounded on the door for what seemed an age, until Jenks slid up a window in his second-floor bedroom.

"Who's down there?"

"It's Quill."

"Oh jeez, Quill, my dog and I been out possum huntin' all night. I just turned in. What is it?"

"Another murder. Will."

Jenks pushed the window down without a word.

Rose peered around for a place to sit on the front stoop while he waited for his deputy, the night excessively dark and still as time in a grave.

A shiver ran through Rose's frame. Overcast nights like this made him feel that the thick, heavy, low-hanging clouds were out to smother him.

Jenks came out the door carrying a lantern.

Rose stared at the light. He shook his head, to clear his mind. "I wasn't thinking. You're right. We'll probably need that."

He forced himself to his feet, and the two went on to the cruiser, Jenks moving toward the left side. "You want me to drive?"

"Yeah, you better."

"Where is it?"

"Rhea Gap."

"Lord, that's in spittin' range of the end of the earth."

"One could say that."

"I mean whoever goes there?"

"Not many people. Can't be more than four families live up in the Gap."

THREE CARS WERE THERE when Jenks drove up, all with their headlights aimed toward a fourth car at the edge of a small tobacco field on the far side of the ditch.

Rose motioned ahead. "Better park out of the way."

Jenks saw a mailbox and a rutted driveway that ran off into the woods. He pulled the cruiser in there and killed the engine and lights.

Someone came trotting up, a flashlight in hand. He put the light in Jenks's face. "That you, Sheriff?"

Rose got out of the far side of the car. "I'm the sheriff."

"Oh, yeah. I'm Bailey Crow. Will and I started out on the patrol together. He told me I should call you if anything ever happened."

"What did?"

"Better see for yourself."

Rose and Jenks followed the state trooper to the other side of the road and down into the ditch.

"So far, it's me, Mike Edwards from the lab and a Knox County deputy." Crow talked while he moved. "Maybe you know him. Kinsey Price? We've got a coroner on the way. You and Will been working on something together?"

"Yeah, a triple murder."

Crow called to the others, "Mike, Kinsey, this is the sheriff from Blount County and his deputy. What's your name?"

"Tommy Jenks."

"Tommy Jenks."

Edwards, the officer on his knees on the seat on the passenger's side of the car, glanced up at Jenks and Rose, then went back to examining the interior.

Price stood to the side, appearing to be doing his best not to touch anything. He looked like he had seen a ghost.

Rose went over to him. "How you getting on, Kinsey? You're a mite pale."

"Threw my guts up when I got here. Never get used to these things."

"Me neither."

"You're kinda out of your territory, aren't you?"

"Only by a couple miles, but we won't get in your way. This is your case."

Crow came over. "Actually, it's ours. We look after our own."

"Guess that's only right."

Edwards called to Rose. "You want to look in through the windshield?"

Rose and Jenks worked their way around to where they could. In the lights held by Edwards and Crow, they saw Will Kaufmann's head at an odd angle against the back of the seat.

Edwards's hand came into the beams as his hand went up under Kaufmann's chin. "Somebody cut his throat—vicious—windpipe, muscles, slashed almost through to the backbone. That's not all."

Edwards's light moved down Kaufmann's chest and to the side. It stopped at the bloody stump of a forearm. "Hacked off his hand. Now why would anyone do that?"

"There's more." Crow gestured for Rose and Jenks to follow him to the back of the car. There he shined his light on the rear window. "See that? 'You wouldn't leave' written in blood. What's that mean?"

Rose looked away. "It's a message to us. How'd he find out about Will?"

Crow gazed at Rose, puzzled. "You know who did this?"

"Yes. We know him, know what he looks like, even had him in jail for a couple days, but we never did get a name out of him."

"You had him?"

"On another matter." Rose tugged at the lobe of his ear. "Tommy caught him near a part of a moonshining operation in the south end of our county. I had reason to want the fella out of the county, so Marcellus Briskey took him for me, put him in his jail. But he escaped."

"How'd you know he was your killer?"

"The day after he busted out, we matched a fingerprint Will had lifted for us to a print on the man's card."

"You still got that print?"

"Yeah. Will kept a copy at the lab, too, somewhere in his files, I suppose."

"That could be helpful."

"Any idea what Will was doing out here?"

"I found a note scribbled in that pad he always carries, that he'd got a call from a sheriff's deputy to come out here and work on a burglary." Crow held up Kaufmann's notepad. He waved it. "You know Will. He'd go anywhere to help anybody on a crime."

"You're right on that."

"But here's the odd thing." Crow gestured to the Knox deputy. "Kinsey's been on the telephone at a house up the way. He called the sheriff and every deputy in Knox County he could, and none of them called Will."

"So it was a setup."

"Appears so. No other explanation works." Crow shoved Kaufmann's notepad back in his jacket pocket.

"Has anybody been by the house to tell Will's wife?"

"I expect that's my job. I suppose it's asking a bit much if you'd like to come along."

Rose glanced at Jenks, and Jenks nodded.

"My deputy agrees, we better."

Chapter 23

The cemetery

> *See that band all dressed in red,*
> *God's going to trouble the water.*
> *It looks like the band that Moses led,*
> *God's going to trouble the water.*
> *Wade in the water,*
> *Wade in the water, Lord,*
> *Wade in the water–*

The choir–young men in black suits, white shirts, black neckties, and equally young women in black dresses, with white scarves around their necks–swayed to the rhythm of the spiritual. At the end of the chorus, the director drew her thumb and forefinger together as a signal for the choir to hum.

An old black preacher rose from a side chair. He shambled over to a woman on the front bench. There he bent down and took her hand in his. He smiled at her, said something, released her hand and moved to the two boys sitting next to her. He spoke to them as well, then squeezed the thick shoulder of older boy and tousled the tight curly hair of the younger.

The preacher stepped back, a man stooped from long years of working in a flour mill for this church could not support him. He looked over the gathering of friends and strangers who filled every bench and chair. Half again as many people stood along the side walls and two and three deep across the back.

He raised an arthritic hand. "We've mourned long enough. It's time we celebrate the life of one we so loved, William Joshua Kaufmann. Ever'body here knew him as Will. He was a great husband to his wife and a magnificent father to his two young boys. He was a loved friend to each of us, one we counted on when life would get difficult, and bein' colored in Knoxville..." The preacher swept his arm over the congregation. "...is difficult no matter what the mayor says in the newspapers."

The preacher gazed out over the heads of the congregation. "Will Kaufmann, he drew his strength from the church—Amen. He drew his strength from his brothers and his sisters in Jesus—Amen."

He picked up the great black Bible from the pulpit and held it for all to see. "Will Kaufmann drew his strength from the book and from his daily walk with our Savior—Amen. He drew his strength from his family, Faith Rebecca, his wife of thirteen years, so solid, so committed to Will and her children, and from his two boys, Samuel and John Mark, filled with the joy that is youth—Amen!"

The choir director gave a downbeat—

> *I heard the sound of the Gospel train,*
> *Don't you want to get on?*
> *Yes, that's my aim.*
> *I'll stand at the station an' patiently wait*
> *For the train that's comin',*
> *An' she's never late.*
> *You must have your ticket*
> *Stamped bright an' clear,*

Train is a-comin', she's a-drawin' near.

If I have my ticket, Lord, can I ride?
If I have my ticket, Lord, can I ride?
If I have my ticket, Lord, can I ride?
Ride away to Heaven in that mornin'—

"Ride away to Heaven in the mornin'." The preacher grew more fervent as he came around the coffin to the platform. "Ride away to Heaven, to be with our Lord, to be where there is no pain and no sorrow—Amen! No sickness, no heartache, no death—Amen!"

It started softly, a few people saying amen with the preacher, growing in volume and numbers with each new shout.

"To be where we can sing of the glories that Jesus said would be ours forever if we would but believe in Him," the preacher rolled on, "as surely we know Will Kaufmann believed—Amen! To dwell forever in the company of our old daddies and mommies, our neighbors who lived down the street, our friends we loved at the places where we worked, our little bitty children who shall be innocent forever—Amen! Ride away on the Jesus train, Jesus, the engineer, the brakeman, and the conductor. Jesus our Savior—"

Steal away, steal away,
Steal away to Jesus!
Steal away, steal away home,
I ain't got long to stay here.

My Lord calls me,
He calls me by the lightning,
The trumpet sounds it in my soul,
I ain't got long to stay here—

"None of us ain't got long to stay here, brothers. None of us ain't got long to stay here, sisters. There's better comin', and it's comin' soon, not here on this sinful, sorrowful, filthy old earth, but in God's great Heaven— Amen! Amen!

"Pray with me, brothers and sisters, pray with me now. Take the hand of the sweet friend beside you. Y'all close your eyes now. Y'all bow your heads. Pray, my children." The preacher raised a hand toward Heaven as he, too, bowed. "Jesus and God, we come before You and all Your angels, giving You the thanks that You allowed Will Kaufmann to dwell among us. Thirty-seven years was a short time, too short, but we know it was enough because You made him a blessing to so many. We thank You that You gave him to Faith Rebecca Greene because out of that union came two fine sons who will carry on the Kaufmann name, bringing new honor to it as they grow into manhood."

John Mark sniffled. He wiped his nose on the cuff of his white shirt. Faith Kaufmann slipped her arm around her youngest boy. She drew him to her and also held Samuel's hand.

"We know that You, through us, will wrap Faith Rebecca, Samuel, and John Mark in a love that will shield them and protect them in these fragile days until their hurt and loneliness have been relieved. All of us, we all thank You now that we can have the confidence that Will Kaufmann has been swept up to be with You forever, that he is there to welcome us when our time comes."

An elderly black woman, rocking in the spirit, repeated, "Amen. Amen."

"There are hard days when it is difficult for us to give You the glory and the honor You so richly deserve. The day Will Kaufmann was taken from us was one of those days."

More rocked with that old black soul. "Amen. Amen."

The preacher's voice filled with power. "But we give You the glory and the honor, even on those hard days because that is Your command to us. Go with us now as we go to the graveyard, there to commit Will Kaufmann's body to the ground, knowing that his soul is already in Your hand. And all God's children said—"

"Amen!"

To the surprise of many in the church, six white men came from a side bench to the plain pine box coffin resting on the communion table. They hefted the coffin to their shoulders, ready to follow the preacher down the aisle—Bailey Crow, Mike Edwards, Quill Rose, Tommy Jenks, Marcellus Briskey, and Jacob Miller, each in a nondescript suit, nothing that would indicate he was a peace officer. That was the way Faith Kaufmann had requested it.

The State Police had offered an honor guard and cruisers to lead the funeral procession from the church to the cemetery, but she refused them. She told Quill Rose, and no one else, why. "The State Police killed my husband."

The pallbearers, outside now, slid the coffin into the back of a battered Model A pickup. Then they climbed up in to sit on the sides of the truck box for the ride to the Oddfellows Cemetery.

A long cortege followed, at the end of which came a Fisk University bus carrying the sixteen members of the choir.

Rose had asked Faith about them.

"You didn't know?" she said.

"Know what?"

"That's how Will and I met, at Fisk. We were both in the Jubilee Singers, toured Europe twice while we were with the choir. The Singers never forget their own."

The pickup bounced through a rut in the cemetery's entrance road and continued on, winding its way back to an old area of the cemetery where dogwood trees and clusters of lilac bushes grew, the lilacs all greened out with great bunches of flower buds not quite ripe enough to open.

It was near one of those clusters that Rose saw a pile of dirt, then an open grave.

The truck stopped and the cars, strung out over a rise toward the front of the cemetery.

No one hurried. It was a warm day, an ideal day for spring when many would rather have been spading up backyard gardens than helping bury a husband, a father, a friend.

The preacher nodded to the choir director.

She raised her hands, then gave the downbeat–

Deep river,
My home is over Jordan.
Deep river, Lord,
I want to cross over into campground–

The preacher stepped to the head of the coffin. He waved his hand that people should bow. "Dear Lord, You who comfort us when we most need it, we know You are here with us. We feel Your presence. Accept now the body of our brother as we place it here in this hallowed and holy ground. Keep his soul safe with You until what we like to call that great gettin'-up mornin' when we all shall join You in Your Heaven. Until then, we promise not to forget this day, this place, or our brother. It's in Your Son's most holy name that we pray. Amen."

The preacher went over to Faith Kaufmann and her boys. He put his arms around them, his touch becoming too much for Faith. She buried her face in his shoulder and wept.

When Faith Kaufmann's tears were spent, the preacher guided her and the children to the side of the coffin.

She wiped at her eyes, then slipped her hand into her pocket. Out came her husband's badge. She placed it on the coffin.

A hand touched her arm, John Mark's hand. "Could I have it, Poppa's badge?"

"No. I never want to see it again." Faith Kaufmann took her boys' hands and moved away from the grave.

Bailey Crow signaled to the other pallbearers. They stepped up to the ropes on which the coffin rested, Quill Rose palming the badge before they lifted the coffin out over the empty grave.

The pallbearers let the coffin down slowly, carefully. When it came to rest on the soil at the bottom of the grave, Crow and Jenks pulled the ropes free. They coiled them and laid them to the side.

The pallbearers stood there in line while the procession shuffled by, friends, neighbors, family. Many stopped at the dirt pile where they picked up a handful of soil and sifted it into the grave.

The mourners shuffled past the preacher and Faith Kaufmann and her boys, mumbling such words of comfort as they could before they went onto their cars.

A man near the end of the mourners' line beckoned to Rose. Rose stepped away and went toward him. But the man walked away.

Rose followed.

The man went past four ranks of graves before he swung around beside a fenced plot where Knoxville businessman and philanthropist Cal Johnson rested, Johnson, at one time a slave.

The man gazed at Rose. "I'm Newell Sanders, a sergeant with the Greeneville Post. I had Bailey point you out."

"How can I help you, Sergeant?"

"Call me Newey."

"Newey," Rose said.

"Will said you might be needing my help. I have the file with his Nashville notes. What are you going to do?"

"I have no idea." Rose stared down, then away, unsure what he should be telling this man.

Sanders hooked a thumb in his belt. "You've got enough here to get warrants."

"Uh-huh."

"Well, we can't just stand around and let this thing go on."

"I don't think it's the right time. A little more booze flowing down the pike isn't going to hurt anybody, and it'll keep some thirsty souls happy for a while." At that moment, Rose made a decision. He looked deep into Sanders's eyes. "Sergeant–Newey–what I think you and I need to do is meet with a wise old judge. How about you come down to Maryville in the morning?"

"I'm on funeral leave. I can extend it."

"Do that. And bring Will's notes."

Sanders extended his hand to Rose. They shook, then Sanders left.

When Rose turned back, the other pallbearers were in the truck, waiting for him, so he stepped his gait up to a trot. After he got aboard, Edwards slapped the driver's door, and the truck rolled away.

Crow hunched forward. He leaned into Rose. "See you met Newey."

"Nice fella. What can you tell me about him?"

"Bit on the crazy side, but a straight shooter. What's he been with us now, Mike, four years?"

Edwards made an okay sign with his thumb and forefinger.

"He come down to us from Kentucky where the patrol sacked him after he turned another officer in for taking bribes. Newey found out the hard way you have to be careful who you make your enemies."

"That's a tough lesson we all have to learn."

"He was with us two years when the captain gave him command up at Greeneville. Went in there and cleaned house. Man, did he ever. His post's now got the reputation of being the best we've got in the Eastern Kingdom. Quill, you can work with him."

Three cars remained at the church when the pallbearers got back, one unmarked toward which Crow and Edwards headed and the cruisers that belonged to Rose and Briskey.

"You coming by the house?" Crow called back to Rose.

"Sure. Tell Faith we'll be there."

The county officers strolled toward their vehicles, Briskey the first to speak. "The only bad thing about a funeral is it's a long time before you can have a chew." He took a pouch of Red Man from his coat pocket and held it out to Rose.

Rose said no as did Tommy Jenks, but Deputy Miller helped himself. Briskey then dug into the pouch. He stuffed a wad in his cheek. "Whatcha doin' next, Quill?"

"About what?"

"This moonshining thing."

"I was talking to a state trooper at the cemetery about that. His name's on Will's list as one of a dozen officers we can trust. Crow's name is there, too."

"Edwards?"

Rose shook his head. "If you want a piece of this, come over in the morning. We'll get together with the judge."

"I can do that. I got three of your drivers and two of your gunners in my jail."

"And for that, Marcellus, I'm ever in your debt. We've got to do this thing right. We make one mistake and they find out we're coming, they'll scatter like geese."

ROSE WAS IN NO HURRY to get away. When the crowd of mourners thinned out enough that a person could find a vacant chair, he wandered over to Will Kaufmann's sons. "How about we go out back?"

"Sure, Mister Rose," John Mark said.

Samuel scuffed at the floor. "Yeah, I can't stand these people crying on me, telling me how sorry they are Pa's dead."

"I think I know what you mean."

The three made their way through the kitchen and out to the back porch where Rose sat on one of the steps and John Mark on his Radio Flyer wagon. Samuel went down in the yard. He picked up a stone and whanged it at the trunk of a pin oak tree.

"Sammy, would you come over here?"

"I'd rather pitch stones."

"I know, but come over here anyway."

The boy kicked at the dirt as he came, not to Rose, but to a porch post. He leaned against it, his hands jammed in his pockets.

Rose folded his hands together. "Sam, John, it's not going to be easy for you. You already know that. Your pa was the world to you, and we buried him today."

John Mark rocked in the wagon. "Why'd he have to go and get killed?"

"I don't know. I may find out someday, and if I do, you've got my promise I'll tell you. I can tell you this, it's the danger of being a policeman. That's why your ma's angry, but it's what your pa wanted to do."

"Mister Rose, you're a policeman. You ever scared?"

"Sometimes."

"You think Pa was scared?"

Rose drew his finger across the step. "I expect he was. But that doesn't stop us from trying to do our jobs."

"I miss him."

"Samuel, you, too?" Rose asked.

"Yeah."

"That's good."

"Why?"

"It means you love him, like your ma loved him. She's going to miss him an awful lot." Rose slipped his hand in his pocket. "Here, I've got something for you."

John Mark brightened.

Rose brought out a badge and held it out to the younger son. "It's your pa's."

John Mark took it. He rubbed his hand over the badge, his fingers memorizing the letters.

"That's to help you to remember your pa. Now it'd upset your ma to know you have it, so you find a place to keep it where she won't find it, a place that's special, all right?"

"Thank you, Mister Rose."

John Mark carried the badge to his brother, to show him. They talked among themselves, then together trotted up the steps and inside.

Their mother caught the screen door before it could bang closed and came out. "You've been talking to the boys, Quill, thank you."

"Some manly stuff, you know. Maybe it'll help."

Faith Kaufmann went to her son's wagon. She sat down and wrapped her arms around her knees, hugging them to her chest. "I find it hard to talk to all these people."

"Uh-huh."

"God, why did Will have to go out there?" The sorrow, pent up for the past two days, burst through for a second time, and Faith Rebecca Kaufmann wept.

Rose sat on the porch without words. He let his gaze inspect the yard worn bare from kids, Will and Faith's and all the children from the neighborhood, playing stickball and football and other children's games. His gaze took in the tire swing hanging from a limb of the pin oak, and beyond the tree, the garden.

After some time, he took a handkerchief from his pocket and held it out to Faith Kaufmann. She wiped at the tears in her eyes, then blew her nose. She crushed the handkerchief in her hand. "I'll wash it before I return it."

"That's all right."

"What are we going to do, Quill? What are we going to do to survive? All Will and I got is this little house, and I don't have a job."

Rose glanced to the side, to Faith. "You've got family and Will's family. They'll help."

"I don't want for us to be a burden."

"Families don't worry about such things."

"It's going to be hard on the boys." The woman, a widow now, peered around. She found herself focusing on the tire swing, motionless there, waiting for some child to come to it, some child wanting to play.

"Faith?"

"Yes?"

"What say you and the boys come down to Maryville for the weekend, stay with me and Martha? Give you a chance to get away, and I'll take the boys fishing."

"They'd like that, but we don't have any way to get there. We don't have a car. And, even if we did, I don't know how to drive."

"Can you take the trolley down to the Southern Depot?"

"Yes."

"You do that then." Rose again cast a sidewards glance at this woman so suddenly alone. "You go to the ticket agent, and he'll be holding three tickets for you for the nine o'clock."

"I don't have the money."

"Faith, you don't need money. They'll be paid for."

"Quill, you shouldn't."

"Your husband was my friend."

CHAPTER 24

The plan

QUILL ROSE AND TOMMY JENKS held down a bench in front of the Sunshine Café, Rose reading the editor's column in the Maryville Times while Jenks wrestled through the pages of the much thicker Knoxville Sentinel, searching for the baseball scores and having no luck finding them.

Rose laughed.

"You see this?" He refolded the paper into a tighter package, the better to show the column. "The editor tells here about the Baptist church starting a Saturday School. To get kids coming, they served lunch."

"Yeah?"

"When the children started through the line, there was a bowl of apples and a sign that said 'Take only one. God is watching.' When the first kids got to the end of the line, there was a bowl of cookies. The editor says one boy said to the next, 'We can take as many as we want because God's watching the apples.' "

A car horn sounded, Marcellus Briskey rolling Louden County's touring car cruiser into a parking spot across the street. He wedged himself out. "Keep you waitin' long?"

"Gave us a chance to see if the editor got the gossip right." Rose folded his paper once more. Jenks did as well, both getting up.

Briskey dodged out of the way of a Gardners' bread truck as he came across the street. "Anybody else coming?"

"One more, and there he is." Rose pointed his paper down the street to a man swinging their way. "Morning, Eskel."

The man waved. "Morning, Quill. Tommy."

"Eskel, I'd like you to meet Marcellus Briskey, sheriff over in Lenoir City. Marcellus, this is Eskel Stinnett."

Stinnett held out his hand.

Briskey gloomed onto it for a powerful shake. "You who I think you are?"

"Could be."

"Tax agent?"

"That's me. Only reason we haven't met is I've not had reason to work your county. Quill keeps me hopping around his mountains and the mountains over in Sevier County."

"Well, I can put you onto a still or two."

"I'm always interested."

Rose opened the café's door. "Marie's holding a table for us."

When the men got inside, the woman at the counter gestured toward a table on which four cups of coffee waited for thirsty souls. Rose and company made themselves comfortable.

"I'm shorthanded back in the kitchen, Quill, so Vida Mae's going to take care of you," the woman said.

"Thank you, Marie."

Another woman bustled over, pencil and pad in hand. "Know what you gents going to have?"

Rose winked at Briskey. "Marcellus, suppose we make it easy on the kitchen."

"Sure."

"Vida Mae, a platter each of johnny cakes, sausage, fried eggs, biscuits, and a big bowl of soppin' gravy. With Marcellus and Tommy here, stack those platters high."

"We can take care of that. Biscuits and gravy's always ready, so I'll bring that first thing." The waitress finished her notes before she tucked her pencil in her hair and left.

Briskey dumped some sugar in his coffee. He stirred it with his finger. "What does Eskel know?"

"Nothing more than this is a horrendous big thing we've got ourselves into." Rose gazed at Stinnett. "Eskel, did you know somebody's consolidating all the whiskeymaking in the south end of the county?"

"I've heard talk."

"I know your ears are as sharp as mine. What have you heard?"

"That there's big money behind it, but no names."

"Anything else?" Rose glanced out the café's window at an aluminum hauler rumbling down the street.

"That you've been hijacking whiskey trucks."

"Hmm, I thought we'd kept that one quiet."

"You had. But I know Oddling, too." Stinnett tried his coffee, then held his cup out and blew across it, to cool the brew. "One day, he was feeling a little proud about what you and him got going, and he let it slip. I figured to lay back in the weeds until you were ready to talk about it."

"Time's come." Rose put a hand on his deputy's shoulder. "Tommy and I know where the manufacturing end is, and the intermediate stop in Nashville and the bottling plant there, too. We can guess, since tankers are hauling to Bristol and Chattanooga, there are bottling plants in those cities as well."

Stinnett tried his coffee again. "What else?"

"The most important thing, we know who the money men are. We found that one out with Will Kaufmann's help."

"And that cost him his life, huh?"

"Would appear so." Rose now stirred his coffee. "We know this group is buying off police officers, probably sheriffs, maybe a judge or two, so they've got protection and ways of finding out what's going on. That's why the three of us here hand pick who we bring into the circle."

"How do you know I'm not on the pad?"

Vida Mae came out of the kitchen with a platter of biscuits, a stack of plates, and a bowl of gravy. She set them on the lawmen's table.

Jenks handed the plates around before he helped himself to the biscuits.

The waitress took eating ware from the pocket of her apron and gave a set to each man. "Everything's coming up fast now. Won't be more'n a few more minutes and I'll have the rest for you."

Jenks reached for the gravy bowl, but his face fell when he saw that Briskey had beaten him to it. The Louden sheriff glanced at Jenks with a grin as he ladled a generous quantity onto his plate and passed the bowl to Stinnett.

Rose drummed his fingertips on the side of his cup. "Eskel, you asked if I know if you've been bought and paid for by the bootleggers. I don't. But I know this, if there's another leak, it's you."

"So why risk it?"

"Because we've got a federal crime here. Sometime you're going to claim jurisdiction, but you do it at the wrong time or in the wrong way, and you're going to spoil this thing for us." Rose took the gravy bowl from Jenks only to discover it was empty. He waggled the ladle at Jenks.

"Sorry, Quill, I'm hungry."

Rose set the ladle on his plate. "Eskel, see why I'm so skinny? I go out to eat too often with Tommy. But as I was saying, the three of us have too much invested in this thing to let anybody mess it up."

Stinnett dipped a biscuit in the gravy on his plate. "All right, what do you want me to do?"

"Listen when we meet with the judge, and don't volunteer to do anything."

"Just sit back?"

"That's it."

Vida Mae came out of the kitchen again. This time she carried a tray with the rest of the breakfast order. Rose swatted Jenks's hand when he reached for the pancakes. "I'm first this time."

Rose helped himself, then passed the platter to Briskey. He also started the sausage and the eggs around, and the butter and the syrup, cane syrup because Marie's husband had a sorghum mill on their son's farm at the edge of town.

Everything went the long way around the table to Jenks, but the breakfast cook had stacked the food high on the platters, so there were no shortages.

"Everything all right?" Vida Mae asked.

Rose cut into his syrupy stack of johnny cakes. "It is now."

"Need more of anything, you let me know." She went back to the counter to take care of a couple men in work jeans and tan shirts who had drifted in.

Stinnett forked a chunk of sausage into his mouth. "You don't know a lot about me, do you, Quill?"

"You've been straight in your dealings with me. Other than that, not much."

"I'm from West Virginny."

Briskey harrumphed. "That's not the best recommendation."

An eyebrow shot up on Stinnett's forehead.

Rose pointed his knife at Stinnett. "Don't pay no mind. Marcellus's wife's family is from back there. Hatfields, I do believe."

"He'll be glad to know I know Devil Anse." Stinnett took something from his pocket. He put it down on the center of the table—a badge.

Rose gazed at it. "Boone County."

"I was the sheriff there for one term. I'm part of your fraternity."

"What happened?"

"I got crossways with the judge executive. Nobody gets elected without him. Price of the office, if I wanted it, was to hire his brother as my chief deputy."

"Did you?" Rose cut his sausage and forked a piece into his mouth.

"Yes. And I fired his oversized butt when I found out he and another deputy were shaking down the businessmen in Robinette for protection money."

"Uh-huh."

"He was my chief deputy, so the old judge ran him against me in the next election. I got all of nine votes."

"That's bad."

"My pap didn't even vote for me."

"That's worse."

"Yup, so when the feds offered me a job, I packed up and left."

Briskey raked a chunk of sausage through the gravy on his plate. "Being sheriff is political, all right. It's et up a fair number of good men. Sorry for ya, Mister Stinnett."

The tax agent picked up the sheriff's badge. "I kept this to remind me I'm free of politics."

Rose sipped his coffee. "Be honest, Eskel, you miss it."

"Naw, just miss working with my neighbors. That part I miss a lot."

Stinnett slipped the badge into his pocket and attacked the fried eggs.

JUDGE LIMKE DRAGGED a long table out in front of his courtroom bench. "Help yourself to chairs where the audience sits," he said to the lawmen. "Bring 'em up here."

Rose grabbed two, the second for Limke. "Judge, you know Marcellus, but you've not met Eskel Stinnett."

Limke held out his hand. "Stinnett? Stinnett? Federal tax agent, I do believe."

"That's right." Stinnett shook the judge's hand.

"Well, sit down, sit down. Quill, I assume Mister Stinnett is all right?"

"If he isn't, he knows I'll jail him."

"I guess then I should trust him, at least somewhat."

"And this man..." Rose pulled Newey Sanders in. "...is a state trooper, Sergeant Sanders from Greeneville. Came down at my request to sit in."

"You're not in uniform, Sergeant."

"I'm not on duty, sir."

"What's he know, Quill?"

"About everything. We got him with the best of recommendations. He's honest."

"Sergeant, that's a character trait we few appreciate." Limke motioned Rose to a chair. "Now what do you got that I don't already know about?"

Sanders handed Rose a file folder as he, too, sat down.

Rose opened it, revealing a page of Will Kaufmann's notes. Rose slid it in front of the judge. "We know who the money men are."

Limke put on his glasses and scanned down the page. "Jesus K. Christ. Are you sure?"

"His name's all over one set of incorporation papers, as is his partner's."

"Your brother-in-law? My God, Quill, I chaired his campaign in the county."

"Are you going to tell him?"

"Not if you aren't."

Rose rolled a pencil on the table top. "Well, I may have."

"What do you mean?"

"When Tommy, Will, and I were in Nashville to check corporation records, I stopped in on Clayton before I knew he was on the papers, and I let a little bit slip."

Limke mopped a handkerchief at sweat beading up on his forehead. "Oh, Quill, my good man, no."

"Judge, I don't think it was enough that he could put it together."

Limke closed the folder. He rapped its edge on the table. "Are you ready to arrest the little bastard?"

"I need warrants."

"Well, we can't go to state court or federal court. We don't know whose side they're on, and I can't issue warrants without indictments."

"So have K.W. swear in a grand jury. Thirty minutes, you'll have what you need."

"Does he know anything about this?"

"Not from Tommy or me."

Limke stamped on the floor, three times.

"What's that all about?"

"Quill, K. Dub's office is right below us. Give him a minute, he'll be up."

A heavy foot sounded on the stairs outside the courtroom, then the door opened. "You want me, Judge?"

K.W. Lingenfelter leaned his girth in, three hundred twenty pounds of fat and gristle, but he masked it with a tailored suit and vest.

Limke beckoned him in. "K. Dub, do you know everybody around the table?"

"Our boys, sure."

"That man who could be your twin there is Marcellus Briskey, sheriff over in Louden, and this other fella is—"

"Eskel Stinnett." Stinnett stood to shake hands with the county attorney.

"He's a federal tax agent outta Knoxville. And this other individual is a state policeman."

Sanders, too, stood to shake hands with Lingenfelter. "Newell Sanders, Greeneville."

"Good to meet you, sir." Lingenfelter came around to Limke. "How can I help you, Judge?"

"Pull up a chair."

The county attorney did, the chair on the puny side for his wide frame.

"K. Dub, you're going to empanel a grand jury and get us some indictments, and the men you select have got to know how to keep their traps shut."

"I can do that. Who're we after?"

"The lieutenant governor and the head of the machine in Davidson County."

Sweat beads popped out on Lingenfelter's forehead. He snatched a handkerchief from his pocket to soak them up. "Jesus, Judge, I voted for Clayton. We were in law school together. What's he done? You sure we've even got jurisdiction?"

Limke gestured with an open hand at Rose.

Rose took that as his cue to talk. "Clayton Johnson and Harmond Watson own the business that bottles and distributes illegal whiskey being manufactured under

Shingle Mountain. Since it all starts here, yes, we can claim jurisdiction."

"How big is this thing?"

"Big enough they're shipping the booze in false-bottom gasoline tanker trucks. Three-thousand gallons at a time."

Lingenfelter puffed out his cheeks at that one. He swept his handkerchief up over his hair and down the back of his neck.

Rose leaned his elbow on the table, his hand in front of the county attorney. "We've only got part of it. They're shipping raw alcohol to Bristol and Chattanooga as well. That means there've got to be bottling plants there, and maybe others involved in the ownership."

Lingenfelter wiped his forehead again. "I'm not telling you your business, but I think we better hold back on the grand jury until you've got the whole package. If we move on the Nashville end, and we don't move on the Bristol and Chattanooga ends at the same time, some people are going to get away."

Rose peered at Stinnett, and Stinnett nodded his agreement. Rose motioned to him. "You want to shadow a tanker to Chattanooga, see where it goes?"

"I can do that."

"Tommy will go along in his pickup. If you split the shadowing duties, less chance you'll be spotted."

"What about Bristol?"

"Marcellus, you want to take it?"

Briskey spit a stream of tobacco juice into a brass bucket to the side of the table. "Hell, our fiscal court's so tight I had to beg 'em just to let me come over here. How about yer Greeneville trooper there?"

Rose turned to Sanders.

"I'm good for it."

Limke leaned back in his chair. "Well, then, are we done for today?"

Briskey caught Rose's eye. He pointed to the judge.

Rose tapped his fingertips on the table. "One more thing."

"What's that?"

"Marcellus has five men in his jail, drivers and guards from the tankers we've hijacked. He can't afford to keep them, and I don't want them over here. Can you give him a transfer order so he can ship them to Brushyfork?"

Limke took off his glasses. He polished the lenses on his sleeve. "Marcellus, can't your judge do that?"

"Well, we're kinda on the outs."

"Outs? So you want me to do the deed." Limke went to his bench where he rustled through drawers until he found the needed form. He signed it with a flourish and handed it to Briskey. "You put the names on it and date it the day you're going to haul them off. I'll call the warden and give him some sort of cock-and-bull story how we need his help holding these fellas until they go up for trial."

"They won't give me their names."

"Bastards think they're tough nuts, huh? Well, just put 'em down as Joe Doe One, Two, Three, Four, and Five. We don't need names to jail 'em or convict 'em."

CHAPTER 25

Shadows

JENKS AND STINNETT only had to wait two days for a tanker to leave the shed by the Little Tennessee for Chattanooga.

Jenks had hunkered down in a grove of chinquapin oaks on a hill overlooking the shed. When he saw a tanker pull out and turn to the southwest, onto State Four-Eleven, he ran to his truck and rumbled it through a rough pasture on the backside of the hill down to a lane that took him to the highway. He saw the tanker in the distance when he made the turn onto the paved road.

Jenks and Stinnett had worked out a relay system. Jenks laid back until he was three miles out of Madisonville, then kicked up his speed, closing the gap on the tanker, the shadows deepening as evening came on. Jenks saw the lights flick on on the tanker as it slowed at the town limits. He saw, too, the Esso station ahead. Jenks was less than a hundred yards behind the tanker when he peeled off into the Esso's lot, pulling up beside Stinnett's car, Stinnett relaxing against a fender, sucking on a cup of coffee.

"That's him that just passed."

Stinnett held his cup out. "Want to finish it?"

"No thanks."

The tax agent dumped the contents. "See you at the Athens Esso."

Stinnett threw gravel as he spun out of the lot and onto Four-Eleven.

Jenks's elderly Dodge didn't have the power to spin its rear wheels, not even on gravel, so he puttered out of the lot, turned west onto Tennessee Sixty-Eight, and ran up through the gears. He got the truck up to sixty miles an hour when the front end began to shake like a frightened horse. Jenks dropped back to fifty-five and the shaking stopped. He held that speed for five miles, then slowed for the turn onto County Three-Oh-Seven and the run on into Athens.

Jenks knew the tanker and Stinnett would go southwest on Four-Eleven to Englewood before they jogged over to Athens on County Thirty-Nine. He also knew that the Athens Esso station had an outhouse. Jenks pushed hard to get there, figuring he could beat the slower tanker by a few minutes if he could hold his speed. He boomed over a hill and spotted the welcoming Esso sign just before the light over it winked out. Jenks hopped his foot from the accelerator to the brake and brought his speed down for the turnoff.

Ahead in his headlights appeared the outhouse. Jenks let his truck roll up beside it. Panicking from the pressure of both a full bladder and colon, he hit the light switch, yanked the ignition key, and ran.

Jenks had hardly dropped his britches when he heard tires on the gravel and a car's horn beep, beep, beeping.

"Oh Lord." He ripped a page from the catalog on the nail, wiped himself, and yanked his pants up. Jenks forced his way out the door, fighting with his belt that refused buckle. "That you, Eskel?"

"You taking a vacation in there, deputy?"

"Hell no."

"He's going down U.S. Eleven."

Jenks wrangled the end of his belt into the buckle and cinched himself in.

"Suspenders would be easier, you know."

"Yeah, yeah, yeah. I'll catch up to him. I'll pass him at Cleveland and wait for you at Ooltewah. I'll fall in behind when you come by."

"Right."

Jenks jumped in his truck. He stepped on the starter button, but nothing happened. "Oh Lordy, Lordy, Lordy. Please Lord, not now—"

"Trouble?" Stinnett called out.

"I got battery, but the starter won't do nuthin'. It's done this to me a couple times."

"Get in my car."

"No, gimme a push."

Jenks and Stinnett shoved the pickup out into the lot so Stinnett could get his Chevrolet behind the truck. After matching bumpers, Stinnett got the two vehicles rolling.

Jenks popped his clutch in less than the length of his truck. The engine fired, and he roared out of the lot, shifting up through the gears, getting up to fifty as he shot past the town's courthouse square.

Eighteen miles on, Jenks spotted the taillights of the tanker as it slowed for Calhoun. He throttled back.

Twenty miles per hour through Calhoun and Charleston, and Jenks brought his speed back up, matching the tanker's forty. Minutes later, he saw the lights of Cleveland and sped up. He swung wide as he passed the tanker.

Jenks slowed for the town, then took his speed up to fifty and held it there until the Ooltewah sign appeared. There he slowed, shifted down, and pulled off on a side street. He killed his lights but not the truck's motor. Jenks only had minutes to wait before the tanker rumbled by. Another minute and Stinnett's Chevrolet.

Jenks backed out onto Eleven and sped after them.

The tanker did not go down into Chattanooga's industrial district as Stinnett and Jenks had guessed it would. Instead, it turned off at East Ridge, rolled through a half-dozen different streets and then into a building that had once housed the Lookout Mountain Wagon Manufactory.

Both Stinnett and Jenks killed their headlights when the tanker turned off into the manufactory's parking lot. Only when the building's doors closed behind the tanker did Stinnett idle closer. He stopped at the driveway. There he turned on his flashlight and aimed its beam around until it came on a sign—Red Dog Feeds.

The tax agent drove on, with Jenks behind him. He stopped two streets away, got out, and walked back to Jenks's truck. "Deputy, the sign back there says Red Dog Feeds. What do you want to do?"

"I'm for going home."

"Why don't you do that? I think I'll stick around, poke around some. I've got a man down here. I'll see him in the morning and see what he knows."

Jenks gave Stinnett a cool look. "If you're going to stick around, I'm going to stick around."

"You don't trust me?"

QUILL ROSE FELT A SHARP STAB in his ribs, a pain that woke him.

His wife rolled away from him, mumbling, "Telephone. You answer it."

Rose threw back the bed covers. He slapped his bare feet down on the cold floor—darn cold he found it—and forced himself up and out onto the stairway and down,

down to the front hall and the telephone that would not stop ringing. Rose gave the phone a pained look as he picked up the receiver.

"That you, Quill?" a voice asked.

"It sure isn't God."

"Quill, it's Od. I got the tanker for ya. Just pulled through town on his way to Bristol."

"You want to go along on this one?"

"Better not. The JP doesn't like me leavin'. Maybe next time if it's a big one."

"It'll be big. I want three tankers going to Nashville."

"Quill, you need to know they've taken to sending cars in front and behind their trucks going to Nashville. Lotsa guns. They don't like it that someone's been stealin' their trucks."

"I'll be back tomorrow. Let's talk." Rose did not put the receiver up. Instead he clicked the hook three times to get the operator. "Yes, May Ella, it's Quill. Get me Greeneville four-five-two."

He snapped on the hall light and looked in the mirror. Just as quickly, he snapped the light off.

"Newey?" he said into the mouthpiece.

"Yeah?"

"Quill Rose here."

"Quill Rose, you know the chickens are still asleep in Greeneville?"

"They aren't up here either. Tanker just rolled through Maryville for Bristol. I'm betting he'll take Eleven-W. It's the only sensible route."

"All right, I'll meet you in Rogersville, in front of the hotel."

"Have 'em make me an egg sandwich, would you, something I can eat in the car? No time for breakfast here. By the time I get my britches on, I'm going to have to drive like the devil's behind me with a pitchfork to catch up with that tanker."

"Eleven-W's a good road. You'll make great time."

"So will he."

"Not likely. He's not gonna drive over forty-five. He don't want to call attention to himself, and he'll probably drop down to fifteen through the towns."

"Hope so."

"You be careful, Quill. Don't hit some farmer's stray cow out there."

"You're the one to be careful. You got that windy road, old State Seventy."

"You gonna talk all morning?"

"No. See you in Rogersville."

This time Rose hung up the receiver. He groped his way back to the stairs and up to the bedroom, finding his clothes where he had dropped them the night before, across a chair. He got into them and into his socks and shoes. Something didn't feel right about his shoes, but Rose hurried on, grabbing for his hat and jacket.

Martha Rose came up on her elbow. "What was it?"

"Going to Bristol. Be back tomorrow, maybe even tonight."

He slipped out the bedroom door, closing it with care so it would make no noise, then clattered down the stairs. Rose had left the cruiser on the street, as if he had expected J.D. Oddling to call. Dew covered the car, so he helped himself to a rag from under the seat and wiped the windshield dry.

Rose liked this cruiser. The model normally came with a little six-cylinder up front, but he requested one of Ford's new V-Eights and got it. He had Clyde Harts make some modifications and found that nothing could outrun the car.

Rose tossed the rag back under the seat and got in. He keyed the ignition, listening as the motor come to life. He liked the sweet, rumbly sound and the slight smell of gear oil.

Rose steered the cruiser through several of the town's streets and out into the country, to County Thirty-Three. This was not a road for making time nor were the streets of Knoxville ahead, but he rolled on.

It wasn't until he reached the far side of Knoxville that Rose stepped down on the accelerator, eating up the miles as he headed toward Blaine.

The sun crept up over the farmland ahead when he crossed the Knox/Granger county line. With the sun, Rose's speed crept up as well–fifty-five, sixty, sixty-five, seventy, seventy-five. He was coming up on Thorn Hill and slowing when he saw the tanker. He slowed more and trailed the big truck through the town. Then, back in the country, Rose kicked up his speed again, closing fast.

He made a decision. Rose steered out into the opposing lane and, when he didn't see any traffic coming his way, stepped down and shot past the tanker, holding his speed until Bean Station. A blink and the crossroads town was behind him.

Rose throttled back now to forty-five, the road ahead wandering, as if the crew that had built it had been drunk. Forty-five, he discovered, was even too fast for some of the twists.

The road straightened out just before Rogersville. The hotel? He couldn't remember, was it on the right? It should be. Rose throttled back, looking, searching.

And there it was.

He pulled off on a side street short of the hotel, made a U-turn, and came back to park at the corner of the side street and Eleven-W.

For the first time since leaving Maryville, Rose relaxed. He stretched and rubbed at his eyes. When Rose got out of his cruiser, he shook the stiffness from his lean body, stiffness from having driven too long, then went off, up the sidewalk, to the stonework hotel's awning-covered entrance. There he came on State Police Sergeant Newey Sanders, in civilian clothes, coming out the door, Sanders carrying a paper bag.

Sanders glanced around. "Tanker go through already?"

"No, I left him miles behind. I was getting hungry."

"Well, here's your fried egg sandwich." The trooper held the bag up. "If you want coffee, I'll go back in and get you a cup."

"No thanks. Coffee's just going to make me have to stop somewheres to pee."

Sanders stared down at Rose's shoes. "You always wear 'em on the wrong feet?"

"What?"

"Your shoes?"

Rose looked down. "So that's why they didn't feel right when I put 'em on."

"Got dressed in the dark, huh?"

"I sure did." Rose took a seat on the hotel's front step. He untied his shoes and pulled them off, switched them from one foot to the other. He wiggled his toes. "Ooo, feels much better."

Sanders handed the bag to Rose. "I'm parked at the next corner. Bring your breakfast with you."

Rose shook one foot like a cat that had stepped in water, then the other before the two lawmen walked on. They conversed about unimportant things while Rose darted his gaze around.

"Looking for a state patrol car?"

"Yeah."

"I didn't take one. Brought my own car. See that black Lincoln up there? Most people think it belongs to a moonshine runner."

Rose whistled. When he got up to the Lincoln, he leaned in through the driver's window. "Take the seats out and you could haul an awful lot of booze in here."

"Guess I could."

Rose patted the steering wheel before he pulled his head out. He set his bag on the roof and dug in, his fingers searching for the sandwich. "Ooo, hot, just the way I like it."

"Hope so. I had 'em splash on some tabasco sauce."

Rose glanced at Sanders, an eyebrow rising. He bit into the sandwich–and choked. Rose's eyes bulged. His mouth gaped open, and he fanned at the fire.

"Not too hot, is it?"

"Hooooyah."

"That's the way I prefer it. You want to ride with me?"

Rose wiped his sleeve under his eyes. "No–heee!– Better double-team 'im. Hooo."

"You sure that's not too hot?"

Rose gasped.

"Maybe some water?"

"No. No."

"About tailing the tanker–"

"How about you take 'im on to Surgionsville?" Rose wheezed, trying to swallow. "Drop back there. I'll take 'im on to Kingsport and pass 'im."

He took a new bite from his sandwich. Rose chewed, and as he did, he mopped at the sweat forming up on his forehead. "You trail 'im through Kingsport–hooo! I'll pick 'im up on the other side–heee! At Bristol, you take 'im."

Sanders aimed a finger to the west. "That him?"

"Looks like it." Rose took another bite from his sandwich.

A tractor and tank wagon came rolling toward them. As the rig passed, both saw the Sunspot signs.

"That's our boy."

"Then I'm on my way." Sanders got into the Lincoln and started it.

Rose stuffed the bag in his pocket. He trotted back to his cruiser, chewing on his sandwich and puffing out his cheeks each time he exhaled more fire.

Rose and Sanders made the hand-offs as they had planned, at Surgoinsville, Kingsport, and Bristol.

In Bristol, Sanders lagging two blocks behind the tanker, saw it rumble across the L&N tracks and into an industrial district. He sped up, only to slow for the approaching intersection. Sanders watched the tanker haul into a parking lot next to a dilapidated warehouse and heard a horn sound.

Warehouse doors rolled open. The truck drove through, disappearing into a cavernous interior.

Sanders stopped. He waited for Rose, and Rose arrived a few minutes later. He left his cruiser to come up to the Lincoln. "He find him a home?"

"The warehouse there." Sanders gestured across the way.

"Want to get closer?"

"I've got me an uneasy feeling about that. How about we take a peek through my bird-watching glasses?" Sanders held up a pair of field glasses.

"You a bird watcher?"

"Hardly." Sanders put the glasses to his eyes. He rotated the focus wheel before he passed the glasses to Rose. "Take a look."

"What are these, ten-power?"

"Twenty."

"Whoa. I guess so." Rose pulled back from the glasses. He blinked his eyes, then stared through the binoculars a second time. "I can tell you the color of the eyes of the people in what appears to be an office."

"That's why I didn't want to get closer."

Rose played the glasses over the building. "A tobacco warehouse, isn't it?"

"That's what they'd like us to think. See the sign over the warehouse door? Now look at the little sign in the window of the office."

"Hmm. DKW Company. Does that mean anything to you?"

"No, but we can sure find out with a call to the Secretary of State's office."

"Uh-huh. Will's cousin works there. She'd look up the records for us."

"How about we get out of here before they get curious?"

Chapter 26

Grand jury

ROSE STUDIED THE MEN in the jury box, silently agreeing the county attorney had selected them well– Buck Harless, Grumble Jones, Homer and Harold Wright, all from Townsend up in the mountains; Luther Click who ran a small farm in Cades Cove; Orville Newcom, the local Ford dealer; Doctor Thomas Milton, from the college; Ebbie White, the pharmacist; Dink Smith, superintendent of the water plant; and Willis Inscoe, the town grocer and captain of the volunteer fire department.

Rose felt particularly good about Click. Click, a distant cousin, operated a still on the sly, but since he never gouged the few customers he had nor poisoned them with bad whiskey, Rose had left him alone. He knew Click would vote for indictments on general principle. The whiskey maker viewed himself as a craftsman, and, as such, despised moonshiners who went in for mass production.

Lingenfelter came over to Rose. "Everybody here we need?"

"Newey's here, sitting in the back." Rose twisted around. He glanced toward the door. "Ahh, here comes Eskel Stinnett, but I don't know who that is with him."

Lingenfelter waved a paper for Stinnett and the stranger to come over. "Eskel, who's this?"

"Simon Grevey, federal magistrate. Figured he'd better listen in."

"Whoa now, we're not giving a show for him."

Stinnett parked the knuckles of one hand on his hip. "Look, I'm going to need seizure orders from this man's court. He can hear the testimony here or I can drag you all up to Simon's courtroom, and don't you think that's going to get more than a little attention?"

"We better see the judge." Lingenfelter glowered, rapping his paper against his fingertips. He went over to the jurors. "Tell some jokes, boys. A matter's come up, and we've got to consult with Judge Limke."

Lingenfelter swept out of the courtroom with Stinnett, Grevey, and Rose in his wake. Rose wiggled his fingers for Sanders to follow.

The five rattled down the stairs to Judge Limke's office. Lingenfelter stopped at the door where he pecked on the door glass.

"Yeah, come in."

Lingenfelter leaned through the doorway. "Enos, we've got a problem."

"Well, come in and tell me about it."

The five crowded into the judge's broom closet of an office.

"Stinnett brought a federal magistrate down to sit in on the grand jury."

Limke wagged a hand at the one man he did not know. "That would be you."

The stranger reached out to shake hands. "I'm Simon Grevey."

"Any other time, I'm sure it would be a pleasure. But Mister Grevey, a grand jury isn't a spectator sport. You can't be in there."

"If I can explain."

"Please."

Stinnett cut in on Grevey. "Judge, we all agree there's a federal crime here."

"We do."

"Well, I'm going to need seizure orders from a federal magistrate when we go in on the still and the bottling plants."

Limke tilted his chair back on its hind legs, crossing his arms over his chest as he did. "Mister Stinnett, I expect you're right."

"If I've got to bring Quill and the state police up to the federal Post Office for a hearing, a pile of people are going to know what's going on, and it's the end of the secret."

"Ah-ha, so you want your magistrate to witness the testimony here where we've got a lid on things." Limke assumed his sage face, a look that suggested he was giving the matter deep consideration. "How do I know I can trust your magistrate to keep his mouth shut?"

Grevey stuck his hand in his coat pocket and jingled some change. "Sir, I'm new here. I've got no ties to the community or even to this state. They shipped me in from Roanoke to fill in temporarily when the old magistrate died."

"Read about it in the paper."

"I've been here less than a week. I can issue the orders on Mister Stinnett's word, but I'd rather hear the case. I don't want some hot new lawyer challenging my orders to my boss."

Limke cocked an eyebrow at Rose, and Rose shrugged.

A frown clouded Limke's face. "Mister Grevey, one word of this gets out and I'll send my sheriff up to drag your butt into my jail."

"Thank you, Judge. I've got the papers with me. I'll fill them out here, file the copies myself. Not even my secretary will know."

Limke came forward in his chair until he could rest his elbows on his desk. "One more thing. Mister Grevey, you're a guest upstairs. You don't interrupt the proceedings. You don't ask any questions. You don't even say a word. In fact, I don't even want the jurors to know who you are."

"I'll sit in the back."

"All right. K. Dub, get to it."

Rose hung back after the others left.

Limke took off his spectacles and massaged the bridge of his nose. "You know, I think that Stinnett fella did a smart thing here. He gets what he needs, and we keep control. Tommy spent time with him. What does he say about the man?"

"He's impressed, and Tommy's less trusting than I am."

"Good." Limke put his spectacles back on. He snatched up his rose-hued fountain pen and went back to the papers before him. "As soon as you get those indictments, hustle on down here, and I'll write you up the warrants. When are you going after our friend in the Capitol?"

"Can I sit a minute?"

Limke waved at an empty chair.

Rose settled in in a slouch that had him tapping the soles of his shoes on Limke's office floor.

Limke stared at him. "You nervous about something?"

"Judge, this is going to rip Martha's heart out, seeing her brother go to jail. She's going to take it out on me if I arrest him. I could end up sleeping on the back porch with the dog."

Limke took off his spectacles a second time and, with the heels of his hands, he set to rubbing his eyebrows into his forehead and his forehead into his scalp. After some moments, Limke peered at Rose, his head tilted. "Have you considered walking away from this?"

"I don't see as how I can."

"Quill, you've done enough. Why not let Sanders and Stinnett finish it up? They're good men, and they've got nothing at stake here."

"Yeah, maybe."

"Look, nobody in the county will hold it against you."

Rose chose not hear that. He gazed out Limke's window at the western slope of Chilhowee Mountain, the smoky blue haze of early summer softening the lines of its ridges.

"Are you listening to me, Quill? You aren't going to do it, are you?"

Rose shrugged.

"So when are you going after the little bastard?"

Rose squared his shoulders. "I expect early next week. They're bunching up the tankers going to Nashville, for protection. I told Od to call me when he's got three going through town. They're our ticket into Sunspot and the bottling plant."

"You best be damn careful. I don't want your lovely Martha being a widow."

Rose pushed his chair back as he got up. "I'm not eager for that, either."

"You want me to talk to her?"

"I'd prefer not." Rose moved toward the hallway.

"All right. Close the door, would you, Quill?"

Rose slipped out. He pushed the door shut, then went on up the stairs. After Rose took a seat in the first row of the courtroom, Lingenfelter called out, "All right, boys, we can go to work now. The sheriff's here." He squared off in front of the jurors, hooking his thumbs in his vest pockets as he did. "We're going to present the facts to you about an illegal whiskey-making business that's operating out of our county. If you think the facts have merit, then it's your job to bring in indictments. Quill, why don't you start 'em out by telling what you know?"

Rose stood and addressed the jurors. "We've got information there's a big factory-type still working up under Shingle Mountain."

Dink Smith raised his hand. "Have you seen it?"

"No, but Tommy's seen the warehouse off Four-Eleven on the Little Tennessee. That's where they load out the tankers."

Grumble Jones put two fingers to his chin. "Tankers?"

"They're shipping the raw alcohol out in three-thousand-gallon loads, in Sunspot gasoline tankers."

"And you know this for a fact?"

"Yes, I've captured three of them."

Smith came forward in his chair. "I want to know why you didn't see the manufactory."

"Dink, I don't like to get shot at. We've got citizens down there who don't like anybody who carries a badge." Rose scratched at his mustache. "Would you go up that road?"

"Not on a bet. But who told you it's there?"

"Sam Berry."

Smith turned to his fellow jurors. "That's good enough for me."

Rose smiled at the comment. "Here it is. I told you I captured three tankers. I delivered the first one to Sunspot's gasoline depot in Nashville. Well, I didn't exactly deliver it. I ransomed it. They paid me three thousand dollars to get the tanker and the alcohol."

Homer Wright shook a finger for attention. "What happened to the money?"

"I put it in the bank. It's all accounted for."

"What about the other two tankers?"

"I ransomed them as well. Then Tommy, Will Kaufmann, and I followed them to the bottling plant on the north side of Nashville."

Jones glanced at Dink Smith sitting next to him, then at Rose. "You get three thousand dollars for each one of them?"

"Yessir. We've scooped up nine thousand dollars of their money so far."

Jones nudged Smith. "This is a good business for the county. If Quill keeps it up, we can get rid of the property tax."

Lingenfelter shook his head. "Gentlemen, please."

Rose took Kaufmann's notes from his pocket. "Will made a search of the corporation records, and here's the chain of companies involved. Sunspot Petroleum Inc. is owned by Harmond Watson of Nashville."

Jones frowned at the mention of Watson's name. "He the political kingmaker?"

"That's the one."

"I've heard he's got his hand in every crooked deal in Nashville."

"He's got his hand in this one. J&W Properties Inc. owns the land and building where the whiskey is bottled. That's a shell corporation. It's owned by New Century Inc., another shell corporation. New Century is owned by Indelmo Corporation. Indelmo is owned by Raines Vendors of Shelbyville, and Raines is owned by Clayton Johnson and Harmond Watson."

Doctor Milton, a philosophy professor, shot a look of surprise at Rose. "*Thee* Clayton Johnson?"

"Yes."

"Sonuvabitch."

Smith raised his hand again. "Can this Will Kaufmann attest to what you're telling us?"

"No. He's dead. Murdered."

Luther Click raised his gaze. He'd been studying the knees of his overalls. "That got anything to do with this, Quill?"

"I think so, but I can't prove it. Not yet. As for attesting, both Tommy and I read the same corporation records. They are as I've told you. We've also located bottling plants in Chattanooga and Bristol. Tommy and Eskel Stinnett, a federal tax agent..." Rose turned toward the back of the courtroom. "...Would you stand up, Eskel?"

Stinnett came out of his seat. He held his hat before him.

Rose took out his own notepad and paged into it. "Tommy and Eskel followed a tanker to Red Dog Feeds. Red Dog is owned by J&W Properties and Old South Inc. Old South is not a shell corporation. It's owned by James Windom of East Ridge." Rose turned back to Stinnett. "Eskel?"

Stinnett cleared his throat. "We've known Windom is a bootlegger, but we'd never found his warehouse. I have an agent down there, following the delivery trucks–damn feed trucks–to see who he supplies."

Rose went back to his notes. "Bristol's the other corner of the triangle. Sergeant Newell Sanders, of the Greeneville State Police post, and I followed a tanker to a tobacco warehouse that's owned by DKW Company. DKW is owned by New Century and Westfahl Fixtures Inc. Westfahl really does make faucets, but in another building in Bristol, not at the warehouse. Westfahl had been owned by the Robert Westfahl family for some forty-five years–highly respected, I'm told–but when the old man died two years ago, the sons sold to Bristol Vendors, and that company is owned by Gordon MacCool. Newey?"

Sanders stood up. "I'd heard about MacCool when I came down from Kentucky, always kind of a shadowy figure. Got his start running cock fights. Went from there to bootlegging untaxed cigarettes. Runs some gambling. For reasons I don't know, we've never been able to make a case on him."

Buck Harless raised a hand. "Sir?"

"Yes?"

"Could maybe he have bought himself some protection?"

"It's been known to have happened."

Lingenfelter planted his hands on the railing in front of the jury box. "Do you see the connections? Watson owns the tankers that move the alcohol. Johnson and Watson own the Nashville bottling plant and run the distribution system there. Johnson and Watson are partners in the bottling plants and distribution systems in Bristol and Chatt with Gordon MacCool and James Windom, neither one of whom will get a stained-glass window in their churches when they die." He shifted his bulk to the side. "It took a lot of money to bankroll this thing, and it's likely, although we can't prove it yet, that the four are partners in the whiskey factory."

Homer and Harold Wright leaned together, whispering.

Lingenfelter gave them the hairy eyeball. "Anything we should know, boys?"

Harold Wright came up straight in his chair. "Seems to my brother and me that there are an awful lot of charges possible."

"True, but the ones we can make stick, if you choose to indict, are the distribution and sale of untaxed alcohol."

Lingenfelter punched his fingers on the railing, like a telegrapher tapping out a message. "Be certain of this, Blount County is claiming jurisdiction because it all starts here with the manufacturing of illegal whiskey. Now, gentlemen, we're going out in the hall for a smoke, so you talk it over. Pound on the door when you're ready. Willis, you've not said much. You be the foreman."

Inscoe signaled his acceptance with an okay.

Lingenfelter gave him the indictment form, then fanned his hands at Rose and the others, to get them moving out the door.

Stinnett and Grevey settled on a bench against the far wall of the hallway. Lingenfelter stepped up to them. "Mister Grevey, did you hear what you needed?"

"I'm satisfied." The magistrate took a fistful of forms from an inside pocket. He opened them and pressed them flat. "Sunspot Petroleum Inc. What's the address?" He aimed his fountain pen at Quill Rose.

Rose checked Kaufmann's notes. "One-twelve South First Street."

Grevey wrote. "Uh-huh, and Nashville. Today's date and my signature, and that's the first one." He handed the seizure order to Stinnett. "All right, number two. J&W Properties, address?"

"Twenty-six Rosebank."

"Street? Avenue? Boulevard?"

"Street."

"Street and Nashville." Grevey dated and signed that order. "Number three, Bristol, DKW Inc.—"

Rose opened his own notepad. "Twelve Tazewell Street."

"Uh-huh." Grevey signed that order large enough that his name could be read from the staircase at the end of the hall. "Number four, Chattanooga, the city beneath Lookout Mountain. Red Dog Feeds—"

Rose looked at his notes again. "Twenty-three Nickajack Street, and that's in East Ridge, not Chattanooga."

"Ah, East Ridge, thank you. I'd hate to send Eskel to the wrong city. All right, two more. The manufactory, what are we going to put down for that address?"

"Shingle Mountain. That's the best we can do."

"All right, big building at Shingle Mountain where alcohol is being made. Today's date and my signature. And number six?"

"Warehouse on the southwest shore of the Little Tennessee River, three miles northeast of Vonore."

"Uh-huh, northeast of Vonore." Grevey signed that order and handed it to Stinnett. "When are you going to get 'em?"

Stinnett stuffed the seizure orders in his coat's side pocket. "The sheriff will tell me. We're going to move on all the places at the same time."

Grevey began writing out duplicate orders for his files. "Mister Lingenfelter, six places, they could arrest a lot of people. Any you don't want to prosecute, send them up to my court."

Lingenfelter gave a quick thought to the offer. "I'll tell you what, other than the principals and the people in my county, why don't you take the lot?"

Grevey glanced up, smiling. "I look forward to it."

A rapping at the courtroom door interrupted. Lingenfelter went to the door.

Inside stood Willis Inscoe. "We're ready."

"We'll be right there." The county attorney motioned to the lawmen to go in first. He held the door open for Rose and Sanders. "Gentlemen, I've got a good feeling."

"Mister Lingenfelter," Grevey said, still writing, "Mister Stinnett and I will be in just as soon as I finish these duplicate orders."

"All right." Lingenfelter strode away into the courtroom and down to the front. "Willis, what's the jury's report?"

"You have your indictment of the four named individuals. We all agreed and signed it." Inscoe handed the form to Lingenfelter.

"Well, gents, I thank you on behalf of the county. Stop by the clerk's office, and Alvie will have a check for five dollars for each of you. Just let me remind you, a grand jury works in secret. Don't talk about what you've done here today with anybody."

Grumble Jones stood and gave his rump a vigorous rub. "Been too long in that chair. K. Dub, you can count on us."

"I know I can. That's why I picked each one of you."

Luther Click shuffled out of the jury box and over to Rose. "When you comin' by to visit with Janey Leigh, me, and the children?"

"Cousin, this is a pretty spooky thing I'm into. Maybe after it all plays out."

"The lieutenant governor, he's your brother-in-law, idn't he?"

"Afraid so."

"Puts you in kind of a tough situation."

"That it does."

Click cast his gaze down at the floor. "You know, I kin help."

"How's that?"

He rubbed the toe of his boot at an imagined spot. "I kin go down to Shingle and find that factory still for ya."

Rose put an arm around his cousin's shoulders. "Luther, those boys under the mountain, they don't like strangers."

"Well, I know a couple of them involved. Don't ask me how. I just do."

Rose scrunched his face. "I wish you wouldn't. But if you go, you be gawd-awful careful."

"I'll get Homer and Harold to drop me at Tallassee. I'll walk in from there, then hike over the mountain to the cove and home."

"No, if you're going to do this, you walk back out to Tallassee." Rose stepped around so Click had to look into his eyes. He leaned down to the little man. "Look, I'll have Tommy and another deputy waiting for you at Woodruff's store. You don't get out by sundown, they'll come in looking for you."

"Quill, those people down there are gonna know something's not right if I backtrack."

Rose folded his arms, listening.

"It'd be better to have Tommy at Happy Valley, the little store there, Brighty's I think it is. They'll expect me to go that way, to cross into the mountains at the gap above Abrams Ridge and take the McCully trail home."

"All right, Brighty's it is." Rose raised a finger in warning. "No later than sundown now, and you stay the night at my house."

CHAPTER 27

The sheriff's spy

JUDGE LIMKE, resting in the swing on Quill Rose's porch, eyed the man pacing before him. "I've got to ask, are you deliberately trying to wear out the floor boards?"

Rose continued to pace. "I shouldn't have let Luther go in there. I shouldn't have done it."

"Come on, nobody's going to bother Luther."

"Wish I had your confidence."

"Look, everybody likes him."

"Everybody who knows him. But, damn, we've got some mean ones down there at Shingle. They don't all know Luther."

Eskel Stinnett stood at a porch post, his arm around it. "So I get the joy of going in there, huh?"

"You're federal. It's a still. It's where they make the stuff."

Martha Rose came to the screen door, Little Nate hanging onto her hand. "Quill, supper's been ready for some time. You've got these hungry men."

"I'm not up to food. Judge, are you hungry?"

"Not particularly."

"Eskel?"

"I can wait."

"All right, I'll keep the supper warm." Martha Rose retreated to the inner recesses of the house, taking the boy with her.

Limke rounced around in the porch swing, as if he were nesting. "That wife of yours, Quill, she's a better woman than you deserve."

"That's for certain. You know what her one disappointment is? We never had children."

"Well, you've certainly got one now."

"But that's only temporary."

"How many months has it been?"

"A few."

"More than a few. Quill, if you and Martha want, I can make the boy a ward of the court, then give him to you to adopt."

Rose scratched at the back of his neck. "She does think of Little Nate as her own."

"So you've given him a name, huh?"

"She has, yes."

Limke slapped his knee. "Then consider it done. I'll do the paperwork tomorrow. Now when are you gonna tell her about Clayton?"

"Not until I absolutely have to."

Stinnett stared off in the distance. "Headlights coming up the street."

"Oh, hey, hear that deep-throated engine, that V-Eight? That's my cruiser, and that's Tommy." Rose hopped the porch rail and ran out to the edge of the yard where a Ford crunched to a stop on the gravel in front of him. Rose jerked open the passenger door, coming near to ripping it off its hinges. He reached in for the little man in the Oshkosh-by-Gosh overalls and hauled him out, wrapped him in a bear hug. "Damn, I worried about you, Luther."

Click squirmed, struggling for air. "You needn't."

Rose slapped him on the back before he let him go. "Where'd you find him, Tommy?"

"'Bout three miles south out of Happy Valley, just this side of Flat Ridge. He was swinging along at the side of the road, happy as you please."

Luther slipped a hand into a back pocket. "Just got to visitin'. Lost track o' time."

"Martha's got supper waiting for us." Rose leaned into the car, to his deputies. "Tommy, Roy Eagle, you come on in, too."

Jenks looked to his partner. "What say, Roy?"

"I'll have to call Mary Lynne."

The deputies clambered out and followed along after Rose and Click.

Roy Eagle Clark, Jenks's fellow deputy, skinny and knot-hard, had been, like Jenks, a lumberjack before Rose picked him up. Rose called back to him, "Mary Lynne won't mind letting you stay, will she, Roy Eagle?"

"We got nine kids around our table. My not being there won't hardly be noticed, but I do want to call home."

Rose held the door. "Phone's right there in the hallway. Martha, three extra plates."

Martha Rose came into the hall from the kitchen, Little Nate clutching onto the hem of her apron. "Husband mine, you're fortunate I expected this of you. You get everybody around the table. Tommy, Judge, will you help me?"

Rose herded Click and Stinnett into the back parlor where a long table had been set for six. Rose counted the guests on his fingers, then dodged into the front parlor for an extra chair.

"Sit, gentlemen, sit," Martha said as she bustled in with the boy beside her. "Stone soup, tonight–"

"–When you get a little unexpected company, you just throw in another handful of stones," Rose said, finishing his wife's sentence. He made room for the seventh chair, then went to the buffet for eating ware and a plate.

"Actually, it's hobo stew. I started it yesterday when Quill told me you might be coming, what with the grand jury and all." Martha set the pot in the center of the table and dipped one bowl full after another as Tommy Jenks handed them to her. Little Nate, watching, went to Rose who picked him up and held him in the crook of his arm.

The judge laid a platter of bread and a bowl of apple butter on the table before he went back to the kitchen for the coffeepot.

Martha filled the last bowl. "It's simple fare, but it'll fill you up. With Tommy and Roy Eagle here, I know that's going some. We've got beet pickles here and cinnamon buns. Judge, if you'd pour the coffee."

Limke did and took the pot back to the kitchen stove, to keep the remaining brew hot. He returned to find one empty chair, at the head of the table. "This is your place, Quill."

Martha patted the chair. "Judge, you don't get over here enough. You just sit down now, and Quill would like you to ask the blessing."

"All right. In my house, we all hold hands, so come on now, join hands."

Stinnett, the stranger to the group, squirmed, but Roy Eagle's mitt swallowed the tax agent's right hand before he could protest.

Luther, shyly, laid his hand over Stinnett's left.

Limke bowed. "Dear and gracious Lord, we thank You for keeping us all safe and for giving us a productive day. We thank You for bringing Eskel Stinnett to us. He appears to be a very fine man. And now this meal that has been prepared, bless it and the dear lady who did all the work. Amen."

Click gazed up at Stinnett. "Yer gonna like these people."

The tax man inhaled the aroma drifting up from the stew before him. "I already do."

"Go ahead, dip yer spoon in. Nobody cooks as good as Miss Martha, exceptin' maybe me."

Stinnett chucked an eyebrow up.

Rose, holding onto the boy, reached for the bread. "Oh, it's true. Luther was a bachelor almost forever, so he got to be a master at the cookstove. I always made it a point to stop by his place at mealtime when I was up in the high mountains."

"And Quill, he's a good eater. Always a pleasure to have him at my table. Except that one night, what was it, Quill, Nineteen and Twenty-Six? Them cousins come by and shot up my house."

Rose, working around Little Nate, buttered a slice of bread and gave it to the boy. "Earl and Bobby Ray, a couple of moonshiners. Eskel, they shot one of your predecessors. Luther found him and packed him off the mountain, and he and Doc Schroeder patched him up. When Earl and Bobby Ray found out Luther had him, they came by a second time and tried once more to kill him. But they didn't know I was there."

Click gathered in the cinnamon buns. "It was the awfullest shootout."

Stinnett sopped his bread in his stew. "What happened?"

Limke looked up from his bowl. "Quill caught them. He drug them to my courtroom, and I sentenced Bobby Ray to twenty years and gave Earl the chair. He'd killed another man."

Rose turned to his wife. "Beet pickles?"

She passed him the bowl. Rose raked some onto his plate while keeping Little Nate's hand out of the bowl. He passed the remaining beets to Roy Eagle. "What did you see today, Luther?"

"Everything."

"I'll bet you did." Rose cut of a small piece of beet and forked it into Little Nate's mouth.

"The place outside Tallassee, where they land the supplies and float out the alkie, had a string of boats tied up there, stacked with barrels. I expect they're floatin' them down river tonight." Click scooped up a spoonful of stew.

Rose waited while Click swallowed it. "They see you?"

"Sure. But they wasn't concerned. Barrels said molasses. They wasn't foolin' no one."

"What else?"

"I walked up the road to the mountain." Click laid his spoon aside. "Quill, you got yer county map?"

"On the hall table. I'll get it." Rose pushed back. He plopped the boy on his chair and hustled out for the map. When he returned, he had it folded open to the section that showed the Little Tennessee River and Tallassee up through Happy Valley.

Click grubbed a stub of a pencil from his bib pocket. He ran the point along the map's road between Tallassee and Shingle Mountain, x'ing three places. "Mister Stinnett, see here? They got lookouts here, here, and here up in the high rocks. Look to have Winchesters."

"Mind if I ask why they didn't shoot you?"

Click chuckled. "Now what harm am I to them, a little mountain farmer like me? I just wave to 'em, and they wave back, and I walk on by. They don't know where I'm goin' 'cept up the road."

"You must have an angel looking out for you."

"Could be, Mister Stinnett, could be. If I do, I try not to make his job too hard." Click went back to the map. He drew a circle. "Here's where the still is. It's a big thing. Building must be, oh, forty-by-sixty. Road dead ends right into it."

"No brush to hide it?"

"Too big. You can't hide a thing like that, so they didn't try, but they did hang an Alcoa sign on the building. Don't think the Alcoa people are gonna be happy about that."

Rose, leaning on the back of his chair, interrupted. "Knowing you, you went in, didn't you?"

"Well, I told ya I knowed some of the boys in this thing, so, yes, I did." Click picked up a slice of bread and buttered it. "Must have been twenty fellers working in there. Got a little exercised when I come in the door until old Beecher Simms calls out, 'Hey, Luther!' Beecher, he's the head distiller and good at his trade."

Click turned to the tax agent, waving his bread. "Mister Stinnett, if you arrest Beecher, I'm gonna stand up fer him at his trial. All he's doin' is tryin' to keep food on the table for his younguns."

Rose cut another part of beet and fed it to Little Nate. "Beecher's a good man. He could have all kinds of jobs if he'd move out of that hollow where he lives, but he just won't do it."

Click took a bite from his buttered bread. "Beecher's like me. That hollow's his home. He grew up there, and he's gonna die there. Now there's three brothers in there I wouldn't give you a nickel for."

"The Hammers?" Rose asked.

"That's them."

"Tack, Ballpeen, and Sledge. Real names are Nance, Arlo, and Garner. Live together, work together, and fight together." Rose wiped up the drool leaking from the corner of Little Nate's mouth. "Eskel, you better figure on killing them because they won't give up."

Stinnett rested his spoon. "What's that road like going in there, Mister Click? Can we make any time driving it?"

"Here's the surprise. The dang thing's paved."

Rose packed a pickled beet in his own mouth and chewed. "State gave us money to pave it last year. I always thought it strange because, as Luther said, that road dead ends. It doesn't go anywhere."

Limke signaled Roy Eagle for the cinnamon buns. "Now you know the fiscal court took the money because it meant jobs. Lot of families staved off starvation for the year because of that road building."

"That's the only value in it. Still I never drove it."

"Road's a little twisty," Click said.

"So the lookouts are going to get off a lot of shots at us?"

"I'd say."

Stinnett toyed with his fork. "Quill, what if I were to commandeer a half-dozen bank cars?"

"All that bulletproof steel and glass, I'd do it. And those cars have gun ports."

CHAPTER 28

Hijack times three

A POUNDING AT THE FRONT door caused Rose to set his breakfast coffee aside.

Martha patted his shoulder as she walked by. "I'll see who it is, dear." Beyond the door glass, when she entered the hallway, she saw a silhouette and hurried to open the door.

There stood a wild-eyed little man, his clenched fist held high as if he intended to pound some more. "Quill up, Missus Rose?"

"He's in the kitchen."

"I gotta see 'im." The man pushed by and ran down the hallway. "Quill! Quill!"

"In here, Od."

"We got 'em! We got us three tankers. Just pullin' through town."

"At last." Rose pushed back from the table. "Guard cars with them?"

"Front and back."

"I've got to make some calls. Od, you have breakfast?"

"Not yet."

"Martha, would you make up some johnny cakes for the constable?"

"Surely. Ham and biscuits, maybe a little gravy to go with that, Mister Oddling?" she asked as she came into the kitchen.

"I thankee. That'd be nice."

"You can wash up at the sink."

Martha went to the sideboard, passing Rose as he strode out to the hallway and the telephone.

He placed five calls in rapid succession–

– to Marcellus Briskey. "Set the trap."

– to Eskel Stinnett. "Get your men for the raid on the still."

– to Roy Eagle Clark. "You lead the raid on the Chattanooga plant."

– to Newell Sanders. "Start your men moving toward Bristol, then catch up with me in Louden County."

– and to Tommy Jenks. "Bring your sawed-off. We're going to Nashville."

Rose became aware of a coolness of the floor only after he hung the telephone's receiver back on its hook. He stared down, then galloped up the stairs for his shoes. Rose pulled them on and tied them, then belted his holster under his right shoulder.

He pulled out his Forty-Four and snapped the cylinder open. His habit was to keep a spent cartridge under the hammer. Now he extracted the dead cartridge and put in a live round.

Rose snapped the cylinder shut. He slipped the gun back in the holster, grabbed his jacket and hat from the closet, and raced back down the stairs, pulling on his jacket as he went.

When he came into the kitchen, there sat Oddling at the table, and, at that moment, it struck Rose how much the constable looked like a chipmunk, his cheeks packed with food, chewing as fast as those small creatures do.

Rose went on to the cabinets. From one of the high shelves, he took down a box of bullets and put it in his jacket pocket. He also took down a box of shotgun shells. He pulled out six and went to the broom closet where he kept a pump Remington twelve-gauge. He flicked the eye hook up and brought the weapon out.

"New gun, Quill?"

"Yes, it is." Rose pushed each of the six shells into the magazine, then jacked one shell into the chamber. "You've got your shotgun?"

"In the car."

"Well, anytime you're ready."

Oddling hopped up from the table, coffee cup in hand. "Could I take this with me, Missus Rose?"

"You certainly may, Constable."

Rose put on his hat. He snapped the brim down and checked it in the glass of the back door.

Martha came to him. "This is dangerous this time, isn't it?"

"We'll go in like Teddy Roosevelt's cavalry. It shouldn't be."

"I won't sleep 'til you get back."

"Maybe two, three days. Why don't you take Little Nate and go over to your sister's and stay with her?"

"I think I'll do that."

"Take Fletch, too. I wouldn't want him to get lonely."

She touched her husband's face. "You care more for that old hunting dog than you do me."

"Not quite. We better go." He took her hand and squeezed it, then hurried down the hallway after Oddling.

Rose found Tommy Jenks at the car, a double-barrel shotgun loose in the crook of his arm, his bedroll on the cruiser's roof.

"Morning, Tommy."

"Morning, Quill, Od." Jenks nodded at the cup in the constable's hand. "See you been dining at the Martha Rose Restaurant. How'd you get so lucky and me not?"

Oddling grinned. "She likes me."

Rose pushed Oddling along. "You want to ride up front? That way Tommy gets the whole backseat to stretch out his bones."

"Fine by me." Oddling went over to his car for his shotgun and bedroll.

Jenks took on the job of packer, pushing his and Oddling's bedrolls and Rose's carpet bag into the far side of the backseat. He next propped the three shotguns on the floor with their barrels leaning against the bedrolls.

Rose reached under the driver's seat for a towel he kept there. He wiped the dew from the windshield, the side windows, and the back window. That done, he slung the towel back under the seat and slid in behind the steering wheel.

Oddling, in the passenger seat, pulled his door closed as gently as he could so as not to slosh his coffee.

Rose waited a couple moments for the motor to warm. He glanced back at Jenks. "You see Roy Eagle?"

"Caught him going out to his truck."

"He call his pap to come over and stay with his family until he gets back?"

"Yup. His pap's a good hand with the children."

"Should be. He raised sixteen of his own."

"Roy Eagle says his pap's ragging him to add to the nine he's got."

"What's he say to that?"

"He just laughs. Says Mary Lynne says nine's the limit. Says if he goes to gettin' frisky, she'll make him sleep on the floor."

Rose started the car rolling while Oddling, at ease gazing out the window, slurped down the last of his coffee. He chucked the empty cup under the seat.

At the town limits, Rose picked up County Thirty-Three, heading north. At Rockford, he cut off on a gravel track that went to Farragut. He stepped down on the accelerator, dust billowing out behind the Ford as it gathered speed. Rose swung wide of the ruts. "Tracks coming up."

Oddling swung his gaze from the fields beyond the side window to the windshield, and his eyes widened. He grabbed for a handhold on the seat as the Ford shot up the grade. It went airborne and banged back down on the far side of the L&N railroad tracks and raced on, Rose holding the accelerator to the floor, not letting off until he came on Farragut. Only then did he throttle back for the stop sign at Kingston Pike.

Rose glanced to the right. "We beat 'em."

Jenks rearranged himself in the back seat. "Beat who?"

Rose motioned past Oddling, toward Knoxville and a train of three tanker trucks trundling their way.

A Packard crossed in front of Rose's cruiser. "Four men, and every man with a gun, I'll bet."

Then the first tanker. "Good. Just a driver. No guard."

The second tanker passed, then the third, and finally a second Packard. It, too, contained four men.

Rose pulled out onto the highway. "Marcellus's deputies should cut that end car off at County Two. I'm to block him in from behind. When I do, I want you boys to get out there and get your guns in their faces before they figure out what's going on."

TWO ANCIENT INTERNATIONAL flatbeds idled at the intersection of County Two and U.S. Seventy.

Louden County Deputy Charlie Davis fretted about his son while he waited. The new baby had a fever and had squalled all through the night.

Davis glanced out his side window at a tanker approaching, and then it was by.

And a second.

And a third.

He tromped the accelerator to the floor.

Deputy Jake Miller did the same from the other side of the highway.

The two slammed on the brakes before their trucks could collide. They bailed out, shotguns in hand.

The Packard driver, booming down on the intersection, threw his car into a skid. Rose, behind him, did the same, eight tires screeching, sliding along the pavement.

Jenks and Oddling kicked open their doors before the cars stopped. They jumped and raced toward the driver's side of the Packard, their shotguns up. They stopped with the barrels pressed against the window glass of the doors.

Davis and Miller ran to the windows on the other side of the car.

Jenks, his chest heaving as he sucked for wind, tapped the glass. He motioned for the driver to bring his hands up, then he opened the door. "Wouldn't mind steppin' out, wouldja?"

The four guards, each with his hands in the air, came out. The deputies relieved them of their guns and shackled them.

Rose trotted up. He, too, held a shotgun. "Got the open cars here, Charlie?"

"Yeah." Davis stuck two fingers in his mouth and let out a piercing whistle.

Moments later, three big-engined Marathon touring cars rolled into the intersection. Rose ran for the rear seat of the first, Jenks the second, and Oddling the third.

"Go!" Rose yelled to his driver.

Louden Deputy Buck Deeds stomped down on the accelerator. "Hang on, Sh-Sheriff! We ga-got seven miles to catch 'em!"

"Can you do it?"

"Wa-watch me!"

Deeds raced up through the gears. He and his drivers behind him held their speed up steep hills and down, swinging wide on the curves, running off onto the gravel to keep from slowing.

Less than a mile from the county line, Deeds popped his car over a hill. "The-there they are! Ta-Time you get down, Sheriff!"

Rose dove for the floor.

Deeds pressed down on the accelerator, closing the distance on the tail-end tanker. He swung out into the opposing lane, the second and third county cars tight behind him.

Deeds shot past the end tanker, then the next, taking his foot off the accelerator only after he came abreast of the lead truck. "Now!"

Rose came up, as did Jenks and Oddling in the cars behind him. They leveled their shotguns at the tanker drivers.

"Pull over!" Rose yelled.

The driver glanced at Rose and, with a sneer curling the corner of his mouth down, swerved his truck toward the car.

Deeds veered away with Rose losing his footing. His shotgun swung up and discharged. Deeds, on the gravel shoulder now, cut back onto the highway, Rose going over the side. Deeds, enraged, brought up his revolver. He fired and the driver's head jerked away.

The tanker again came toward Deeds. He slammed on the brakes, spinning the steering wheel to the left to get out of the way, but the tanker caught the rear of the car and flipped it off the highway, into a ravine.

The tanker continued on, weaving, wandering, then it, too, careered off, jack-knifed, and plunged down. The tanker rolled over, hit the bottom of the ravine, and exploded.

Rose came scrambling up out of the ditch. He ran toward where Deeds's car had gone off and side-hopped down the slope to it, steam billowing from a broken radiator, Deeds still behind the steering wheel, shaking.

Deeds turned to Rose, his eyes pleading. "Oh da-damn, Ma-Marcellus ain't ga-gonna like this. The-this is his ba-brother's car."

Rose yanked on Deeds's door but it wouldn't open, so he climbed into the back seat and over into the front. There he kicked at the passenger door until it gave way. Rose got hold of Deeds's arm and hauled on him.

"Oh Ga-God."

"What?"

"Think I ba-busted some ribs."

"That's not all. Your forehead's gushing blood."

"Hell, I th-thought it was sweat. Ma-Musta hit the windshield."

"Come on, you gotta help me get you outta here, Buck."

Deeds worked his legs. He slid on his butt and slid again until he was clear of the steering wheel.

Rose got his hands under Deeds' shoulders and lifted, Deeds grimacing, but Deeds kept working his legs, kept pushing as Rose pulled.

"My ga-gun—"

"What?"

"I la-lost my gun."

"Where?"

"Ga-gotta be in the ca-car."

"Can you stand?"

"No. La-Lean me against the back door."

Rose eased Deeds around and braced him against the side of the vehicle. He then went back into the front seat and there ran a hand in the crevice between the seat and the seat back.

Nothing.

Rose gazed over the floor on both the driver's and the passenger's side.

Nothing.

Finally he scrunched down for a look under the seat. "I see it."

"Ca-can you ga-get it?"

"Yeah." Rose reached under. He fished with his fingers until he grasped the gun butt. Rose pulled the weapon out and held it up for Deeds's inspection.

"Tha-Thanks. We ga-gotta buy our own ga-guns, you know."

"Same in my county. Let's see if we can get up to the road." Rose locked arms with Deeds, and they climbed, slipping, grabbing for scrubby bushes to keep from falling back.

"Sha-sure hope this sta-stuff ain't pa-poison sumac."

"I'm just glad they're not pricker bushes."

Deputy Henry Thornton, on the edge of the highway's shoulder, side hopped down the ravine. "You all right, Buck?"

"Not ca-cloggin' tonight, ba-buddy."

"He busted some ribs."

"Sheriff, I saw you go out of the car. You look pretty beat up yerself."

"Nothing a hot bath and a change of clothes won't fix."

Thornton got a hand on Deeds's belt. He hauled away, with Rose pushing Deeds, to the top of the ravine. There Thornton slapped a handkerchief over the gash in Deeds's forehead and put Deeds's hand over the handkerchief. Thornton followed that by ripping the sleeve from his shirt, for a tie bandage.

"Ha-Henry, I da-don't feel so good."

"Let's get you sat down. Sheriff?"

Rose took one of Deeds's arms and Thornton the other. Working together, they helped injured lawman down to the pavement. "Sheriff, you watch him, won'tcha, while I get my car? I'll get Buck to the doc's office."

"Sure thing."

Thornton dashed down the highway toward the car he had abandoned near the second tanker.

A black Lincoln came rocketing from the east, slowing as it came on the tangle of cars and trucks choking the highway. The driver wove through until he got to Rose and Deeds.

Newell Sanders leaned out the window. "What the hell happened to you two?"

For the first time Rose noticed the rips in his coat's sleeve and the leg of his trousers. "Tanker driver didn't want to give up. Tried to run us off the road. I got thrown out."

Deeds began to shake. "I, I sh-shot him."

Sanders got out. He secured a blanket from the trunk of his car and draped it over Deeds's shoulders, snugged it around him. "This man's going into shock."

Thornton backed his car in and shoved the passenger door open. "Get him in. I'll take him to Doc Mullens."

Sanders and Rose hoisted Deeds to his feet and helped him shuffle to the Marathon. After they got him in the seat, Sanders tucked the blanket more tightly around the deputy. "Driver, it's more important you keep him warm than hurry."

"If you say."

"I do say." Sanders pushed the door closed, and Thornton drove off.

The trooper stood there, staring well ahead at smoke roiling out of a ravine on the other side of the road. "That fire the tanker?"

"It's gonna be scrap when it burns out."

"Driver get out?"

Rose rubbed at his bruised leg. "Don't know. Haven't been up there yet to look."

"Get in my car. I'll drive you there."

"Appreciate it. Think I've done my walking for the day."

Rose forced his body to move around to the passenger side of Sanders's car. He turned to gaze up the highway when he heard a second car drive off. Jenks, Oddling, and a Louden deputy came hustling his way.

"Hubey Smith's takin' our drivers to jail," Jenks said. "Quill, you all right? I saw you go out of the car."

"I'll live, but don't you go telling Martha what happened."

"I never talk about the job."

"My hat and my shotgun are somewheres back there. Would you see if you can find them? Newey and I are going up to see about the burning tanker."

"Lost your weapon, huh?" Sanders asked after Rose got in the car.

"Shotgun, yeah. Brand new, too. Only had it a week."

"Isn't that always the way it is? You have something old, nothing ever happens to it. You get something new, it disappears or gets broke."

Sanders idled along the hundred yards or so to the tanker and parked his car on the far side of the road, away from the inferno. Smoke and the stench of burning fuel and alcohol billowed up from the ravine. It rolled across the highway, at moments engulfing the car. Sanders backed up a short distance. "Pee-yew, stinks," he said as he got out.

"Yeah."

Sanders reached back in for a bandana. "That's one hell of a hot fire."

"You surprised? Thousand gallons of gasoline, three thousand gallons of two-hundred-proof alcohol."

"Well, you stay here. I'll go look."

Sanders pressed the bandana over his mouth and nose and scuttled away, into the heat and down into the ditch, holding an arm up to protect his face. The trooper stayed there only seconds before he clambered back up and out. "He's cinders, Quill."

Rose pushed the door of the Lincoln open. He leaned out and retched. When there was nothing more for him to throw up, Sanders passed Rose his bandana.

Rose spit the last of breakfast from his mouth. "Gawd, I'll never get used to death."

"It's best you don't. You don't want to get like those cold bastards we have to haul in."

"I suppose."

A Model T touring car rattled its way in from the west. It, too, pulled to the side of the highway and stopped. Sheriff Marcellus Briskey and his driver got out, Briskey waddling over. "Quill, Sergeant, looks like we missed one helluva party."

Rose mopped at his face. "Wasn't any fun."

"Never is when they go wrong." Briskey parked his bulk against a fender of the Lincoln. He took out a tobacco pouch and stuffed a wad in his mouth.

Rose pushed Sanders's bandana into his pocket. "One dead in the fire. Your brother's car's wrecked."

"Buck?"

"He got pretty badly beat up. Henry took him to Doc Mullins."

Briskey spit a stream of tobacco juice toward the ditch. "Doc'll fix him up. How about you?"

"I'll be all right."

Briskey chewed for a moment. "My brother's gonna be mad."

"About his car?"

The Louden sheriff spit again. "Yeah."

"Why don't you confiscate the two Packards, give one to your brother and keep the other for a cruiser?"

The corners of Briskey's mouth lifted. "That's a right good idee."

"Marcellus, we could talk all day, but you better get on up the road if you're going to lead the Bristol raid."

"Oh, now that I look forward to."

Sanders came over. "I've got six men at the Kingsport post. You meet them there. They know where to go. The feds will have a tax agent there, too."

Briskey squinted at Rose. "Seven plus Jacob and me, think that's enough?"

"It'll have to be."

"Well, all right then."

Rose brought out some papers from his inside pocket. He handed them on. "Blanket arrest warrants. The tax agent will have the seizure orders." He dug into his trousers' pocket for a roll of bills and peeled off one hundred dollars. "A little moonshine money for gas and expenses. Marcellus, I know your how broke your county is."

"I'll keep a tab."

"Don't bother."

"What time do you want us to hit 'em?"

"Plan for ten tomorrow morning. If we all go in at the same time, none of the bad boys get to call one another."

Chapter 29

Surprises

TENNESSEE SERVES two clocks. Blame it on the cabal who invented railroad time, Rose thought whenever he drove west, but then Standard Time was better than every town maintaining its own clock. Nonetheless, here he and Sanders were in the Central Zone, and a couple miles back, they had been on Eastern Time.

Rose was still ruminating when Sanders pulled to the side of Crossville's main street. He stopped his Lincoln in front of a clothing store.

Rose glanced up to see Sanders motioning at the building. "They've got what you need, my raggedy friend." Sanders took out a pocket watch to check the time.

Rose tapped the watch's face. "That's not right."

"Pardon?"

"We're in the Central Zone. Set the hands back an hour."

Sanders twisted on the stem of his watch, to roll the hands to the correct time. "Are you going to sit here while I'm doing this or are you going to go get yourself some new duds?"

"Guess I could." Rose vacated his side of the car.

Sanders slipped out his side as he pocketed his watch.

Two gasoline tankers rumbled up the street. Rose waved to Jenks in the lead tanker and gestured ahead. "Find a diner!"

Jenks tipped his hat and drove on, the second tanker close behind.

Rose moved on up the store's steps, Sanders with him. Sanders opened the door. "So you're getting hungry."

"Yeah, got rid of my breakfast back there."

The clothier on duty turned away from a display of shirts he was straightening, swivelling to the lawmen. "Welcome to Lebbeck's, the finest haberdashery in middle Tennessee. My name is Cerroll–Lebbeck, of course. How may I help you gentlemen?"

Rose peered around. "I guess I need some new clothes."

"Ah-ha." Lebbeck scanned Rose from toe to head and back down again, clicking his tongue at Rose's torn and dirty outfit. "I believe I have just the thing for you. Come this way."

He guided his customers into the center of the store. There he took a three-piece business suit from a rack and held it out. "You will look superb in this, I guarantee it. And it comes with an extra pair of pants."

"No, just tan trousers and a canvas jacket, and maybe a new shirt–white. And I'd better get a hat while I'm here. I lost mine."

"If you don't mind me asking, the condition of the clothes you're replacing, what happened?"

"I fell out of a car."

The wrinkles in Lebbeck's forehead deepened. He cast a glance toward Sanders, and Sanders nodded.

A shudder ran through the clothier's frame. He moved away to a table stacked with trousers. There he pulled out a pair. Then he went to another table for a shirt and took a jacket from a display rack. Lebbeck brought them to Rose and led him to a change room.

While Rose got out of his tattered clothes and into the new togs, Lebbeck laid out a selection of fedoras. "What do you think of these?" he asked Sanders.

"You wouldn't happen to have a top hat, would you?"

"With work pants and a jacket?"

"Slip it in there. Let's see if we can get a rise out of my partner."

Lebbeck shook his head, yet he went to a tall glass-fronted case next to the store's mirror. He brought out a black opera hat.

Sanders chuckled when Lebbeck put it in with the mix of hats he wanted Rose to consider.

Rose came out of the change room, admiring his new clothes. "Pretty good fit."

Sanders tipped a finger at the open fly.

Rose looked down and blanched. He pushed the errant corner of his shirt inside his fly and buttoned up.

Sanders leaned on the clothier's shoulder. "I swear, I can't take this man anywhere without him embarrassing me. Quill, I would have gone for the business suit."

"I've got one. Bought it ten years back." He perused the selection of hats Lebbeck had set out. "Wear it to church."

"And you'll likely be buried in it."

"I expect so, but I'm not planning on it being soon."

Rose went straight to the opera hat. He picked it up, spun it around, and swiped his jacket sleeve across the top as if he were dusting it. Rose lifted the hat to his head. "Mister Lebbeck, your mirror?"

"Right this way." The clothier led Rose to a set-up with a full-length mirror and two smaller side mirrors.

Rose admired the image of the hat as he adjusted the tilt. "Newey, you like it?"

"Stunning."

"It's yours." He sailed the hat to the trooper and went back to the table for a tan fedora. Rose tried it for size. "This one I'll take."

"An excellent choice. Now to complete the look, you need a necktie." Lebbeck shot over to a display rack and sorted through the choices. He discarded a half-dozen shades of blues and browns, selecting instead a red-and-black mottled necktie, a subdued red. He slipped the tie under Rose's collar and worked it into a four-in-hand knot. He snugged it up under Rose's Adam's apple before he led Rose back to the mirror.

Rose studied himself and the necktie. "What do you think, Newey?"

"It won't show blood."

He chuckled. "Mister Lebbeck, how much?"

"It's free. The pants, shirt, jacket, hat, seven dollars twenty-six cents."

"And that stove pipe for my friend?"

Sanders, a pained expression on his face, dropped the hat on the table. "I don't want this."

"Sure, you do. I'm buying it for you."

Lebbeck gave off a knowing smile. "It's expensive."

"Nothing's too good for my friend from Greeneville."

"I can let you have it for eight-fifty."

"Sold."

"Maybe you'd like some new socks?"

Rose shook his head. He pulled his roll from his pocket and counted out twenty dollars. This he handed to Lebbeck and waited for his change.

Sanders stopped Rose when the two got outside. "Why didn't you get the suit?"

"A suit coat shows a shoulder holster unless you have the coat specially tailored, you know that. A loose jacket like this, I can hide an armory under it. What say we catch up to Tommy and Od, and you can show them your new hat?"

"I'll die before I'll ever put it on." He opened the passenger door for Rose, then went around to the driver's side. There he tossed the opera hat in the back seat before he got behind the steering wheel. "Shoulder holster, huh?"

Rose pulled out his long-barreled Colt.

"Lord, you could go hunting bear with that."

"Up to a hundred yards, it's as accurate as a rifle."

Sanders peered at the gun for a long moment before he glanced in his side mirror for traffic. A Model T rattled his way. After it to pass, he and Rose drove on until they came on the Sunspot tankers parked at the side of a truck-stop restaurant. Sanders saw something else, a black Buick on the far side of the street, the car aimed east toward Knoxville, not west toward Nashville. "That car, that was behind us when we were grinding up the Plateau."

"So?"

"In the creeper lane?"

"You're sure it was that car?"

"Or its twin."

Sanders pulled in beside the tankers. Once out of his car, he trotted across the street to the Buick and laid his hand on the hood. "Engine's warm," he called back to Rose.

Sanders pulled out a notepad and pencil. He wrote down the license number before he hurried back to his own car. There he recovered the opera hat from the back seat. Sanders put the hat on and adjusted it to a jaunty angle. "I'm ready."

"I thought you said you'd never wear that."

"I've changed my mind."

Inside the restaurant's front door, Sanders banged on the wall.

Men at the counter twisted around, and those at the tables also looked up.

"Anybody own that Buick across the street?"

No one spoke.

"Whoever car's it is, I dented your fender."

All went back to their meals.

"Not here, I guess."

Jenks waved from a table halfway down the restaurant.

Rose waved back and moved Sanders toward the table.

"What was all that about?" Jenks asked when Rose and Sanders pulled out chairs.

"There's a car across the street. Newey thinks it's been following us."

"Oh, if I wore a hat like that, I believe I'd think everybody was following me."

Sanders tilted the hat forward, over an eyebrow. "You don't like it?"

"I do. Stylish, real stylish." Jenks gathered in his cup of coffee. "Od's having a hamburger and fried taters, but I ordered smothered steak and the same for you two, if that's all right?"

Rose pulled over a handwritten menu. "Newey, what do you think?"

"Fine by me."

Jenks nodded toward the kitchen and the waitress coming through the swinging doors with a tray above her shoulder. "Good thing 'cause here it comes."

The waitress brought the tray down to the edge of the table. As she did, she dealt out the plates. "Hamburger and country fries for you, Mister Oddling, and smothered steak for you, Mister Jenks."

She gazed at Rose and Sanders. "These the friends you were waitin' on?"

"Uh-huh," Jenks mumbled as he hacked into his steak.

"Smothered steak all right for you gents?"

"Looks like what my momma used to make." Rose rubbed his hands in anticipation.

Sanders, though, pushed back from the table. "Start without me. I've gotta visit the toilet."

"I like your hat, mister. Don't let any of our wiseacres knock it off." The waitress, her eyes twinkling, pointed toward the back of the restaurant. "See that door? Right through there and down the hall."

Sanders nudged Rose's shoulder. "Maybe I should leave my hat with you."

"I'll put it right here on your chair."

"If you let anyone sit on it, I'll haunt you. And if you let your deputy eat my steak, I'll haunt you double."

"I'll guard both with my life."

Sanders handed his opera hat to Rose and strolled to the back of the restaurant. He reached for the doorknob only to find the door opening and a man on the other side wanting to come through. The two did a two-step to get around one another, the man mumbling something before he slipped into a booth by the back wall.

SANDERS STARED at his side mirror. "That damn car's back there again."

Rose twisted away from the woods and farm fields he had been watching to look through the back window. "You sure it's the same one?"

Sanders topped a hill and started down the far side. "Been with us the last three miles. One way to find out."

He swung off on a farm drive, stopped, then backed his car around so he was headed east. Sanders roared back up the hill. He let off on the gas when he topped the crest. "Where the hell did he go?"

The road ahead was as empty as it would have been on a Sunday morning during church time.

Rose jacked a pointer finger at a side road. "He could have gone that way. Probably just someone going home."

Sanders continued on. At the side road, he turned the big Lincoln around and sped off to the west, to catch up with the tankers.

THEY CONTINUED ON through the afternoon and early evening, the lawmen having agreed to stop in Lebanon for the night.

Jenks, in the lead, was the first to see the town limits sign and a row of tourist cabins beyond. He turned off the highway, then Oddling. They wheeled their tankers around behind the cabins as a black car passed Sanders and Rose when they slowed for the turnoff.

Sanders swore.

"What?"

"There he is again."

"Are you sure?"

"Quill, I saw his license plate."

"It wasn't well lit."

"I tell you I saw it."

"Whoever it is, he's gone now. That doesn't seem to suggest he's got any interest in us."

"Maybe. Maybe I've just been a trooper too long."

Sanders followed the dust of the tankers, then changed his mind and aimed the Lincoln toward the café that doubled as the office for the cabins. The sign in the café's window told travelers everything they wanted to know–'Uncle Ed's Barbeque, Gas, Tire Repair and Tourist Court.'

Jenks and Oddling came up as Rose and Sanders left the Lincoln. Rose pulled Oddling in. "How's that tanker drive?"

"My oh my, it's a boneshaker."

"Aside from that?"

"Pretty good. I do grind the gears some, but by the time we get to Nashville, 'spect I'll be a pro-fessional driver like Tommy here."

Jenks put his arm around Oddling's shoulders and squeezed. "You tryin' to get in good with me so's I'll let you have the bed tonight?"

Uncle Ed Marling put on an impressive spread for his guests. He also gave them two of his best cabins. Best or not, Oddling didn't get much sleep. Jenks rounced around so much that he pushed Oddling out of the bed, twice.

The second time Oddling hit the floor, he crawled over to his clothes, gathered them in, and went on outside to sleep in the cab of his tanker. Not comfortable, either. A spring had pushed up through the seat. It jabbed at Oddling whenever he moved the wrong way. Yet he did manage to drift off.

A pounding on the truck door woke him.

Oddling sat up. He rubbed at his eyes and yawned. When he opened the door, there stood Tommy Jenks.

Jenks jiggled his truck's key in his hand. "Wondered where you got to. Woke up this morning an' you was gone. Well, come on. Don't just set there waitin' for the Second Coming of Jesus. Quill and Newey got your breakfast ordered, an' mine's gettin' cold."

Oddling rescued his hat from the floor. He beat it into shape and plopped it on his head. Then and only then did he climb down from the high seat. Jenks slammed the door shut before Oddling could reach back for it.

As the two walked toward Uncle Ed's place, Oddling burred out, "Bed hog."

"What did you say?"

"You heard me. Bed hog. You pushed me out."

"Did not."

"Did, too. Twice you did it."

"Well, you shoulda woke me."

"Con sarn it, Tommy, I tried, but you sleep sounder 'an a dead man. Exceptin' for all that thrashin' around you do, one would think you was dead."

"Well, I'm sorry."

"Ferget it. But I'm ain't sharin' no bed with you again."

"Aw, next time you take the bed. I'll sleep in the truck."

"Tommy, we get shed of these trucks today. There ain't gonna be no truck fer ya to sleep in. Wherever we stop t'night, you sleep on the floor."

"Od, that's cruel."

They opened the door and went into the café.

"That's survival, for me at least. Big bear of a feller like you, you roll over on me in the bed and you'd squash me like bug."

Rose looked up from his breakfast coffee. "What are you two yammering about?"

Oddling threw a hand in the air. "Nuthin', nuthin', nuthin'."

Rose took a sip from his cup. "Didn't sound like nothing to me."

"Well, if you gotta know, Tommy pushed me outta the bed last night."

"Did not."

"Did too."

"Did not."

"Did too."

Rose raised his hand. "Boys, I sure hope we can get home without you killing each other."

Oddling sniffed. "I survived. I slept in the truck. Although there was this dang spring kept jabbin' me in the back."

"Od, eat your eggs and grits before they get cold."

Oddling stared down at the plate in front of a vacant chair, a plate heaped with food. "Glory be, this is gonna be a gooder day, ain't it?"

He sat down. As he did, he reached for the biscuit on Jenks's plate. "You waddn't gonna eat this, was you, Tommy?"

"Not now that you've got your fingers all over it."

Rose waved to the man behind the counter. "Can we have more biscuits and coffee?"

Oddling broke open the biscuit. He scooped gravy over the two halves. "What's the plan fer the day, Quill?"

"We should hit Sunspot at nine o'clock. Od, I'm going to drive your truck and you ride shotgun. Newey's going to get the gate man and cut the telephone wires. You and me and Tommy, we bag whoever's in the office."

Sanders leaned in. "A State Patrol paddy wagon will come in right behind us. From Sunspot, we go to the bottling plant. A half a dozen troopers and a federal tax agent will be waiting to go in with us."

Oddling packed his cheeks with biscuits and grits and chewed with vigor. "The buildin', how do we get in?"

"They're expecting the tankers, so we beep the horn. They open the doors, and we drive right in."

Oddling tossed back a mouthful of steaming coffee, Rose grimacing.

"What?" Oddling asked.

"That coffee's scalding."

"Really? Didn't notice."

Rose pushed his chair back and stood up. "Well, if you and Tommy have inhaled everything, I think we ought to be going."

Oddling raked his sleeve across his mouth. "Toilet stop fer me. See ya at the truck."

After Rose paid the bill, the three lawmen went on outside, a shiver moving through Rose's lean frame as he peered up at the graying sky. "Sure hope it doesn't rain."

Sanders gazed up as well. "It could be to our advantage if it did."

"Maybe. Still, I don't like the idea of getting wet. God intended men and their dogs to lay by the fire on days it rains."

Rose went around the tanker Oddling had been driving, kicking each tire to make sure none had gone flat. He despised the prospect of having to change an inside tire on a dual and, worse, having to do it in the rain.

Rose opened the driver's door. He grabbed the frame and hauled himself up to the seat. "Newey, you'll watch our rear end?"

"That's my job. Want your shotgun?"

"Guess I better have it."

Sanders went to his Lincoln. There he opened the trunk and took out two shotguns. When he saw Oddling trotting his way, he gestured to him to take Rose's weapon. The other he laid on the passenger seat in his car.

At the truck, Oddling opened the passenger door and shoved his and Rose's shotguns under the seat. After he hoisted himself in, Rose wiggled his fingers at him.

"I 'spose ya want the key, huh?" Oddling giggled and thrust his hand in his pants pocket where he sorted through a collection of nails, washers, and coins until his fingers felt the shape of an ignition key. He pulled it out and handed it to Rose.

Rose then fired up the engine. He pressed on the accelerator a couple times. When he was satisfied with the sound of the big motor, he shifted into super low and started the big rig creeping away from the tourist cabins.

At the road, Rose stuck his head out the side window, looking for traffic. An Old Dominion semi whooshed by followed by a much slower Dodge pickup, a boy in the box holding onto a dog struggling to lean out into the breeze.

Rose eased the tanker up onto the pavement and shifted up through the gears.

It was an easy thirty-five miles through rolling countryside to Nashville. Rose did not take notice of the black Buick that had fallen in behind his convoy when they came through Hermitage. He throttled back and shifted out of road gear when he came on the first twenty-mile speed zone, then shifted down again. "Od, this truck's been jostling my breakfast coffee through me. Man, I gotta pee."

"There's a truck stop up ahead. How 'bout there?"

A crack of thunder shook the cab. With it, raindrops seemingly the size of dimes splattered against the windshield.

"Looks like we're in for it." Rose shifted down to second and made the turn into the Ace High parking lot. He ran the tanker around back, but this time he searched for a parking slot in the first row and found one.

Jenks wheeled his rig in next to Rose's tanker.

Sanders pulled his car across the rear of the two and stopped.

Rose leaped from the cab and ran before Jenks could get his door open.

"Toilet stop," Oddling called out.

"Guess I'll wait in the truck then." Jenks ducked back inside the cab of his tanker.

Sanders had his car's door open, too, and one foot on the ground when Rose raced by, hollering, "Gotta go bad."

"Quill, I think I saw that car."

"Later." Rose whipped the Ace High door open. He plunged into a gaggle of truck drivers loafing around the gas counter and pushed his way through. When he broke free, he ran for the back hallway and the toilet, the place rank with the smell of urine and deodorizer blocks, strips of fly paper hanging down over the sinks. There he dashed into a stall, latched the door, and dropped his pants.

"Whooee, thought for a minute I wasn't gonna make it," Rose said, talking to himself.

"Gettin' bad out there?" a voice asked.

"Huh? Oh, a thunderstorm about to let loose."

"Where you drive in from, the north?"

"East. Maryville."

"Nice town I'm told."

"We think so."

Rose wiped himself. He pulled his pants up, buttoned his fly, then opened the stall door. As he cinched his belt, something hit him in the forehead, and he fell.

A man reached down for Rose's left wrist. He snapped a handcuff on it and pulled Rose up enough that he could fasten the other cuff to the handle on the stall door.

The man flicked open a long pocketknife. He stroked the blade on his pant leg as he reached down for Rose's right hand.

"Hey! Whatcha doin'?!"

The man jerked around to a truck driver in the doorway and a second trucker behind him. His blade slashed across Rose's wrist as he scrambled to his feet. The man threw himself into the first driver, knocking him and the other driver back against the hallway wall. He rolled to the side and raced away.

The drivers pushed themselves up and plunged into the toilet.

"My gawd, lookit the blood. Andy, git that towel outta the towel machine." The first driver slid to his knees. While he pulled off his belt for a tourniquet, the second driver ripped the towel machine off the wall and tore the roll of toweling out of it.

The first driver wrapped his belt around Rose's arm, just above the biceps. He pulled the belt tight while the second driver slapped his bandana over the wound, then wrapped the towel around it and the wrist, two, three, four times.

He cut the towel and tore the end so he could tie it over the wrist.

The first driver glanced at the handcuff as he worked. "What the hell's he doin' manacled in here?"

"I got a tire iron in my truck. I can bust that handle loose."

"Better get it."

The second driver ran out. He danced around another man making his way toward the toilet. "Fella in there's hurt."

The man–Tommy Jenks–pushed on in. "Ohmigawd."

The first driver looked up. "What is it?"

"It's my boss."

"Somebody was tryin' to cut him when me an' my partner walked in. Sliced his wrist, but I think we got the bleedin' stopped."

"You see the man?"

"No, not really. He knocked me down, gettin' the hell outta here."

The second driver pushed back in, holding a tire iron above his head. "Outta my way."

He wedged the bar into the door handle and pulled hard, splintering the wood. He pulled a second time, and screws popped. The handle fell away, Rose's arm with it.

The three men rolled Rose onto his back. In the process, Rose's jacket fell open.

"He some kinda goon?" the second driver asked, bug-eyed at the shoulder holster and revolver.

"No, a sheriff. I'm his deputy." Jenks fumbled in his pocket for his badge.

Rose moaned.

"He's comin' 'round."

"Jesus," Rose whispered.

"You been hurt," Jenks said.

"I know. My head."

"Your wrist. Somebody cut your wrist. These men, they stopped the bleedin'."

Rose opened his eyes. He blinked, trying to make them focus first on Jenks, then the others. "Thanks."

He attempted to raise himself on his elbow. "Oooo—"

"Maybe you should lay still a minute, mister."

"Tommy, get me outta here."

Jenks slipped an arm under Rose's back and the other under his knees. He lifted. "Get the door, boys."

The second driver pushed the door to the hallway open and held it. "You better get him to a doctor. He needs serious help."

"Plow a path for me, wouldja? We got a car outside."

CHAPTER 30

Raids

JENKS STUMBLED out the door, carrying Rose. Sanders saw them and bolted from his car. "What the hell happened?"

"Somebody cut him. We gotta get him to a doctor."

Sanders wrenched open the back door of his car, and Jenks worked at pushing Rose inside, but Rose braced his good hand against the door frame. "I go in your truck. We've got a schedule."

"Hell with the schedule. You come first."

"Dammit, I didn't come this far to have this thing fall apart."

Oddling hustled over. "What happened?"

The worry lines in Jenks's face deepened. "Quill's hurt."

"Od, Tommy's driving lead. I'm riding with him. You drive the second tanker. For gawdsake, let's go. I'm gettin' wet."

Jenks stared at Sanders, rain water dripping down his face. "Newey, whaddaya think?"

The muscles in Rose's jaw tightened like steel bands. "Do it my way."

Sanders waved toward Jenks's tanker, and Jenks ran for the passenger's side. Oddling got there first. He opened it, and the two horsed Rose up and inside.

"Don't you fall behind now, Od. You keep on Tommy's bumper. Run red lights if you have to."

"I'll keep up, don't you worry." Oddling slammed the door, then raced toward the second truck.

Jenks, now in the driver's seat, started the engine.

"Tommy, button my jacket, wouldja, about half way? Stick my arm in the opening. The jacket can be a sling."

Jenks worked three buttons into the holes. "About here?"

"Yeah. Now my arm. That's right. That's right. Good. Now my gun. Get it out, put it on the seat."

"You're going to get out of the truck, aren't you?"

"Damn right."

Jenks reached under Rose's right arm for the Colt and laid it beside Rose.

"Come on, get us out of here."

Jenks shifted into super low, to get the truck into a lane leading to the street. Once in the lane, he shifted up to first, glancing in his side mirror as he did. "Od's with us, and there's Newey. How long can we go with that tourniquet?"

"Doc once told me twenty minutes at most. If we don't loosen it by then, my arm's gonna start to die."

"It'll take that long to get to Sunspot."

"If nothing messes us up."

Jenks rolled out onto Lebanon Pike. After he shifted up through the gears, he located the switch for the windshield wiper, a single blade on the driver's side, and turned it to on. He listened to the small vacuum motor sweep and reverse the blade. "I don't have this on my truck. Mine I've gotta move the blade by hand."

Jenks turned onto First Avenue. The rain increased, and, in contrast, the traffic thinned. He worked at holding a respectable speed in spite of the stop signs and traffic lights. "There's Woodland and the bridge."

"Od still with us?"

Jenks glanced at the side mirror as he shifted down. "Yeah."

He caught a green light and made the turn onto Woodland, but the light clicked to yellow, then red for Oddling. The constable hammered his horn and bulled his way into the intersection, cutting off a city bus.

On the bridge, traffic slowed, then stopped.

Rose craned his neck to see ahead. "What's got us blocked?"

Jenks rolled down his window. He leaned out into the rain, scanning as far ahead as he could. "Can't be sure."

"Pull out. Pass 'em."

"Quill, there's traffic coming."

"They'll get out of the way."

Rose reached across Jenks. He slammed his hand down on the horn button and held it down while Jenks wheeled the tanker out into the opposing lane, Oddling behind him.

Jenks set his jaw and plowed on while Rose held the horn button down, on past a pileup near the end of the bridge. Jenks swerved back into his lane. He shifting up into third only to throttle back for the turnoff onto First Street. He made the turn and held his speed for a few moments, then shifted down for the turn onto the terminal's gravel drive.

Rose motioned with his good hand at the guard shack. "Give him a thrill."

"Glad to." Jenks cut the tanker toward the shack. He clipped the corner, spinning the shack off its foundation.

Oddling drew his tanker up beside Jenks's, both slowing as they rolled on toward the office.

Sanders, behind them, jumped from his car and dashed after someone trying to extricate himself from the guard shack.

Jenks came to a stop at the office. He threw his door open and ran through the pelting rain, his pistol out.

"Take the front, Tommy!" Rose hollered. He forced his door open and called out to Oddling, "Od, you get the back!"

Oddling came out of his truck with his shotgun and galloped around the building.

Jenks kicked the door open.

In a hurry now to get out of the truck, Rose slipped. He fell and rolled to the side, with his revolver out and trained on the doorway. Splashing came from behind him, and Rose whipped his gun around.

Sanders threw up his hands. "It's me!"

"That was close."

"You're telling me? I saw your finger on the trigger."

"Help me up."

The trooper grabbed hold of Rose's good arm. He hauled Rose to his feet, and together they splashed through the puddles to the steps and on inside. There they found Jenks and Oddling, their guns trained on three men with their hands in the air.

Rose mopped muddy water from his face as he peered at one of them. "Matthew, is that you there? It is, isn't it?"

Matthew Shutts twisted a cigar along his lips. "If it's money you want, you bastard, it's in the safe. Take it and get the hell out of here."

Rose laid his revolver on the sole desk in the room. He took out his badge and thumped it down beside his gun. "Tempting, but I'm here to arrest you. And you, too,

Ralph," he said to the second of the three men. Rose brought out several folded papers from his shirt pocket. "Newey, these might've got a bit wet, but they should be legible, warrants for Matthew and Ralph and a third one that's blank that you can use for the other two. I'm done in. I'm gonna sit down."

Two state troopers, in black rain slickers, ran in through the open doorway. Sanders handed the paperwork to them. "You've got three men here and one handcuffed to the fence. Names of two are on two warrants. You write the names of the other two on the blank warrant."

"Sarge, you've got all our work done."

"You dump 'em as fast as you can, then come out to the warehouse for another load."

One of the troopers stepped up to the three prisoners. "All right, boys, put your hands out. We've got jewelry for you you're just gonna love."

The troopers manacled the three and herded them out the door.

Jenks came to Rose, Rose, his teeth clenched against the pain in his wrist. "We have to get that tourniquet loosened."

"Just for a couple minutes, then we've gotta get outta here."

JENKS, ODDLING, AND SANDERS pulled off on Porter Street where two State Police cars idled in the rain.

Sanders ran to the cars, waving for the officers to get out. "Boys, you're going to get wet. I want three of you on the back bumper of each tanker. You're going to ride on inside and bag everyone in sight." He pulled one of the officers aside. "You're with me. We cover the backside in case anybody tries to come out that way."

Three troopers hunched up and dashed for the rear of Jenks's tanker, another three for the rear of Oddling's. Sanders and his new partner jumped in the Lincoln and sped up beside the cab of Jenks's tanker, Sanders beeping his horn and motioning for Jenks to start moving.

Jenks rammed the transmission into first. He got the tanker back on the street and made the turn onto Rosebank, rocking the rig across a set of railroad tracks and on into the Old Hickory lot.

Rose, from his place on the passenger seat, slammed his fist down on the horn button. He hit it again and again until the building's doors swung open.

Jenks rolled the tanker inside. Two officers jumped from his bumper. They grabbed the men at the doors. The third waited until Oddling's tanker was well inside, then he, too, jumped. The officers from Oddling's tanker joined him, and they raced toward the men working the bottling equipment.

Jenks opened the door of his cab. He stepped out on the running board, raised his shotgun and jerked the trigger, the blast blowing a hole in the roof. "Police! Get your hands up!"

A whiskered man on a loader cut his machine toward the trucks. Oddling shot out the tires, then ran for the driver.

Someone slipped out of an office above the work floor, a pistol in his hand. Rose saw him and came out of the cab, his own weapon out. He crouched, used the fender to steady his aim, and fired.

One shot.

The man dropped.

Several troopers broke away from the others. They worked their way further back into the building, searching for anyone who might be hiding among the stacks of boxes and crates. One trooper heard running feet

and twisted around. "Sam, someone going toward the
back!"

"I'll get him!"

An officer broke into a run. He leaped over boxes in
his way.

A car engine started, and tires squealed. The car—a
black Buick—crashed through the rear wall. It careened off
a rear fender of Sanders's Lincoln and skidded away
around the corner.

Sanders and his new partner stumbled out of the car
to find themselves without a shot. Sanders swore. He
threw his hat at his car, and it skipped across the hood to
land in a puddle on the far side. Sanders stalked after his
hat. Only when he had recovered it did he see the damage
to his car. "Jesus K. Christ."

"You all right, Newey?" his partner called out.

"Yeah, but the sonuvabitch caved my fender in."

The officer splashed his way around to Sanders,
Sanders kicking at his car.

"Hey, hey, hey! That doesn't solve anything. You
want to drive it, right?"

"Sure."

The officer stepped up to the damaged fender. He
studied it for a moment, braced a foot against the tire,
grabbed the fender with both hands where it pinched in,
and pulled. The metal gave. A second pull and it gave
some more, enough that the tire wouldn't rub against the
fender. "How's that?"

"Edgar, you're one strong man."

"I wrestled in the Grand Nationals back in college."

SANDERS COUNTED THEM while Jenks loosened the
tourniquet on Rose's arm. "We bagged eight men, nine if

you count the dead one upstairs. Quill, we've got to get you to a hospital."

"Not yet."

"The tough guy, huh?"

"Not by choice. How much whiskey did we get?"

"Edgar estimates six thousand gallons bottled, boxed, and ready to go."

"Any delivery rigs?"

"None. The federal agent thinks there may be four, maybe five on the streets, making runs to the saloons." Sanders pulled off a shoe. He poured water from it. "We're gonna keep the lights on here until they come back. Once we bag them, he's gonna dynamite the place. It'll be a helluva fire."

"Newey, get the trucks out. You can sell them."

"My men will see to that." Sanders pulled off his other shoe and dumped water from it as well.

Rose peered up at Jenks. "Tommy, cinch my arm up. I'm losing too much blood."

Jenks pulled the tourniquet tight. "Can you move your fingers?"

"Not much. Stick my arm in my jacket. Time we visit Clayton." Rose's face twisted as Jenks lifted his arm.

"Newey can do that without ya."

"Tommy, you and me, we've ridden this horse from the beginning. We're going to ride it to the end—all the way. Help me to Newey's car."

Jenks slipped his arm under Rose's left shoulder and lifted.

Rose, with Jenks's help, moved along, keeping a tight grip on Jenks's jacket to steady himself, but still he stumbled.

Sanders came hopping alongside, trying to get his foot back in his second shoe. "You can't do this."

"Tommy's not gonna let me fall. Just need a little rest. I can get that in your car."

"And you're going to bleed all over my seat, aren't you?"

"Probably. Od, collect our shotguns and our bedrolls. We're not coming back here."

"Right." Oddling took off at a trot for the two tankers.

"Jesus Christ, Quill, you can at least let me get my car over here." Sanders gestured to a trooper to bring the Lincoln into the warehouse through the shattered back wall.

"Wanna sit a spell?" Jenks asked Rose.

"I better."

He eased Rose down onto a crate of empty bottles, Rose steadying himself. "Gawd, I'm thirsty."

Sanders laced up his shoe. "You've got a world of moonshine here."

Jenks shook his head. "He don't drink it. I've got a couple bottles of root beer in my bedroll."

Rose perked up. "The sweet stuff you make?"

"Yeah."

"Tommy, it'd be awful good."

Sanders's Lincoln came to a stop in front of the men. Sanders opened the trunk and helped Oddling toss the bedrolls in. Jenks recovered his and pulled out the two bottles.

Rose stared at the buckled rear fender. "Newey, you restyling your body?"

"That guy in the Buick hit me, the Buick you insisted wasn't following us."

"You get him?"

"Hell no, but I've got his license number from yesterday. It's gonna give me a mountain of pleasure to run him down and clamp him in irons."

Jenks helped Rose into the front passenger seat. He opened one of the root beers and put it in Rose's hand. Then he and Oddling—Oddling with his collection of shotguns—climbed into the back seat. Under Jenks's bulk, the rear of the car settled low over the axle.

Sanders clapped one of his officers on the shoulder. "Edgar, we look like hell. Pick three men in clean uniforms and follow us to the Capitol."

"What's going on, Sarge?"

"You'll see. I need you for show."

"Siren?"

"Only if we have to bust through traffic. You stick to my bumper." Sanders slipped behind the wheel of his Lincoln and pulled the door closed.

Edgar Wilson, a ten-year veteran of the Patrol, called out to three others as he ran for his cruiser. "Clint! Eddie! Bob! You're with me!"

Rose raised the root beer to his lips and sucked some of the contents down. "You expecting trouble?"

"Not at all. I just want to make it clear to everyone who sees us drag the lieutenant governor out, kicking and screaming in handcuffs, that nobody in this state messes with us."

"I'm sure glad you're on our side."

ROSE DRAINED the last of his root beer as Sanders swung his Lincoln around a city bus. Rose handed the empty over the seatback to Jenks. "That was good stuff."

"Want the other?"

"Maybe later."

"How's the arm?"

"Hand's tingly."

"You're gettin' some color back."

"Just needed to sit awhile and get something in my stomach."

Sanders crushed his car's brake pedal, and everyone came forward, Rose jamming his good hand into the dash to keep from being thrown into the windshield.

Sanders ground his teeth as he stared ahead at a snarl of construction and car traffic around Public Square. He rolled down his window and windmilled his arm for Wilson to pull up beside him. "Put on your siren and get us the hell through this!"

Wilson flipped a switch up. His siren cranked up from a low moan to a high scream during the moments it took him to force his cruiser into the lane ahead of Sanders.

Sanders smiled. "Just like Moses parting the sea."

The cruiser and the black Lincoln sliced through the traffic, weaving from lane to lane, the drivers slowing only for the hard turn onto Third Avenue and the equally hard turn onto Cedar. They barreled up Cedar to Seventh, then up and around the Capitol building to the rear entrance. There they banged their cars over the curb and stopped, each with one tire on the sidewalk.

The siren's pitch wound down as the lawmen left their cars.

"Quill, want yer shotgun?" Oddling asked.

"No. It's enough you and Tommy've got yours."

"We need shotguns?" Wilson called over to Sanders.

"No. Square up your uniforms. This is the Capitol."

The eight men pushed their way through the massive oak doors, up to the first floor, rain water dripping from their pants cuffs and squishing from their shoes.

A REPORTER from the Nashville Tribune saw the front quartet enter the rotunda, wet, mud-spattered civilians with four uniformed troopers behind them. He hurried over but stopped when he saw two of the civilians toting shotguns.

The reporter's better sense told him to dive behind the information desk, but he bucked up his courage. "Hey!" he called out, waving his notepad.

Sanders recognized him. "Harvey, you want a story, stick with us."

The reporter grabbed his photographer.

An assistant doorkeeper, stationed at the information desk, stood up when the strange assemblage came his way. "You can't come in here with guns."

Sanders held up his badge and kept walking. "The lieutenant governor in his office?"

"The Senate chamber. He's presiding today."

The group continued their march to the grand staircase. Rose slipped on the steps, but Jenks caught him.

Sanders got a hand on Rose's belt. "You gonna make it?"

"Yeah."

"Just another couple hundred feet."

"I know."

Sanders and Rose—Rose with Jenks's help—topped the stairs and continued on toward the Senate chamber. They pushed through the doors.

The Senate doorkeeper and the sergeant-at-arms wheeled on the strangers. "Only legislators permitted—"

Two troopers braced them against the wall before the sergeant-at-arms could finish his sentence.

A gaggle of senators, conversing near the doors, glanced up as Sanders and Rose brushed past them and into the center aisle. They strode toward the podium, Jenks and Oddling behind them, the stocks of their shotguns resting on their hips. Two troopers completed the detail, the Tribune reporter and photographer dashing up a side aisle.

Clayton Johnson turned from the secretary with whom he was talking. "You can't come in here," he said when he saw Rose and Sanders.

Rose pulled papers from his shirt pocket. "Clayton, I have warrants for your arrest signed by Blount County Judge Enos Limke and U.S. Magistrate Simon Grevey. Do you want me to read these to the Senate or do you just want to come along?"

Sanders held out a set of handcuffs to the lieutenant governor.

"Touch me and I'll have your badge." Johnson banged his gavel on the lectern to get the attention of the senators. "Excuse me, gentlemen! Excuse me. Some business has come up that I must attend to. The leader of the Democratic majority, Senator John Albert from Perry County, shall assume the gavel."

Johnson straightened his suit coat as he came around to the aisle. When Sanders reached for his arm, Johnson jerked away, snarling, "You sonuvabitch."

Johnson, ever one to be at the head of a parade, led the detail of lawmen out of the chamber.

The photographer ran ahead, turning back to snap a flash picture of an angry lieutenant governor, a gaggle of lawmen, and a passel of perplexed lawmakers with the flags of the State of Tennessee and the Tennessee Senate behind them.

The reporter remained behind, scribbling notes about what he had witnessed. When done, he dashed after the others, catching up with them at the stairs.

Rose sat there, on the top step, leaning against a banister post. "I'm done, Newey."

Johnson, three steps below, wheeled around. "You sonuvabitch, to think you can do this to me. I'm blood for God's sake."

A shotgun came up, but Rose put his hand out. "It's all right. Clayton, you shouldn't have got into the booze business, and you sure shouldn't have got into it in my county. Darn right we're family, so you should of known I'd have to come after you. You, you're going to Brushyfork, and me, I'm going home to explain your mess to your sister."

Chapter 31

No heroes at home

QUILL ROSE EASED himself out of the backseat of Newey Sanders's Lincoln, his arm in a sling and a patch bandage on his forehead. "Get my bag and my shotgun, would you, Tommy?"

Sanders watched Rose. "You be all right?"

"I expect so, but I won't be winning any foot races for a while." Rose leaned on the car to steady himself.

"Do you want me to come to the house with you?"

"No, you've got your own family waiting on you. You better get on home."

"Quill, it sure was an exciting time."

"Yeah, now I've got to tell my wife we jailed her brother."

Tommy Jenks came around, his bedroll and Rose's carpet bag under one arm and a shotgun in each hand.

Sanders fiddled with the shift lever. "How do you think she'll take it?"

"Not good."

"I can come in with you."

"Tommy will protect me."

"I hope it don't come to that," Jenks said.

"Well, all right then." Sanders moved the shift lever into first. He let out the clutch and the Lincoln, with its well-bent rear fender, rolled out into the street and into the lengthening shadows of evening.

Rose hauled off his hat. He stuffed it in his damaged hand so he could finger-comb his hair. "I don't know how I'm going to explain this, Tommy."

"You want me to do it?"

"No."

Rose, in his muddied and water-stained trousers and jacket, new three days before, moved up the walk with Jenks ambling beside him. The two made it to the porch, but not to the door before Martha Rose opened it. She did not step toward Rose. Instead, she took root in the doorway, with the child hanging onto the hem of her apron, gazing up at her. She kept a hand on the boy's shoulder. "Quill, are you all right?"

"You heard."

"It was on the radio, and the judge called."

"Anyone else?"

"My sister-in-law, Clayton's wife."

"You know everything then."

Her face twisted. "He's my brother, Quill. How could you do that?"

Rose studied Martha, trying to read her. Which emotion had taken the greater toll in the last hours, worry or anger? Anger he decided. "Now don't get mad at me. Clay's the one who broke the law. It was not like it was an accident. It was deliberate on his part."

"That makes no difference. You should have warned him."

"I couldn't do that."

A hardness came into Martha Rose's eyes. "No, you couldn't, could you? You never bend. With you it's black or white, right or wrong. It's the law or nothing. I used to admire you for that, but no longer."

"I'm sorry."

"Sorry don't feed the chickens." Venom dripped from each word.

"I'm tired. I want to go in, sleep a bit."

Martha Rose stepped back, taking the child with her. She retrieved a suitcase and a second carpet bag and dropped them in front of Rose. "Go sleep under the trees or on Tommy's back porch. I don't want you in my house."

"Martha, we married for better or for worse."

"And this is the worst." She slammed the door.

"GAWDDAMMIT, Quill, what the hell were you doin', running all over the state, when you got business here in the county you were elected to do?"

Rose slid further down on the hard oak chair that the county fiscal court had set out for him.

Flecks of spit flew from the corners of Judge Executive Mitch McMahan's mouth as he roared on. "Hijacking whiskey trucks! Arresting the lieutenant governor! What in God's name got into you?"

Rose pulled a white handkerchief from his pocket. He raised the handkerchief over his head.

McMahan reddened. "That kind of smart shit isn't going to get you anywhere."

"Well, then, let me know when you're finished."

"Why?"

"So I can tell you how much money you made."

"Money? What money?"

"Are you done, Mitch?"

"No."

"Okay."

Silence seeped into the room.

McMahan glared at Rose. He held back until he could hold back no more. "What money?"

Rose cleared his throat. "Mitch, I know how broke you're always telling me the county is."

"Yeah?"

"So I took advantage of my good office to make us a chunk of money, maybe take the pressure off the budget and off me in the process."

"You sure as hell can talk your way around Robin Hood's barn. Get to the point."

"The point is, Mitch, the Maryville State Bank stands ready to deposit eight thousand, one hundred eight dollars and seventeen cents in the county's general fund."

"Why?"

"Mitch, would you stop interrupting. It's money for you to spend in whatever way you see fit."

McMahan turned to his fellow court members, then back to Rose. "Is this legal? You're giving the county government money we can spend?"

"Of course, I'd like some for the sheriff's department, raises for a couple deputies."

McMahan leaped to his feet. "You blackmailing bastard."

"Mitch, you're just mad because I arrested your friend."

"Gawddammit, if we coulda got him elected governor, there woulda been all kinds of good things in it for us." The cords of McMahan's neck stood out. His jaw cut a sharp line.

"He's a crook, Mitch."

"Yeah, but he was our crook."

"Careful how loud you say that. The newspaper editor's sitting outside the door."

McMahan blanched. "Jens?"

"Yes."

"You ask him here?"

"I did."

McMahan opened a drawer. He rummaged in the contents for a moment, then brought out an army Forty-Five pistol. He placed it on the table, the barrel pointed at Rose.

The other fiscal court judges scuttled back in their chairs, wide-eyed. They stared at McMahan.

Rose pulled his Colt Forty-Four long barrel out of his shoulder holster. He laid the gun on the table, the barrel directed at McMahan. "I'll see you—and raise you one." Rose brought out a Thirty-Eight Special from his jacket's side pocket. He set the weapon on the table as well. "Now are you going to let me talk?"

McMahan sat, apparently considering his options. He swished his fingers to the side.

"Mitch, you say I hijacked some whiskey trucks. You're right. Five to be exact. It would have been six, but that last one burned in a crash. Three of the trucks I ransomed for three thousand dollars apiece."

"Three thousand dollars?"

"Yes, I put that money in a special account at the bank, and I had Avery Moore keep books on it."

McMahan ran the arithmetic. "Three thousand each for three trucks, how come we ain't talkin' about nine thousand dollars here?"

Rose reached for his revolver. McMahan saw it and shifted back in his chair.

"Mitch, we had expenses. I provided a complete accounting to Avery. He's certified the expenses, and here's his report." Rose placed a paper on the table next to his gun. "Now you approve the report, and Avery transfers the money to the county's general fund. Then I suggest you can call the editor in and take credit for saving our taxpayers a wad of money through good government."

McMahan wiggled his fingers at Rose.

Rose responded by sliding the paper up the table.

McMahan caught the paper. He twisted it around and scanned down the numbers. "What's this money for the Louden sheriff?"

"It's all there. Marcellus gave a lot of help when his county was broke. He needs every cent of that."

"I don't know."

"Aw, Mitch, for once in your life, do the right thing. Take the money for the county. I could have kept it for myself. You would have."

"Watch your mouth."

Fiscal judge Amos McCander raised a finger bent by arthritis.

McMahan scowled at him. "What is it?"

"I think we ought to take the money."

The judge executive aimed two fingers at Leland Appleton, the third member of the fiscal court. "Leland, whaddaya say?"

"Take it. If we don't and my wife finds out about this, I'm gonna catch hell at home."

McMahan drummed a pencil on the table before he looked at Rose. "Two to one."

"Oh, go for it, Mitch. Make it unanimous. Be a hero to those who had the lack of foresight to vote for you."

"You bastard. But you're not getting anything out of this."

"I don't want anything other than raises for Tommy and Roy Eagle. They went way out on a limb on this because I asked them to. They've earned it."

McMahan peered at McCander and Appleton. Both nodded.

"You've got it, but, gawddammit, that's all you get."

"How much?"

"Five dollars a month."

Rose got up from his chair. He put his revolver in his shoulder holster and his Thirty-Eight in his side pocket. "I thank you for them, Mitch, Amos, Leland. I'll send in the editor, and, Mitch, you take all the glory now."

After Rose got outside the meeting room door, he leaned down to a man sitting on a hall bench, flicking playing cards toward an up-turned hat.

Rose jerked his thumb toward the door. "Big story inside. Come by and see me when you're finished."

Wallace Jens stood up. The editor of the Maryville Times brushed the wrinkles out of his trousers before he picked up his playing cards. After he had corralled the last of them, he recovered his hat and went in to find out what the fiscal court had done that was newsworthy.

Rose continued on to the stairs and down to his office.

Tommy Jenks hung up the telephone receiver when he saw Rose come in. "Quite a bit of yelling up there?"

"About the usual. I've got to start stuffing cotton in my ears before I go up to meet with the old dragons."

"Pretty rough, huh?"

"Amos and Leland aren't so bad, but, my gawd, that Mitch is a misery."

"They ask about yer arm?"

Rose brought his arm up and the sling that held it. "I don't think they even noticed."

"You know you're lucky you didn't bleed to death."

"I do, but we got the job done, didn't we?"

"What're we gonna do now to keep the dust curls from settling?"

Rose picked up a fistful of mail from the secretary's desk. He carried it to his own and flopped in his chair. "Tommy, Tommy, Tommy, I'd just as soon go fishing and let the dust curls settle back under the bed, let those curls get so big people think they're turkey nests."

"Fishin' and you is only good for a day."

Rose sliced open an envelope. "Maybe so. By the way, you've got a raise. And when Roy Eagle comes in, tell him he's got one, too."

"Well, with his brood of children, he needs it."

Hezzy Radcliffe sat filing jail reports. "How about me?"

"Sorry, you know how hard Mitch squeezes a nickel. That poor old buffalo on it is lame for a month once he lets it go. I couldn't get anything for you nor a penny for me. The best I could do was a ten-dollar bill for Tommy and Roy Eagle to split."

Jenks laid his Thirty-Eight on a newspaper open on his desk and brought his cleaning supplies up from the drawer where he kept them. "That old pinchpenny. Quill, why don't you run for his job?"

"If I was to run and win, then I'd be the old pinchpenny. It's Mitch's job to protect the taxpayers' money, and I hate to say it, but nobody does it better."

"He sure burns your britches every chance he gets."

"Yup, well, it's better than him beating his children."

Hezzy whirled around. "He beats his children?"

"No, he doesn't. I'm just saying if he wasn't beating on me, maybe he would or he'd take to kicking dogs. What's this?" Rose looked a second time at the letter he had removed from its envelope. "A note from Newey. Says his captain's asked him to gather evidence on the six troopers on Will Kaufmann's list and arrest them. Asks we don't talk about it until he's done."

A knock on the glass of the sheriff's department door interrupted. Rose twisted around to find Wallace Jens waiting there.

The newspaper editor stepped in. "Got some time for me, Quill?

"Absolutely." Rose hooked an empty chair with his foot and pulled the chair over to his desk. "Sit yourself down."

"I do an awful lot of that when I come to the courthouse."

Jens, on the plump side, had come to Maryville from Bristol where he had burned out on a daily newspaper. He found a county weekly suited him better, that it gave him time to sit in on lectures on medieval history at the college.

Rose beckoned to his secretary. "Would you bring a cup of your fine coffee over here for our fair city's outstanding newspaper editor? He's been up with the fiscal court. I expect they dried him out."

"Take it black?" Hezzy asked as she filled a blue china cup.

"Is there any other way in these hard times?"

She brought the steaming cup to Jens.

"Thank you. Hezz, you're too wonderful a woman to be looking after these ruffians. If it wasn't for being married, I'd come courting you."

"Aren't you the sweet one?"

"That's what my wife says." Jens changed the subject. "What do you have for me, Quill?"

"What did they tell you upstairs?"

Jens snickered as he took out his notepad. "The tallest gawddamn tale I ever heard about a bunch of money falling from the heavens, only you and I know it's not true."

"We do?"

"Quill, you had a big hand in that money coming here. Od told me."

Rose gazed away.

"You're not the only person I talk to, Quill. When I sniff out something, I go around until I find some soul just bursting to tell me the details. So little happens in Od's life that he really feels good about, I cannot tell you how tall he's walking since you all came back from Nashville. And, yes, I know what happened to your arm."

Rose rapped the end of a pencil on his desk top. "Wallace, you can write anything you want about my arm and about Nashville, but you don't write anything about my part in the money."

"Why not?"

"You and I kick old Mitch in the bee-hind every chance we get. It's time he got a little glory for keeping this county from being broke. You print exactly what he said."

"Quill, there are those who know what he says is a lie."

Rose poked the point end of his pencil in front of Jens's face. "They're not going to talk about it. And after I visit with Od, he's not going to talk about it either. So when you write what Mitch says, your story holds as God's gospel truth."

"I don't know."

Rose dropped the pencil back on his desk. "Look, I don't do this job to get my name in the paper. Sometimes it happens, and there's not a heckuva lot I can do about it. But this is one story you don't hang on me. Hang it on Mitch. And if you write about Nashville, you spell Tommy's name right and you spell Od's name right. Those two did a helluva job keeping me alive. Without them, you'd be writing my obituary."

"You're a hard man, Quill."

Rose leaned forward. He thumbed to Jenks. "I only want what's right for the people who work for me, and for my friends. Is that too much to ask?"

"No, I guess not. Now about Nashville—"

"Wallace, why don't you take Tommy to lunch? He knows everything that happened."

Jens glanced at Jenks.

Jenks turned his hands palms up. "I eat an awful lot."

CHAPTER 32

Making peace

QUILL ROSE, his arm no longer in a sling, sat on the steps of the back porch, rubbing the ears of his black Labrador, Fletch. "Missed you, old boy. How're you getting on?"

The water dog, his tongue lapping at Rose's wrist, pounded his tail on the grass.

"Yes, it's a tough life when you've got no vocabulary."

Martha Rose came out from the kitchen. "What're you doing here?"

Rose kept his gaze fixed on his dog. "Came by to see Fletch."

"And the boy?"

"And the boy."

"Pretty presumptuous of you."

"That's me, always presuming."

"Tommy throw you out?"

"No." Rose raised his right hand above his head. "Doc took the stitches out of my wrist this afternoon, threw my sling away. Figured–"

"You'd just stop by and see your dog and Little Nate."

"Yeah."

"He's inside, taking a nap." Martha leaned against a porch post, the wisteria vine beyond it in fragrant bloom. She turned away from Rose, to her garden.

"You want that dog?"

"I was just thinking–"

Both spoke at the same moment, one over the other, aware too late of the other.

Martha peered at one of her tomato plants. "You first."

"No, you." Rose shifted on his step.

"You know, Quill, you're a lot like your old dog." She glanced at her husband from the corner of her eye.

Rose stroked Fletch's head. "How's that?"

"You always come dragging home after you've run yourself ragged, expecting somebody to feed you and give you a warm place to sleep for the night."

"That's pretty harsh."

Martha leaned on her hands on the porch railing. She rocked. "You hurt me, Quill."

"Would it help to say I'm sorry?"

"Not much. It's just that you get so wrapped up in what you're doing, you don't think about me. The last few years it's gotten to be like we weren't married at all, just sharing the same roof to keep the rain off until the sun comes out. Are you listening to me?"

Slowly, Rose nodded.

"Could you change?"

"I could try."

"Probably wouldn't be much, would it?"

"Probably not, long as I carry a badge."

"And you won't give that up, will you?"

"What would I do?"

"Sell insurance, something."

"Huh."

"Look, you sell yourself to the people of this county every two years."

"That's because I believe what I do makes a difference."

Martha glanced again at Rose. "You really believe that, don't you?"

"Yes."

"Quill, I don't know—"

"Is it my turn?"

"I guess."

Rose stroked the long bridge of Fletch's muzzle, the dog closing his eyes in sweet pleasure. "You know what I thought the day we got married, when I saw you coming down the stairs of your momma's and your daddy's house, you in your grandma's wedding dress?"

Martha took a lace handkerchief from the pocket of her apron and touched it to her nose.

"I thought, my Lord, what an amazingly beautiful woman, and me, all tall, gawky, and homely as a mud fence, how lucky I was that you agreed to share a life with me. And I was scared, too."

"Why?"

"What'd I know about being married, other than it seemed to work for my dad and my ma. You know they held hands in church? Every Wednesday night and Sunday, until the day Dad died. Not a cross word between them that I can recall. Remarkable."

"And we've had cross words."

"Well, I brought that on myself."

"Yes, you did. The judge told me he gave you a chance to walk away, to let Newell Sanders run that thing in Nashville."

"It just didn't seem right."

Silence seeped in between them. After some time, Martha Rose broke the silence. "You want to hold my hand?"

Rose nodded.

She came to the steps. She moved down them so slowly, as if time were suspended, then she sat down beside Rose, her hip and her shoulder touching his.

In the wordless quiet that followed, Fletch placed his head on Rose's knee, and Rose reached his hand for Martha's. Their fingers touched, tentatively, then twined together.

"Old man, what am I going to do with you?"

Chapter 33

The trap

ROSE HELD his right hand high over his head for all to see as he came through the office door. "No more stitches. Doc Stanley says now I can play the fiddle as good as I ever could."

"Hey, hey, hey!" Tommy Jenks called out from the counter where he sorted old arrest reports. "Hezzy, look who didn't come home to my house last night."

Hezzy Radcliffe glanced up from her typing. "You make peace with Martha?"

"I think I did."

"It's about time. You were getting to be miserable to have around."

"Thank you for your good wishes."

Jenks reached for Rose's wrist. "Let me see that. Hmm, by the scar, looks like your hand was sewn on by Doc Frankenstein instead of a high-paid surgeon in Nashville. You really play the fiddle?"

"No, but at least I'll be able to throw a baseball, and I can hold a fry pan over a campfire. What are you working on?"

"Hezzy's been after me to shape up these reports so she can file 'em." He held out one. "This one still bothers me, the mystery guy I caught by the river. He broke jail in Lenoir City, you remember? Oh, you've got a note here."

Jenks went to his desk. He dug through a mass of papers until he found the sheet he needed and handed it out to Rose. "This woman called. Wants to talk to you."

Rose read the note, all three words of it—Mildred, Sunshine Café. "She say what it was about?"

"Nothing more than it's important."

"The Sunshine? Well, I feel a hankering coming on for a piece of raisin pie. I do believe I'll go on down."

The Sunshine was a short two blocks from the courthouse. Maryville residents went there because they could count on getting the biggest dime hamburger in town and the deepest nickel cup of coffee, and the pies that Marie Waxman made, newspaper editor Wallace Jens once effused in his 'Window on Main Street' column, you had to order a week ahead to be sure you'd get a wedge.

Rose found, when he crossed to the café's side of the street, J.D. Oddling leaning on the hood of a Chevy coupe, scribbling out a ticket. "Catch you another scofflaw?"

Oddling looked up, his lazy eye wandering off while his good eye focused on Rose. "Oh, it's just Doc Stanley again. He knows he's not supposed to park here."

"He won't pay."

"Never does, but it's my job to write him up." Oddling tore the ticket from his book. He reached through the open side window and laid the ticket on the dashboard.

"I'm going for pie, Od. Want to come along?"

"Oh my, it's been a frightful long mornin' since breakfast. I'll just take you up on that. See yer arm's outta the sling."

"Yes, I'm thinking of going up to Fountain City, see if I can pitch hard enough to get a slot on the ball team."

"Quill, yer like me. Yer too old for that."

Rose slapped his shoulder. "Oh, I think I still have a bunch of strikes left in this arm."

"Well, if ya want to get yer fanny beat so bad, why don'tcha go over to the college? You kin pitch some practice innings there. They got a couple juniors that kin just whup that ball fer a mile."

"How do you know?"

Oddling stuffed his ticket book in his back pocket. "Quill, ya know the nice thing about being town constable? I kin go over to the college an' watch their games an' pretend at the same time I'm doin' my job."

Rose opened the door to the Sunshine. He held it for his fellow lawman. When Rose got inside, he pointed to the cup that had his name on it on the shelf above the cash register. He also gestured to Oddling's cup.

Marie Waxman took them down. "Your usual booth?"

"Yup. Raisin pie today?"

"One just out of the oven not ten minutes ago."

"A piece for me and a piece for the good constable. And put some of that sweet vanilla ice cream on it to cool it. Is Mildred here today?"

"You know her?"

"I heard you had somebody new. If it's who I think she is, yes, I know of her."

"She's in the kitchen. I'll send her out with the pie and ice cream."

Oddling snatched off his cap. "Yer lookin' mighty fine, today, Marie."

"Yes, I know." She primped her hair. "But you two still pay full price."

Rose led Oddling to the back booth. They had hardly gotten seated when Waxman came up with two cups of coffee. "Mildred's scooping up the ice cream. She'll be here directly."

Rose put his hand out for his cup.

"See you're out of your sling. That's good."

"He wants to pitch some baseball. I think I got him talked into goin' over to the college an' pitchin' some practice innings there."

Waxman set the cups on the table. "My son's over there, did you know that?"

"No, I didn't." Rose pulled his cup to himself.

"It's his first year."

"Is he going to be a preacher?"

"I got my hopes. Here comes Mildred, so I'll get out of the way." Waxman stepped aside for her waitress and went on up to the front of the café.

The woman slid one plate in front of Oddling and the other in front of Rose. "Same order for both of you?"

"Yeah."

"Missus Waxman says you're the sheriff."

"That's right."

Rose gazed at the woman who stood at the side of the booth. She was a bit hunched, he thought, deep worry lines in her face, hair showing tinges of gray. "It's been a lot of years, Mildred. Od, this is Mildred Whitlow."

"I'm Mildred Conable now, although my husband's been dead for three years. Maybe you heard I moved back a bit ago. Needed a job, and here I am." The waitress pushed an errant strand of hair back behind her ear.

"Business looks a little slow. Won't you sit down and join us?"

"I better stay on my feet."

"You called?"

"I heard you got cut bad."

"It wasn't my best day."

"I know who did it."

Rose peered at Oddling, and Oddling stared at his coffee.

"How do you know?" Rose asked.

"It was my brother. He come to me the other night. He told me."

Rose tried to bring the face back from the far recesses of his memory. "Your brother?"

"Yeah, Jimmy."

"I thought he died in the war."

"So did we, Ma an' Pa an' me." Conable fiddled with her order pad. "Just tore the soul outta Pa."

"Well, where's he been all these—what, sixteen years?"

"I don't know. He wouldn't talk about it much."

"Where's he now?"

"Hanging 'round our old farm." The waitress shifted, squaring around more toward Rose. "Sheriff, Jimmy scares me. He's got this big old knife he keeps wipin' on his trouser leg."

"Where are you staying?"

"I got a little house at the edge of town."

"Marie!" Rose called out.

"Yes?" Marie Waxman left her work at the front counter and hurried to the back booth.

"Marie, this woman's not safe where she's living. Can she stay the next couple nights at your place, with you and Teddy?"

"Sure."

Rose touched Oddling's arm. "Od, I need you in on this. I want you and your night deputy to keep an eye on Marie's place. Any men come around you don't know, haul them to jail and I'll sort it out later."

Mildred Conable rubbed a finger on the side of her order pad. "Jimmy's not the skinny kid you remember,

Sheriff. He's thickened out, powerful built now. Got a slash on the side of the face, said he was cut by a German bayonet."

Rose raised an eyebrow. "Mildred, I've seen him. I even had him in my jail, but I didn't know him at the time. Now I know who I'm looking for."

TOMMY JENKS backed a rusting Model A pickup down to the porch of the Whitlow farmhouse. After he stopped the truck, he forced his bulk out of the cab and went around to the back to unload. He wore the tired clothing of a sharecropper and Quill Rose's sweat-stained slouch hat.

He pulled off boxes and barrels and carried them in the house, then came back for a table and two straight-back chairs and a spring bed. He carried these in, as well as a table and chairs for the kitchen and a bed frame and a corn shuck mattress for the back bedroom.

When Jenks returned for the last time, only one item for the house remained, a large trunk. He wrestled that in through the door and set it down in the main room. After Jenks closed the door, then and only then did he open the trunk. "You all right in there?"

Quill Rose threw an arm over the edge. He hauled himself up. "This isn't the easiest way to get around."

"You think he'll come?"

"If you make enough noise like you're living here."

"Well, I got a crate of chickens to let loose in the yard. That ought to look good."

Rose gazed around the room, then up at the loft. "Tommy, up there, that's where I'll be."

Jenks went outside. The sun was sliding down toward the Tennessee River when he released the chickens. He threw out a couple handfuls of shelled corn to keep them busy while he parked the truck at the side of the house.

Jenks took a box of hand tools from the cab and made a show of carrying the box to the barn. By the time he came back, the chickens were strutting around beneath the trees, looking for one in which to roost.

Jenks went in. He lit lanterns and stirred about in the kitchen, preparing supper, cooking enough for two people. When he had it ready, he carried a plate and a cup of coffee into the main room and handed them up to Rose.

Rose, in the loft, sampled the chopped ham and fried potatoes. "Not bad. Melting the cheese over it, that's a good idea."

"That's the way my ma always made it, and, of course, we made our own cheese."

"You lock the kitchen door?"

"Yup." Jenks buttered a chunk of crackling bread.

"Nail the windows shut, too. That way he's got to come in the front door, and I'll know he's here long before he gets close to you."

Jenks, his head bobbing, bit into the bread. "That eases my mind some."

JENKS READ FOR SOME TIME that night, after he had put up the dishes. When he tired, he made the rounds of the several rooms, rattling the kitchen door one last time and checking the windows, to be sure the nails he had tacked in held tight.

He took a lantern to the front door and around outside to the outhouse.

Some minutes later, Jenks returned. "G'night," he called to Rose as he went through the main room and on into the back bedroom where he turned out the lantern.

Jenks kicked off his shoes and rolled in under the covers, the bedsprings making music as they stretched.

THE HOURS PASSED. Rose knew his deputy had drifted off when he heard a soft snoring coming from the direction of the back bedroom. The only other sound that came his way was the occasional hooting of an owl in a nearby tree.

Rose fought hard to keep awake and was about to succumb when the pressure of his bladder too full hit him. He agonized before he gave up and swung his feet over the edge of the loft. He felt for the ladder, got a foot on a rung, and worked his way down and across the floor to the door. Rose eased it open.

He listened.

Hearing nothing other than the owl and the deep rumble of bullfrogs in the distant creek, he slipped through and dashed for the outhouse.

Rose had torn a page from the catalog that hung from a nail when a yell and a pistol shot brought him off the bench seat. He yanked up his trousers and ran, falling when he missed the porch step at the house. Rose scrambled to his feet. He ran on through the doorway, into the main room and the bedroom beyond.

He saw a form at the window and whipped his revolver up.

"It's me, Quill!"

"Tommy?"

"Dammit, he cut me, but I got off a shot. He could still be here."

Rose edged around until he felt a lantern on a side table. He found a box of matches, got one out and struck it. He touched the flame to the wick. The weak light flickering up revealed Jenks on the far side of the room, clutching his shoulder, a revolver in his hand.

Rose, still with his own long-barreled Forty-Four out, scanned the room as he worked his way around the bed toward his deputy. One step and he went down, grabbing for the bed. Rose caught himself and, pulling up, worked his way back for the lantern. He brought the light over by the bed. "Damn, there's a hole here, a trapdoor."

"You sure?"

"I'm looking at the thing."

"I didn't know there was no trapdoor in the place."

"Me neither." Rose knelt down. "Look here. See this rag rug? It must have been over it, and we never bothered to kick it aside. Tommy, our man had to go out this way. If you can take care of yourself, I'll go after him."

"Go."

Rose set the lantern on the floor. He lowered himself through the hole, then brought the light into what appeared to be a small cellar room. Rose estimated four people could hunker down in this dirt-floored, dirt-walled space. "Tommy, I see something."

"What is it?"

"A tunnel. It's leading out." Rose got down on his knees. He pushed the lantern into the hole and gazed beyond. "Tommy? I found the escape. I'm going after him."

"Be careful. He could be waitin'."

Rose pulled the lantern out of the tunnel. He set it on the floor, then wriggled into the low, narrow hole, keeping his gun out ahead of him.

All he could see was blackness as he crawled along. Rose lost track of time, wondering how far he had gone, wondering where he might be when, ahead, it began to grow less black, more the velvety color of night, and he was out, out somewhere where water splashed over rocks. He could hear the sound. Rose glanced up in time to catch the last sliver of the old moon as it slid behind a skiff of clouds.

Now on his feet, he stumbled along, one foot slipping, sliding every few paces, splashing into what had to be a stream.

Rose stopped when a fence blocked him. He got a hand on a post and climbed the fence wire over into a ditch next to a poorly graveled road.

He set off at a trot, hoping he was going toward the Whitlow place.

The moon sliver came out from its hiding place and illuminated the road jogging off to the right. Ahead, Rose saw it, lights in the windows of a house.

He kept up his pace, slowing only when he got to the porch. He plunged inside, into the main room and beyond, into the kitchen, to Tommy Jenks leaning on a table, holding a blood-soaked rag against his shoulder. "Find him?"

"You see him with me? He came out into Pistol Creek. The tunnel ends there."

"It does?"

"Where he went from there, I don't know. How're you doing?"

"Not good."

"Lemme see."

Jenks took the rag away. Blood flowed from the wound.

"He carved your shoulder like a Christmas ham. I need a couple towels."

Jenks clamped his rag back over his shoulder. "Box by the sink."

Rose found two towels where Jenks said they were. He folded one down to a square and packed it over the wound. The second he wrapped over the square and around the arm. He tied it and pulled the knot down tight, Jenks wincing.

Rose helped Jenks outside to the truck and drove him to Maryville, to Doc Stanley's house where a thunder of banging brought the doctor, in his nightshirt and feet bare, to the door.

"Got a wounded man for you." Rose pushed Jenks ahead of him into the front hallway.

Stanley led the late callers toward his kitchen. He snatched his bag from the hall table as they hurried by. "Jesus, Quill, this is an honest man's bedtime."

"That's where we ought to be, but we were trying to catch a killer."

"Get him in a chair now. Thank God, Bess keeps a pot of water hot on the stove all the time. She does love her tea." Stanley reached for the kettle. He poured its contents into a basin and brought the basin and towels to the table. He nodded at Rose's makeshift bandage. "Untie your wrapper."

Rose did, and Stanley sponged at the clotting blood. "Know who did this?"

"That we do."

Stanley opened the slice. "Lordy, Tommy, that's deep. I've got to clean it, and it's going to hurt like hell."

"Do what you have to do, Doc."

Stanley took a sterile pad from his bag. He slapped the pad over the wound. "Quill, hold this while I find my bottle of iodine."

Stanley rummaged deeper in his medical bag. He found the bottle and splashed the contents onto a second pad. Stanley pulled the first pad away. He spread open the wound and raked the iodine-soaked pad through it, Jenks howling.

"Tommy, I wish there was something easier, but there isn't." Stanley closed the wound and placed the iodine pad over it. "You hold this while I thread me a needle. I'm gonna practice my stitchery on you."

Jenks, gritting his teeth, forced his hand over the pad.

Stanley took a needle from a bottle of alcohol and poked a hank of thread through the eye. He tied the thread off, then made the first stitch, Jenks yipping when the needle pierced his skin. Stanley tied off the stitch and snipped the thread. "So who do you think it is?"

Rose watched Stanley pierce Jenks's skin a second time. "A man I thought had been dead for sixteen years."

"How's that?"

"Jimmy Whitlow. He came in by way of a tunnel under the Whitlow house. No stranger's going to know that tunnel's there, so it had to be Jimmy. Had to be somebody who'd lived in the place."

"I suppose."

"Doc, he grew up playing there. He'd know about it."

Stanley started another stitch. "Didn't I hear years back he never came home from the war?"

"Makes you want to believe in ghosts."

Stanley tied off the stitch and began another. Again Jenks yipped. "Tommy, quit that. My God, you're not some little child."

"It hurts."

"It's just a pin prick. Quill, I've never heard of ghosts wielding knives, leastways not one that cuts like this. What're you gonna do?"

"Wish I knew. One thing's sure, and I'd bet Tommy's pay on it, Jimmy's not going to make it easy for us."

ROSE DELIVERED JENKS to his home. After he got him bedded down and the lights out, he left and hustled off toward Harper Street, toward Marie and Teddy Waxman's house.

He slowed when he saw a Model T coupe parked near the Waxmans'. It wasn't so much the car, but the cap Rose saw through the rear window, the cap on the passenger's side. He eased up, moving like a Cherokee in moccasins.

Rose stopped by the rear wheel. He glanced around. From near the side window he said in a low voice, "Evening, Od."

The man in the car bounced up, a newspaper flying to one side, a porcelain cup out the window.

Oddling twisted around, all the color drained from his face. "Quill Rose, scare a body to death."

"Just checking to see you're on the job."

"Lordy, Quill."

"Anybody come around?"

"Just a couple dogs to pee on my tires, and now you."

"I need to talk to Mildred."

Oddling motioned at the house, his hand shaking. "Lights been out a couple hours."

"Looks like I'm going to wake them."

"You want me to come along?"

"No, you keep watch. I'm not the only one out tonight." Rose slapped the car door. He continued on to the Waxmans' house, a rambling old home built by someone who had expected to have a lot of children. Rose rapped on the front glass until light from a lantern came into the upstairs hallway and down the steps.

A man in long johns opened the door.

"Teddy, I'm sorry to wake you."

"That's all right. 'Nuther hour I'd be up anyway." Teddy Waxman yawned. "'Bout time I got to building a fire in the beehive oven. It's my morning to bake bread for the café."

"I need to talk to Mildred."

"Teddy! Who's down there?"

"It's the sheriff, Marie," Waxman called up the stairs. "Says he needs to talk to Mildred."

"Is it bad, Sheriff?"

"It is."

"I'll wake her."

Waxman, yawning again, rubbed at his ribs. "Quill, won't you come in? Got some sweets in the kitchen I brought home from the café. I could even fix you a sandwich if you like."

"Maybe a little something to nibble on." Rose stepped into the front hall. He followed Waxman's lantern through to the kitchen in back.

Waxman went to the breadbox by the stove. "Got this awful good peach pie. One piece left."

"Don't tell Od about this or he'll be upset I didn't let him come in."

"Oh, I took a piece out to him and stoked up his coffee before we went to bed." Waxman lifted the slice of pie out of the box. He put it on a saucer and passed the saucer and a fork to Rose. "It's nice of him to keep watch."

"Yes, I feel good with him out there."

Hurried footsteps came down the stairs and up the hallway, the footsteps of Marie Waxman and the Waxmans' house guest. Mildred Conable came in the kitchen first, her hair mused from the bed pillows. She pushed at her hair with one hand, while with the other, she clutched closed a well-worn wrapper. "What is it, Sheriff?"

Rose held his fork poised over the pie. "Jimmy showed up at the farm tonight."

"You catch him?"

"He got away, out through the tunnel. Tommy and I didn't know there was a tunnel."

Conable, her eyes filled with worry, turned to Marie Waxman, then back to Rose. "I hadn't thought about that tunnel for years. Papaw told us tales about it, said his daddy dug it in the Civil War so's the family could hide when the Carolina raiders come over the mountains."

Rose pushed the pie away. "Well, it sure worked for Jimmy. Do you know where he'd likely run?"

She put a trembling hand on a chair back to steady herself. "You think he might be 'round here?"

Rose shook his head. "If I was him, I'd run for the mountains."

"Not Jimmy. He was never much for living off the land." Conable slipped into one of the Waxmans' straight-back chairs. She pulled the sugar bowl to her and absently toyed with it. "What'd he say to me? Something about the aluminum plant? He was rambling. I don't know what he meant."

"The aluminum plant? Alcoa?"

"Maybe. There's the reduction plant down in the south end of the county. Could be that, too. I'm just not much help, am I?"

QUILL ROSE FLIPPED his coat lapel back, revealing a badge, and shouted to make himself heard over the roar of machinery. "You have a James Whitlow working here?!"

"Whitlow?" the mill foreman shouted back. "No!"

"Maybe about five-feet-eight, mustache maybe, scar along his face." Rose drew his fingertips along his cheek. "Graying hair. Coulda hired on in the last month!"

"Past month?"

"Yeah!"

The foreman cupped his hand beside his mouth. "Sounds like a guy we call Renee!"

"Come outside!" Rose motioned toward a door that led away from the banging of aluminum ingots being dropped on the rollers at the far end of the mill. The rollers shiushed the ingots down the line, rolling them into ever thinner sheets until they came off the end, an eighth of an inch thick.

Once outside, the mill noise dropped off. Rose turned back to the foreman. "A man could go deaf in there."

"It's got its advantages. When I get home at night, I can't hear my wife. This man you're looking for–" The foreman braced his knuckles on his hips.

"Whitlow."

"As I said, sounds like Renee. He done something wrong?"

"Killed somebody."

"You sure? Renee's pretty quiet, a good worker, about as nice as they come."

"Can I talk to him?"

"Sure."

"Got a place inside where he wouldn't think nothing of it if you told him the boss had to see him?"

"Yeah." The foreman motioned toward the upper part of the building. "There's a second-floor office that overlooks the mill floor. My boss works up there some. Everybody knows that."

"Where's your boss now?"

"In a production meeting with the superintendent. Won't be back 'til after lunch."

"So his office is empty? No one's there?"

"Right."

"Would you point it out to me, then ask this Renee to go up? I'll follow behind."

The foreman shrugged. He led Rose back inside and waved at a stairway against the far wall leading up some sixteen feet to a catwalk that ended at a room, the top half of which was glass.

The foreman wove his way toward the interior of the mill. He disappeared among clusters of men pushing aluminum stock from one set of rollers to the next. Minutes later, he emerged, gesturing toward the far wall.

Rose squinted. Yes, someone was starting up the stairs. Rose dashed for the steps. He took them two at a time when he got there, until he reached the top. There he slowed. Ahead, beyond the grimy glass of the office window, Rose saw a man sitting in a chair, his back to the glass.

Rose moved with the silence of a morning's mist across the catwalk but needn't have concerned himself about any sound his shoes might make on the gratings, not in the din of the Alcoa mill. He eased the door open.

The man turned.

Rose came on in. He pulled the door closed, more to shut out some portion of the racket than for privacy.

The man cocked his head to one side as he studied Rose. "I think I know you."

"Jimmy Whitlow?"

"Yeah?"

"You're Jimmy Whitlow?" Rose asked again.

The man peered down at the floor, at the grit that was there. "Few people have called me that for a lotta years."

Rose slipped past the man, to the swivel chair behind the desk. He sat down.

Whitlow continued to keep his gaze on the floor. "Mister, it was Nashville, waddn't it? I shoulda killed you there. Then I just wanted your hand."

"My hand?"

Whitlow raised his eyes. "I collect hands, don't you know?"

The workman leaned forward, his hand going down to his boot top. He brought out a weapon some eight inches long that he laid on the desk, the point toward Rose.

Rose's hand went inside his jacket. He brought out his Colt Forty-Four and laid it on the desk, the muzzle toward Whitlow. "Stone breaks scissors."

Whitlow gazed at the gun. "S'pose you want to know why."

"Why what?"

"Why I trailed you? Why I collect hands?"

"The trailing part's easy. You worked for that moonshine factory. I expect you were their bush guard, only my deputy caught you. When you busted jail, I figured you ran back to Shingle Mountain."

"I did. Then somebody started stealing our trucks. They sent me out to find out who it was and stop 'em." An easy smile came to Whitlow's face. "Imagine my surprise when I caught you in the toilet."

"But you didn't kill me."

"I figured you'd bleed to death once I took your hand. You'd be dead. That's what my boss wanted, and I'd have your hand. That's what I wanted."

"But why? Why my hand?"

"When I came back, long, long after the war, you know what?" Whitlow eyebrows squeezed together, until a harsh furrow formed between them, as he peered at Rose. "I found out my pa had lost his hand in a wood choppin' accident."

"He did, didn't he?"

"That's right."

Rose leaned back in his chair. "I'd forgotten that."

"Pa couldn't work no more after that, so the bank said they was gonna take his farm away." Whitlow, with his index finger, doodled in the dust on the desktop. "I was told Pa give up and died."

"Seems I remember."

What had been a relaxed hand drawing who knows what in the dust balled into a fist. "That damn lawyer, that gawddamn lawyer come along and bought our farm for the back taxes. He moved my ma off, and she was old." Whitlow raged at the past. "That was Pa's home, Ma's home. Them people had no right to be there."

It was Rose who now rubbed a finger in the aluminum dust on the desk. "Your ma, she's still living?"

"At the county poor farm. I seen her."

"She remember you?"

"No. She don't even know where she is nor who she is. She should be home, mister. She should be home." Whitlow's face twisted. "So I decided if Ma couldn't live there no more, nobody could. So I started me a hand collection—right hands—like the hand my pa lost." Whitlow leaned forward. He studied Rose. "You see that man back in the spring?"

"At the farm?"

"Yeah."

"That wasn't the lawyer."

"Yeah, it was."

"Jimmy, it was just a poor tenant farmer who'd moved on the place. You killed him, and you killed his wife. But what I want to know is why you killed the little girl?"

Whitlow thrust himself back. He moved on his chair as if he were hurt, glancing at Rose, his voice a whisper, then rising, "Because she screamed. She wouldn't stop screaming. I couldn't stand the screaming. The screaming was like all those poor boys in my company, wounded, dying, screaming for somebody to help them. It all come back on me. And this factory—"

"The noise?"

"The noise. They drop an ingot—boom—like a shell exploding. So gawddamn many dead." Jimmy Whitlow sobbed, his shoulders shaking beneath his work shirt silver with aluminum dust.

"You're not dead."

"Gawddamn shell killed three of my buddies, tore me to hell." Whitlow gasped. "The French, they told me in notes they found me wanderin' on the battlefield. They sent me off to a hospital. My ear half blowed off, they sewed it back on."

He wiped his sleeve under his eyes. "I couldn't hear for the longest time. I couldn't talk. I didn't even know who I was. So they give me a name. Renee. Can you believe that?"

Whitlow laughed. "They thought I was French. It was years before I remembered."

An ingot slammed down on the rollers below. It hit with such force that the tiny second-floor office shook. Whitlow jerked around, terror in his eyes. He screamed.

To Rose, the next moments were a confusion. It appeared to him that Whitlow levitated from his chair, and he heard the shattering of glass.

Rose remembered throwing himself out of his own chair.

He remembered racing around the desk.

He remembered seeing Whitlow go over the railing. He remembered him plummeting, plummeting down, down into the machinery, the hungry machinery that pulled everything into its rollers.

Rose wanted to remember no more.

ABOUT THE AUTHOR

Jerry Peterson created Quill Rose as a minor character in a novel he wrote 20 years ago. Really good minor characters often insist on their own stories, and Peterson obliged Rose with this one. Peterson will tell you writing–creating worlds where none had previously existed–beats teaching high school English, working in public relations, and editing newspapers, all of which he has done in previous lives. Today he lives and writes in his home state of Wisconsin, the land of brats, beer, and good books.

UPCOMING TITLES

Coming next in the *Wings Over the Mountains* series, book 3, *Rooster's Story*.

Survival is the theme of *Rooster's Story*. Rooster Wilhite is a deeply conflicted person who lost an arm in a work accident. However, in his mind, he lost more than an arm; he lost his worth as a man. How will he recover his worth?

The book also is a story of flying the airmail in the 1920s, flying the mail at night when that was a new and dangerous and sometimes deadly venture.

Get a taste for it here, well, on the next several pages, chapter 1 of *Rooster's Story*...

Rooster's Story

A Wings Over the Mountains
Novel
- Book Three -

CHAPTER 1

The singing saw

NOTHING, Rooster Wilhite told himself, not even if he lived to be a hundred, could have topped that day.

That day he had flown the lead airplane, barnstorming in a blue and silver Jenny, stunting and looping high above the largest crowd he had ever seen.

"Did you see when that smoke burst from my engine?" A grin wreathed his face.

Another pilot–Homer Wright, co-owner of the sawmill where the barnstorming crew worked–poked Rooster. "Buddy, I thought sure you were gonna crash."

Another man–a crewman, Willie Joe Brown–elbowed Rooster. "The women down there, they screamed."

"That's what I wanted."

Rooster's wing walker–Harold Wright, Homer Wright's brother and partner in the sawmill ownership–set his sandwich aside. "How did you do that anyway?"

"I just rigged up a little bottle of oil, so when I jiggered this wire, it'd drip on the manifold. I started it at the top of the loop and cut the smoke at the bottom."

"You sure didn't warn us."

"Do you tell me everything you're gonna do? And then in that last stunt, you fall off my top wing. You flop right in the cockpit, right smack on top of me. I'm

grabbing for the control stick, but it's up your pant leg."
Rooster's head snapped back in laughter.

Harold snickered. "Yup. For a bit there I thought you
was getting fresh."

"I was just trying to get hold of the damn control
stick. And you, you're yelling, 'Quit it, quit it!' "

"Yeah, and you're yelling at me, 'I can't see around
you! Where the hell are we?'"

"I sure was, wasn't I? How the Billy Dickens we ever
landed that airplane is beyond me." Rooster raised a jar of
sweet tea to Harold.

Harold held up his coffee cup, returning the salute.
"I'm just glad you caught me or I woulda been splattered
all over Elkmont's main street."

Brown slapped the wingwalker's knee. "That woulda
ruint the Labor Day parade fer sure."

Rooster roared with laughter until tears coursed
down his cheeks. Between gasps, he glimpsed the others
of the sawmill crew also crumpled up, Brown staggering
away.

Homer Wright mopped at his own tears as the hoo-
haas ran down. "Boys, we're gonna be telling this story to
our grandchildren, but for now, let's get to it. We've got
lumber to cut."

Brown, still snorting, gathered up his lunch pail and
helped Rooster to his feet. The two shambled back to the
bandsaw, Rooster ripping off with a new gale of laughter.
He rubbed at his ribs. "Damn, my sides ache. Too much
of this funny stuff."

THE WRIGHTS heard the engine start that powered the
saw. Up came the machine's speed and with it the whine
of the blade. The whine descended as the carriage pushed
a log through the blade and rose again when the first slab

fell away. The brothers knew Bill Hansen—Big Bill, everyone called him—was there to catch the slab and carry it away to the scrap pile.

There was a rhythm to the work. Homer and Harold could be engrossed in working through the details of orders and deliveries while they strolled along to their office, the crisp smell of newly cut lumber mingled with engine exhaust drifting around them, but they knew without paying any mind to the howling bandsaw just when the carriage slid back for the next cut, just when Willie Joe Brown rammed his peavey under the log and wrestled it onto its flat side, just when Rooster engaged the clutch that rolled the carriage and the log it bore forward into the saw.

Homer sensed the crew had missed a beat.

He glanced up, puzzled by Rooster's delay in engaging the clutch. Before he could say something to Harold, someone screamed.

The brothers jerked around. They ran for the sawing shed.

Rooster came racing away, toward them, grabbing for an arm that wasn't there, blood spurting from a severed artery. He slammed into the Wrights, and the three went over in a jumble.

Rooster kicked hard, but Homer got a hand on the sawman's belt. He yanked Rooster over on his back, swung a leg across the sawman's chest, and pinned him, Rooster writhing, screams piercing his sobs.

Homer jabbed his brother. "Gimme something to stop the blood."

Harold whipped a bandanna from his pocket. He shoved it into Homer's hand, and Homer clamped the bandanna over the bleeding stump.

"It's not enough." Homer glanced up at the crew running from the shed. "Willie! There's a strip of leather on a post by the saw. Get it!"

Rooster yelled and wrenched himself around in an effort to get free. Homer swung his fist hard into the side of Rooster's face, and the sawman went limp.

Brown ran up with the leather strip. He thrust it at Homer, and Homer whipped the strip around Rooster's arm, above the wound. He tied it. "Saw an ambulance driver do this on a battlefield, squeezed off the blood." Homer looked up at Hansen sobbing. "Get me all the cobwebs you can find."

Hansen stumbled away to the shed.

Homer hauled down hard on the leather strip as he tied a second knot. "Willie, I need some clean sawdust."

Brown dashed off.

Harold Wright stood watching, the knuckles of one hand braced on his hip. "How can I help?"

"Your shirt. I need it."

He stripped out of his plaid flannel and thrust it to his brother.

Hansen ran up, snuffling at his tears, holding a broom out rich with webs that spiders had spun among the shed's trusses.

Homer raked the cobwebs off. He packed them over the wound. "Civil War thing my grandpap told me about. Don't know how it stops the bleeding, but it does. Sawdust!"

Brown dumped a shovelful by Rooster's shoulder.

Homer packed massive handfuls onto the wound. "Bill, get down here. Put your hands over this mess for me. I need you to hold it together."

Hansen hunkered down and slipped his hands under Homer's.

Homer, with his hands free, folded his brother's shirt into a more manageable size. He placed it over the oozing mass of cobwebs, sawdust, and flesh.

Hansen moved his hands around to a new position, to hold the mass more stable.

Homer glanced up at Harold. "You're not gonna like this, but I need your pants."

"My pants?"

"Don't argue. I've gotta have something to tie this mess off with and your pants'll do it."

Harold rescued the spectacles he and his brother shared from his bib pocket, then shucked himself out of his overalls' shoulder straps. He let them and the work trousers drop. "Why the Billy Dickens couldn't I have put on clean shorts this morning?"

"Get your feet out of your pants."

As Harold stepped away, his boot snagged on the denim, and he fell. Brown snatched the pants by the cuffs and yanked them away.

"Willie, hold the legs out and whip the bib around the crotch a couple times." Homer Wright motioned how to do it with his hands. "You've got it. You've got it. Now give it to me."

He placed the doubled-over bib against and around the stump end of Rooster's arm. With Hansen lifting Rooster's shoulders, Homer pushed a pant leg under the sawman. He wrestled the pant leg to where he wanted it and tied it to the other pant leg, creating something of a pressure bandage. Homer raked the back of his bloody hand across his forehead. "Now comes the hard part. We've gotta get Rooster to Doc Schroeder's or we're gonna have us a funeral ahead of us."

Brown broke away. He ran for the company's Reo truck. While he backed it in, Hansen muscled Rooster up into his arms.

Harold Wright clambered up onto the truck bed. He reached back down for Rooster, but Hansen shook his shaggy mane. "You might drop him. I don't want him hurt no more."

Homer moved in beside Hansen. "Bill, you've got to hand him up. We've got to get Rooster to the doc. Harold will sit down here on the edge."

He motioned to his brother to sit down on the tailboard. "Bill, you lift Rooster into Harold's lap. I'll see that he's all right. Then you get up on the truck and you take Rooster back. You hold him. I want you to hold him all the way to Townsend. "

"Your word, Homer?"

"My word."

Hansen choked back his tears. With the gentleness of a mother caring for an injured child, he placed Rooster in Harold's arms, then swung up on the truck bed and took Rooster back.

Homer Wright caught his brother's hand and pulled himself up. He guided Hanson toward the front. "If you get down here behind the cab, both of you'll be out of the wind. Come on, sit down here now. It'll be easier for you to hold Rooster."

He and Harold held onto Hansen while he slid down behind the cab.

Homer, crouching, laid his fingers on Rooster's forehead. "Damn, he's getting cold. Willie? There's a tarp next to you on the seat. Hand it up here."

A tarp came out the truck's window. Harold Wright grabbed it.

"All right, Willie, get us the hell out of here."

Brown jammed the Reo up through its gears. He rocketed the big truck out of the mill yard and onto the main road. While he drove, the Wrights packed the tarp around Rooster and Hansen, Hansen stroking Rooster's hair, whispering, "Yer gonna be all right. Yer gonna be all right."

Harold, the wind whipping around his skinny legs, took up a position behind the driver's side of the cab. With one hand, he held onto the top of the door, with the other he beat on the roof. "Faster, Willie! Drive like the devil was after ya!"

Made in the USA
Charleston, SC
13 June 2014